PAMELA NISSEN

Rocky Mountain Redemption

Steeple
Hill®

Published by Steeple Hill Books™

STEEPLE HILL BOOKS

Steeple Hill®

ISBN-13: 978-0-373-82857-9

Recycling programs for this product may not exist in your area.

ROCKY MOUNTAIN REDEMPTION

www.SteepleHill.com

Printed in U.S.A.

"Your brother told me to find you."

The words fell from Callie's lips, stiff and measured and loaded with things unsaid.

Ben faced her. "What do you mean? Max sent you here?"

"That was his last sentiment." The words sounded as if forced from her lips.

"His last words were about me?" Rubbing his temples, he dragged in a deep breath.

The nod she gave was slow and painfully measured. And seemed meant to sever any further inquiry he might have.

"Tell me what this is all about, Callie. Why are you here, anyway?" His voice had risen a good notch. "Because, had I not come along when I did, you likely would've frozen to death on my doorstep. Why would you put your life at risk like that?"

When she slowly rolled away from him, he knew he'd pushed too far, too fast.

"I'm sorry. I'm just glad that you turned to me."

When he pivoted to leave the room, he could've sworn he heard her whisper, "You were my last resort."

Books by Pamela Nissen

Love Inspired Historical

Rocky Mountain Match
Rocky Mountain Redemption

PAMELA NISSEN

loves creating. Whether it's characters, cooking, scrapbooking or other artistic endeavors, she takes pleasure in putting things together for others to enjoy. She started writing her first book in 2000 and since then hasn't looked back. Pamela lives in the woods in Iowa with her husband, daughter, two sons, a Newfoundland dog and cats. She loves watching her children pursue their dreams, and is known to yell on the sidelines at her boys' football games, or cry as she watches her daughter perform. She relishes scrapbooking weekends with her sister, coffee with friends and running in the rain. Having glimpsed the dark and light of life, she is passionate about writing "real" people with "real" issues and "real" responses.

And we know that for those who love God
all things work together for good, for those
who are called according to his purpose.
—*Romans* 8:28

In loving memory of Mom

Your laughter delighted
Your generous love deeply motivated
And your courage…your courage inspired

Chapter One

Help Wanted...

Callie blinked against the wind-whipped snow that swirled in curling waves onto the small porch where she huddled. She fastened her weary gaze to the simple black and white placard, staring at those two words: *Help Wanted*.

She'd gladly snatch up the job her brother-in-law, Doctor Ben Drake, advertised in the front window of his office. He certainly wouldn't mistake her sudden appearance here for some heartwarming family connection.

Clamping her teeth against their chattering, she scanned down the road to the heart of Boulder. Only a few horses stood tethered to hitching posts, their broad, saddled backs flocked with fluffy, white snow. Apart from the welcome lantern's glow spilling from a few windows into the dark of night on this early October evening, the town seemed as if caught in a dreamy, blissful slumber.

So where in the world was Doctor Ben Drake?

She'd never even met the man and already had a mountain of bias against him. The two long days she'd spent journeying from Denver to Boulder on foot, she'd recoiled at the thought of asking Ben Drake for charity like some beggar.

The idea of another debt hanging over her head sent repulsion snaking through her veins. If she could offer her services and get paid…now that was far more appealing.

Perhaps there existed a slim thread of hope in her frayed life. A second chance. An opportunity to start over and find some peace.

Callie gave a solid knock on the door, her icy cold hand throbbing as she waited for him to answer. She gave another determined knock then, with frozen-to-numb feet, hobbled left a few paces to the long window. Cupping trembling hands around her eyes, she peered inside. But there was no sign of life, just like the hollow, dark look in her husband's eyes when he'd died in her arms six months ago.

Images she'd just as soon lay to rest swirled into her mind. Max, wracked with pain and delirium from a gunslinger's fatal shot. His inconsolable groan for help, when it was clear he was beyond help. On a ragged whisper and dying breath, he'd said, "Find my brothers. Find Ben. He'll see to you."

Even then, in the midst of Callie's frantic fight to keep Max alive, those words had stunned her as much as they did now. He'd wanted nothing to do with his brothers, so why would he drive her to their doorstep with his last breath?

Battling back the haunting memories, she peered inside the office again. No oil lamp flickered to life. Not even the weighted sound of hurried footsteps advanced this way.

Shaking and frustrated, she drew her lightweight wool cloak snug around her shoulders in a vain attempt to shield herself from the storm that barreled through the quaint mountain valley. The small, covered porch gave no protection from the sting of icy snow. The cast-off satin dress she wore from the brothel did precious little to insulate her from even the whisper of a breeze.

Even so, this didn't seem half as bad as the uncontrollable hardships of the last seven years. At least now she had some control over her future, and if she froze to death, it would be because she decided to do so.

When a harsh cough tore through her lungs, she braced her pounding head against the siding. Irritation mounted with each frosty breath in winter's threat.

"Where are you, Ben Drake?" Her words sputtered between chattering teeth.

Maybe he'd landed in some saloon, drinking and gambling away the night, just like his brother, Max.

Shivering, weak and exhausted, Callie slid down the thick clapboard. She tugged her cloak tighter and pulled in a deep, steadying breath to calm her irritation. When the bitter air hit her lungs, a spasm of wrenching coughs doubled her over, threatening to cave in her resolve.

Still, she closed her eyes and pictured herself snuggled before a warm, crackling fire. A soft groan escaped her lips as she imagined her hands cradling a steaming mug of cider—or cocoa, maybe. Nestling deeper beneath the thick luxury of a cozy quilt and sleeping till she could sleep no more.

A mean gust of wind whipped across the porch, slapping reality in her face once again. She didn't have the job yet, and until she rectified the situation that loomed like some noose before her, she was a prisoner to her past, a slave to her present and a hostage to her future.

With a stuttering sigh, she closed her eyes. She should probably be angry that Max had left her standing alone down one of life's dark dead ends, but really, she just felt numb. The irony of that sunk deep as she shivered, slipping slowly into sleep. Yes, she was definitely numb—she could barely feel her arms, her legs, or her heart.

"Ma'am?" A deep, mellow voice stirred her senses. "Are you all right?"

"Ma'am?" Ben Drake tried again, keeping his voice low.

The woman raised her head, sending a wave of relief washing over him as a stark curtain of snow lashed across the porch.

She was alive—that much was good.

When he'd arrived home just moments ago and had spotted a dark form huddled here on his office porch next door, a sick sense of dread had roiled in the pit of his stomach. The thought of someone seeking him out for help, only to die waiting for his return, would likely haunt him for the rest of his days.

"Come on…let's get you out of the cold." He scooped up her rail-thin frame.

With a grunt, she stiffened arrow straight, squirming out of his arms. When her feet met the floor with a dull thud, she sliced a sharp breath through her teeth. "Oww…"

"What's the matter?" He hunkered over to get a look at her as she sagged against the building. "Are you hurt?"

From beneath a tattered hood, the young woman peeked up at him. "My feet. They're cold as ice." The woman's unfamiliar, raspy voice hit him square in the heart.

"Well, then, let's get you inside." He made quick

work of unlocking the door. "I'm sorry I wasn't here sooner."

"Are you Doc—Doctor Drake?" Her teeth chattered.

"Yes, I'm Ben Drake." When he braced an arm at her back, she dodged it as though he meant to hog-tie her. "Have you been waiting long for me?"

"Long enough," she muttered, shuffling inside, each shivering, wobbly step piercing his heart more than the last.

She pulled her cloak tighter, but the way it puddled on the floor, hanging like a big, old drape, he wasn't quite sure how she'd managed to maneuver ten feet in such a garment.

The lingering feel of her thin, quivering frame and her wariness to his touch sent compassion thrumming through his veins, especially when she produced a harsh cough.

"That cough of yours sure doesn't sound good."

"It's nothing," she answered, her teeth chattering. "Just an everyday kind of cough, that's all."

"Well, it sounds like more than that to me. Good thing you came when you did. Follow me," he said, leading the way through the dark waiting area into the exam room where he lit a lamp. "I'll get a fire going so we can get you warmed up."

When he wrapped two warm quilts around her quivering frame, he had to hold his confusion in check when she shrugged them off as though they were some disease-ridden rags. She possessively clutched her arms around something as though he might snatch it away, and he tried not to react. This woman was mistrustful and guarded and set against a little help. She eyed him as though she'd seen his face plastered on some Wanted poster.

"Why don't you sit down here by the woodstove so you'll be close to the heat?" Gesturing to a chair, he barely contained a wince when she avoided his outstretched hand as though he meant her harm. "It shouldn't take long for the place to warm up."

She sat on the edge of the chair. Bunching her shoulders up tight, she made a valiant effort to stop shivering, but as long as she kept that thin and wet cloak on, she'd likely never warm up.

While he banked the coals and loaded fresh kindling in the stove, he stole furtive glances at her shadowed, pale face, looking for signs of bleeding. Or broken bones.

She coughed then grabbed her side, and Ben's blood ran cold through his veins. His hair prickled at the back of his neck. That she might be another unfortunate bride of some no-good excuse for a husband, who treated his wife worse than his livestock, made him push back a ready curse.

When her whole body heaved with a sudden cough, he hunkered down next to her. "Easy, now. That sure doesn't sound like an everyday kind of cough. How long have you had it?"

At her dismissive shrug, he gently laid the back of his hand against her forehead, concern mounting at the heat that his touch met. "You're fevered, too. That's not good. I hope you'll forgive me for not coming sooner."

She flicked her gaze to him, cagey as a mouse in a barren field. Edging away, she angled her focus downward, intent on unknotting tattered ties that held her cloak together by mere threads.

His heart squeezed. He had to bite back a groan

of sympathy at the sight of her shabby, wet shoes that poked out from her cloak. When she tipped her head back, nudging her hood off a mat of auburn waves, his throat grew tight.

And when she glanced up at him with the most beautiful almond-shaped blue eyes he'd ever seen, he struggled to gather his wits. She looked like an ethereal waif who'd been to the depths of darkness and back.

The glassy-eyed look veiling her gaze quickly snuffed out his fascination.

He struggled to find his voice. "I think you could use some hot tea about now."

Her focus skidded to a halt at him, her lips lifting at one corner with the faintest look of pleasure.

Ben swallowed hard, then set to work measuring out a dose of sassafras tea he kept with his medical supplies. When he set the kettle on to boil he was thankful to find heat already radiating from the woodstove.

"So, what's your name, ma'am?" Straddling a chair directly across from her, he silently tallied her respirations, unable to miss the way she breathed in shallow, raspy rhythms.

"Callie."

"Callie…" he prompted.

"Just Callie."

"I'm Ben Drake. I'm the doctor here, but then I think we already covered that." He offered her a reassuring look. It was nearly killing him to take up precious time with niceties, but as skittish as she was, he didn't want to risk having her walk out the door. "Are you from around here, *just* Callie?"

She shook her head. "No, I'm not."

"Well, how can I be of help to you? You must've come about that cough, am I right?" He dipped his head in an unsuccessful attempt to catch her attention. "How long have you had it?"

"Not long." Callie slowly rose from the chair, the dingy flour sack grasped firmly in her hand. A wince, so slight he almost missed it, crossed her face as she stood ramrod straight, her chin held high, a heartrending contrast in vulnerable fatigue and determined strength.

"So, you must be in need of a doctor?" he attempted again, inward alarm mounting at the unhealthy flush of her sunken cheeks. "You came to the right place. I'll do whatever I can to help."

Her perfectly shaped brows creased in a stern look over red-rimmed eyes. "I'm not here for medical attention. I—I want to speak with you about something of *pressing* importance."

Smoothing a hand over the day's growth of stubble on his chin, Ben bit back the sympathetic look that was close to surfacing. There was just something about her show of strength, about the way she wore bravery like a suit of armor five sizes too big that tugged at his heart.

"Well, whatever it is must be important for you to seek me out in a snowstorm like this." He resisted the urge to stand when she stared at him as though he was some wily predator. "So tell me, how can I help you?"

She coughed, and a definite wheeze threaded through the harsh sound. Turning, she shrugged her cloak off and laid it on the chair along with her sack, then faced him once again. "I'm here to offer my services to you."

Ben slammed his gaze down to the floor. Fumbled to cover his shock, but the sight of her standing before him…it was nothing short of shocking.

He braved a glance up again to see a ruby-red satin dress hanging on her thin frame, the gaudy ruffles and lace worn almost beyond repair in places. And the scoop neckline—he swallowed hard—plunged way too far down to be considered appropriate.

Ben averted his attention to the floor again. Frowned in confusion. What could this woman possibly offer him?

When he sneaked another glimpse and took in her tattered but risqué appearance, he had to steady himself as a ghastly glimmer of understanding enlightened him.

Did she mean to sell herself?

Gritting his teeth, he prepared to set her straight right here and right now. He may be a twenty-nine-year-old bachelor, but he hadn't ever, nor would he ever, resort to using a woman like that.

"I'm sorry. But I'm not interested in that kind of thing, Miss…Miss Callie." He forced himself to meet her cautious gaze as she clutched something at her neck. "If it's money you need, I'm glad to give you some. But I would never think of paying for female companionship."

Her red-rimmed eyes widened as though she'd been scandalized. "Doctor Drake, you misunderstand me." She squared her shoulders. Grasped the front of her dress, yanking it up in an awkward, unnatural angle for such a garment. "I'm here to inquire about the job. You do have a sign at your window advertising for such, am I right?"

Her bravado ended on a fit of coughing that sent him bolting to her side.

"I do." He forced his hands to remain at his sides when she instantly sidestepped. "But for the life of me, I'm trying to figure out why you'd inquire about the job this late at night. In a blizzard. And in such poor health. I am looking for help, but I think that before we discuss anything like that, we should *first* get you well."

On a wheezing breath, she slapped him with a reproving glower.

She was proud—that was for sure.

He inwardly kicked himself for saying what he had. But she'd dressed the part—though now that he thought about it, her skittish behavior and repulsion to his touch didn't correspond with a woman of that line of work.

But her dress...

"I'm here about the sign you have in your window, Doctor Drake." She nervously toyed with some trinket at her neck. "I can start working immediately, if that suits you."

"First of all," Ben began, glancing at her neck. He expected to see some worthless bit of whatnot hanging there, but when his tired gaze settled on a small silver locket, an icy chill doused his weariness. His heart ground to a stuttering stop. His breath caught.

He'd recognize that locket anywhere.

It was one of a kind. Handmade for his mother by his father who'd dabbled in jeweling throughout the years. The locket had been a priceless treasure. A gift deeded to Ben by his mother shortly before she'd passed twelve years ago.

Memories surfaced with breakneck speed, shooting up from a miry depth he'd tried to ignore all these years.

The constant run-ins he'd had with his brother, Max. The way Max would milk Ben's compassion for his own ill-reputed gain. The way Max would venture off for weeks at a time, returning with tales of some young harlot. And then that night seven years ago, when Max had come home thoroughly drunk. It had been a final, awful conflict. Max had destroyed anything he could get his hands on, furniture, dishes, relationships...

After Max had forced a lewd, unwanted kiss on Aaron's sweetheart, Max and Aaron, the fourth in a line of five Drake brothers, had gotten into a terrible fight. By morning, some of the money Ben had set aside for medical school had come up missing. Along with the heirloom locket. And Max.

A sharp stab of betrayal cut deep as he stared in disbelief. Max had stolen the locket and now here it was, hanging on the neck of some woman who was dressed for more than just baking bread.

Was this the young harlot Max had told them about? The one who'd likely lured him away for good, leading him into a sordid lifestyle of gambling and drinking?

Callie lifted her chin a notch, her slender fingers clamping around the silver locket. "The job, Doctor Drake… What about the job? I can assure you that I would be a good—"

"Where did you get that?" He took one step closer, craning his neck to get a better look. The fine, detailed filigree and etched scrolling shone even in the dim light, a testament to his father's talent.

She slid back a step. "Get what?"

"The locket." He nodded toward the object, forcing himself to remain calm.

"This locket is no concern of yours." She flattened both hands over the locket, her dress slipping down to a brazenly improper draping.

He clenched his jaw tight, furious that his dear mother's locket hung from this woman's neck.

"And it certainly has nothing to do with my being here. Like I said, I'm here about the job."

"Oh, it doesn't?" He gave a sarcastic laugh, infuriated at her bold censorship. "Funny thing, that locket. It looks just like one I once had."

"I'm afraid you're mistaken. This was a gift given to me. There's no way it could belong to you." She coughed again, glancing over her shoulder toward the door. "Now, about the Help Wanted sign."

He shifted his focus to the door, suspicion creeping up his spine, and setting his hair on end. What if Max lurked out there? Waiting for her? Maybe this was all just some ploy to make off with more money.

That possibility had Ben's blood boiling red-hot.

Resisting the urge to open the door and see for himself, Ben stepped closer to Callie. "Forget about the job for now, ma'am. *Where* did you get that locket?"

She balled her fist around the locket, inching away. "I told you, it was a gift."

He pinned her with an intense stare. "Who gave it to you?"

When her sunken eyes widened with the smallest hint of fear, a subtle sting of remorse pricked his conscience. He'd never spoken like this to a woman—ever. Even if she was a conniving thief sent by Max, she was a thin, sickly, delicately beautiful one, and he could've gone a little easier on her.

She drew her lips into a silent, grim line.

"My mother gave me that locket twelve years ago," he said evenly, determined to remain controlled. "On her deathbed."

Her fine features creased in a frown.

"The last time I saw it was just before my brother Max took off with some harlot over seven years ago. Do you know Max? Is he out there now?" he probed with a brisk nod toward the door.

Callie opened her hands. Slammed her gaze down to the silver locket, and for a split second he thought he saw her perfectly shaped lips quiver.

That worked the slightest bit of unwanted softening in his heart. He'd rather disregard the vulnerability he saw there, but try as he might, he couldn't banish the pathetic image of this woman huddled on his porch. Clad in nothing more than dirty rags. Doomed to freeze to death had he not come along.

"Let me put it this way." He took a step back and held his hand out. "That rightfully belongs to me."

Panic shuttered her eyes. "But I—"

She blinked with deliberate concentration, once, twice, her face paling as white as the stark snow whipping through the valley. She sidestepped. Teetered like some piece of fine china hanging over the edge of a high shelf.

When her eyes began a slow roll back, Ben lunged forward, catching up her light frame just before she hit the floor.

Callie draped limp in his arms, her hand slowly slipping from the locket and flopping down toward the floor. From the way her body burned with fever, she'd be here for a while. And despite her interest in the Help Wanted sign, he was positive that she hadn't come here for a job.

Chapter Two

Callie struggled to force open her heavy eyelids. She stared through a fuzzy haze up at the ceiling. Pain pounded her head. Her eyes burned, but still she inched her gaze around the room, trying to remember where she was.

Bits and pieces came to her… Trudging through the snowstorm, huddled and waiting on a porch. Strong, capable arms holding her…

A strangely familiar man, tall and dark-haired, came into focus next to her.

She shot up in bed. Regretted it instantly when her head spun and her stomach roiled.

"Whoa there, miss." Ben eased her shoulders back to the feather mattress. "Not so fast."

"I need to get up." She weakly wriggled from his unsettling touch.

Sighing, he crossed his arms at his chest. "I would strongly advise against doing anything of the sort. You're in no condition."

When she looked up at him, the world spun out of control. She closed her eyes and hoped he wasn't obser- vant enough to notice her condition, because the absolute *last* thing she wanted was to look feeble and needy in front of this man.

"Seeing as how I'm not your patient, I believe that I'm more than capable of making my own decisions." She pulled her chin up a notch, wincing at the thin, raspy sound of her voice.

"Like it or not, you're my patient now."

Averting her focus from his steel-blue gaze, she recalled fainting. And just before that, she'd been arguing with this man over—

"My locket! Where is it?" Dragging herself up to her elbows, she scanned the room. "And my box! Where did you put my things?"

When she spotted her box snuggled in the old flour sack atop the bureau, she tried to quell the frantic beat of her heart. But the idea that this man could've taken the few possessions she had left in this world seized her heart with utter, unexplainable panic.

At the cool touch of silver against her chest, she discovered the locket was where it had always been and dropped back to the pillow.

"You see." Ben drew his mouth into a grim line. "The locket's still there. Around your neck."

Peering down at her chest just to make sure, she screeched. "My dress!" She jerked the quilt clear up to her chin, being clad in nothing more than her paper-thin chemise and threadbare drawers. "Did you—"

A violent cough had her bracing herself, but she still managed to glower at him. "You undressed me without my consent? How dare you!"

His steady gaze didn't flicker an ounce. "Your dress was soaking wet, ma'am, and the weather prohibited me from summoning my sister-in-law's help as I usually would have."

"But still, I—"

"You're not the first woman I've tended to and you won't be the last. It was in your best interest that I get you as warm and dry as possible. And I can assure you that I honored your modesty in every possible way." He emphasized the last three words, his low, rich voice reverberating right through the layered quilts and chemise, to her bare skin.

Huddling tight beneath the covers, Callie turned and stared at the fresh cream-colored wall. A wash of shame spread through her like some dread disease. She hated reducing herself to this kind of ungrateful behavior, but she didn't even know this man.

Max, though no saint himself, had never spoken one kind thing about his family—especially Ben. Callie didn't have a single reason to like him. After all, Max's bitter edge surely didn't exist simply because of some innocent family sparring. He'd had a long list of reasons that fed his loathing.

She grasped the locket, recalling Ben's adamant claim that it belonged to him. Apparently this was one of those situations that Max had referred to...when his brothers would edge him out of something for their own gain. She'd like to give Ben a dressing-down about that, but since she had nowhere else to turn, and desperately needed the job, she decided to go for a more mild-mannered approach.

Plastering on an awkward smile, Callie attempted a pleasant look. But it felt so odd and she was pretty sure her expression didn't come off pleasant at all.

The sting of his words—that Max had married some harlot—came racing back, barging into her mind and producing instant outrage.

A harlot?

The very reason she'd come crawling to Boulder had been to avoid becoming just that—a harlot. She'd had nothing else to wear, but the cast-off dress Lyle Whiteside had thrown in her direction six months ago when she'd started working as a housekeeper at the brothel. He'd burned her other dress, saying that he didn't want some lowly-looking scullery maid walking his halls, scaring off the paying customers.

Callie could almost feel her eyes darken with indignation. "It seems there's some confusion about this locket," she tried to say sweetly, but failed miserably.

He quirked one dark eyebrow. "There's no confusion as far as I'm concerned."

She stifled a ragged cough, her ire kicked up a notch at the sight of his steady, grating calm. Regardless of the fact that she needed this job, she nailed him with the most threatening glare she could muster. Held his penetrating gaze for a lengthy moment.

The man was wily, of that she had no doubt. Probably as clever and intimidating as the oldest, meanest wolf living in the Flatirons.

"Look, let me make this easy for you." He crossed his arms at his broad chest. "I can prove the locket belongs to me."

"How?"

"There's an engraving on the inside."

Prickly heat crept up her neck. Her pulse slammed in her ears as she grasped frantically for some argument. "How do I know you didn't inspect the locket while you were—while I was unconscious and you *undressed* me?"

"You don't, I guess," he managed with an insignificant shrug.

"Exactly." She swiped at a wayward, fever-induced

tear rolling from the corner of her eye. "How do I know what went on then, Doctor Drake? I mean, having been dead to the world as I was, I would've been none the wiser had you sniffed and pawed through my things."

She grappled for control, but, horrifically, felt it slipping through her hands.

"The engraving says *All for Love*." The oddly tight and low sound of his voice arrested her attention. "It was something my father used to say to my mother."

Swerving her focus to the ceiling, a memory staggered into her mind. Shortly after she'd met Max, he'd given her the locket as a pledge of his love. She remembered the gloriously heady feeling she'd had as she'd stared at the romantic engraving.

She'd loved Max.

Even in the darkest hours of their seven-year marriage, she'd loved him. She'd held out hope that he'd change, and return to the wonderfully adventurous Maxwell Drake she'd fallen in love with. Before bitterness ruled his moods. Before he'd taken to gambling, drinking and the other things that followed.

Hot tears pooled in her eyes. She could only hope that they would pass off for a fevered symptom instead of betrayal's bitter sting.

She'd been deceived. Again.

She could stubbornly stand her ground regarding the locket, but even as a lame argument began forming in her mind, she felt her feeble case sinking beneath unsteady footing. She'd love to believe that this was all just some innocent mistake, but she knew she'd stumbled onto another one of Max's lies, and for some reason the discovery wasn't any easier than the last time.

Or the time before that.

Or before that.

Disgust knotted her stomach tight. Just moments ago the locket had hung as a precious symbol of first love. Now it burned with dishonesty's harsh reality against her skin. It took every bit of poise she possessed to resist the unrefined urge to rip it off.

The sound of Ben dragging a chair across the room jerked her from her thoughts.

He sat beside her bed, looking almost as tired as she felt. On a yawn, he dragged a hand over his face. "We can talk about this another time, Callie. You need to rest."

The concern filled way he responded tugged at her heart. It could easily be her undoing if she let it. But she wouldn't. Couldn't.

He definitely was not safe. He had a way of getting to her that was nothing short of a threat to her strong resolve.

When a deep cough tore through her throat, she winced at the merciless pain. Squeezing her eyes shut, she drew quivering hands to her neck, scrambling for a foothold with this bothersome sickness.

And this man.

Before she knew it, Ben had his strong arm wedged behind her shoulders as he held a glass to her parched lips. "Here, try to drink some water."

As much as she didn't want his help, she just didn't have the strength to spurn his gesture. Especially as the cool moisture touched her lips and slid down her throat.

"There you go. That's the way," he soothed, settling her against the pillow again. "Better?"

She nodded, feeling a small bit of relief. Blinking hard, she avoided Ben's penetrating gaze and instead lugged her focus to the gleaming dark hair that dangled loosely over his brow.

He scooped up her wrist and monitored her pulse. Though his eyes were watchful, his touch was gentle and respectful, even kind.

Uncomfortable with his attention, she struggled to push herself up again. If she set her mind to it, she could make herself get out of this bed.

With a slow shake of his head, Ben eased her back to the mattress. "Would you *please* just lie still? You have no business getting out of bed."

He smoothed a lock of hair from her face, the simple gesture bringing her a foreign sense of comfort.

Sighing, he gently tucked her arm beneath the thick layer of quilts. "It's three in the morning and the snow's coming down harder than ever. And you are very, very sick. If you have plans to move on in the middle of this blizzard, you might as well walk out there and dig your grave in the nearest snowbank," he added, biting off a yawn. "Though, frankly, I think you're too stubborn to die."

"I can't be sick." Squeezing her eyes shut, she felt stuck. Trapped. Dratted sickness! Why'd she have to fall ill now, of all times? "I have to work. The job. Is the job filled yet?"

He gave a tired chuckle. "If you mean, has someone else ventured over here tonight in the middle of a heavy snowfall to interview for this job…" He furrowed his brow as if trying to recall. "No."

"So does that mean you're hiring me?"

"Tell you what, Callie…" The tired droop of his eyes almost made her feel sorry for him. "We'll talk about the job when you're feeling better. All right?"

"I'm feeling fine now. Really," she rasped, her voice catching on a cough that wrenched her entire body.

The calming weight of his hand on her arm sent a small, soothing rush through her.

"I'm not sick," she argued, noticing the rugged, masculine scruff of dark beard growth on his face. "It's nothing. Just a bad cough."

After a long, unreadable look, he stood and walked over to the window. He parted the lace curtains that bracketed the cloudy, paned glass and leaned his arms against the frame. "A bad cough *and* a fever that'll be the death of you, if you don't get adequate rest. I'll repeat it again…you're in no condition to get out of bed."

Callie stared at his broad, strong back, then she sliced a glance to her dress on the bureau, an unwanted prickle of sensitivity working through her. In spite of the way he felt about her dress, he'd folded it. Neatly.

She tried to brush the feeling aside. Within a year of marrying Max she'd learned that she was better off not expecting anything in the way of care or loving concern. She'd buried her needs and feelings right along with her dreams. Couldn't allow things, good or bad, to affect her. She would've never managed the past seven years, otherwise.

She blinked hard. She had to get better soon or Ben might hire someone else, since he certainly hadn't made any move to hire her. Yet.

Had she any other option when she was back in Denver, she would've taken it, but given Max's history, she had little chance of getting a decent, wage-earning job. When she'd married Max, any bridge to her father's good graces had been burned. Even the church had turned away from her when she'd inquired about a position in the orphanage. Though she'd never once partaken in Max's sordid hobbies, she supposed that in their eyes she was guilty by association. She was the shunned widow of a *sinner*.

And for all she knew, God must look at her that way, too. Because since she'd disobeyed her father and married Max seven years ago, her life had been one hardship after another.

Coming to Boulder had been out of necessity alone. Without a job, she'd have no money and no hope to escape what awaited her back in Denver if she didn't pay up.

Max had barely been cold in the ground when Lyle Whiteside had come knocking on Callie's door, hanging the significant gambling debt like a noose before her. Since then she'd been working feverishly to pay it off by cleaning his saloon and brothel, but the payback hadn't been fast enough to suit him. Three days ago he'd stared her down with those snapping black eyes of his, demanding that she pay off the rest upstairs on her back.

He'd vowed to be her first customer.

She could not—*would not*—slide her neck into that rope and drop to that low a level, no matter how desperate the situation. No matter how risky it was to run out on such a powerful man.

"I'll be up and moving by tomorrow." Her hoarse voice barely sounded. "I'll make sure to compensate you for your doctoring. And room and board."

He came to stand next to the bed, peering down at her with a certain compassion that had her averting her gaze. "If it's money that has you concerned, don't worry about that right now. It'll all work out. I won't charge you a thing."

No matter how destitute she and Max had been over the years, she'd never taken charity.

Callie gripped the bedsheets when another deep, brutal cough commanded her strength. Maybe she was flirting with death to even think about getting out of this bed. The way her head and body ached, she couldn't imagine walking twenty feet.

"I have nothing to pay you with." She set her jaw. "But I don't—won't—take charity. You can just subtract what I owe you from my wages."

"Your wages?" he echoed on a bemused chuckle.

"Yes, my wages."

When she absently set a hand to the locket, she caught herself, suddenly wishing that she'd never been given the gift.

She lifted her head from the pillow and fumbled for the clasp. If it belonged to Ben Drake, then she'd promptly return it because the lovely piece of jewelry had obviously never belonged to her. Or Max.

His brow furrowed. "What are you doing?"

"I'm giving this back." She steadied her fingers enough to undo the clasp. "Like you said, it belongs to you."

His hands lightly grasped hers, stilling them, his face a mask of confusion. "No. Please, don't take it off, Callie."

She couldn't move, couldn't look at him. Inside she was in an all-out war for control. She was deeply hurt, betrayed by Max, though he was six months gone. And Ben wore self-assured confidence like some fine evening coat fitted to a T. Yet he showed concern and compassion.

"It's not mine," she declared, weeding out any sign of self-pity from her voice. "It never was and I—"

Her words died on another violent fit of coughing that paled all others. It wrenched her chest, her shoulders, her head. Every muscle convulsed.

She was barely aware as Ben slipped an arm behind her shoulders. She felt his strong arms cradle her as he whispered soothing words while she fought to gain her breath. When he pulled her closer to himself and wedged another pillow behind her head, his warmth seeped into her. And much needed relief slowly settled over her as he lowered her to the pillow.

"That really didn't sound good." Ben hunkered down to eye level with her. "At all. I'm very concerned."

"I'll be fine," she rasped, with painful effort.

She wasn't sure if her throat felt like it was closing up because of her cough and sore throat or the emotion his tender care evoked. For the first time in a long time, she might be experiencing what it was like to have someone care about what happened to her. To care for her.

But how could that be? Max had done nothing but speak ill of his brothers—especially Ben.

She pushed away from Ben, thinking about how Max must've been wronged and how things could've been so different if only…

The bitter sense of betrayal and pain and unfulfilled dreams stripped her bare. There was no way to change the past, but she could be unwavering in her quest to carve out a future of her own making.

After she'd paid off the debt.

Her eyelids drooped heavily, blatant fatigue demanding every bit of her attention. She could barely hold a coherent thought, but as she drifted closer to the blessed brink of sleep, Ben's face flashed in her mind.

He deserved the truth about his brother. Especially

if she was going to be working for him. It was only right.

Forcing her eyes open, she yawned. Coughed. "I need to tell you something if I'm going to be working for you," she managed, her words sounding far away, though Ben's presence felt almost as near as her next, ragged breath.

He leaned in just a bit closer.

"That woman Max ran off with…that was me. I'm your brother's wife." She gripped the sheet as she worked down another painful swallow. "I was married to Max."

Ben's strikingly handsome features creased in a disturbing wash of pain and anger. "Was? What do you mean, *was?*"

She quickly stuffed down the raw emotion. "Max was shot in an alley for double-dealing. He died six months ago."

Chapter Three

The news of Max's death echoed in Ben's head like a gunshot in a deep mountain canyon. He'd not heard one thing. Not one thing.

When Callie had uttered the words a few hours ago, his emotions had warred between deep anger and grief. The death was an utter waste of a life so young.

And a mark of shame for Ben.

If he'd been able to turn his brother around, Max might still be here.

Ben let out a stuttering, remorse-filled sigh. He hadn't realized he'd been holding his breath, and tried to relax his tight muscles, calm his beating heart, but it seemed useless. His entire being had been drawn into a knot of unrest and regret in hearing the news.

He would've questioned her further had she not drifted off to sleep. He wanted some proof of marriage or of Max's death, but the longer he sat here staring at her—his brother's widow, a young woman whose brow even now furrowed in pain—the more he questioned his need for evidence.

He didn't know one thing about Callie. Had no reason

to trust her. Still, she didn't strike him as someone who'd lie about something so severe.

Ben had a volume full of unanswered questions regarding his wayward sibling. Twice as many misgivings. If he could learn even a little about what had transpired in the past seven years, then maybe, just maybe, Ben could put to rest the painful remorse.

He doubted he'd ever find peace about certain things, though. With Max dead, there were some bitter words Ben had said that could never be taken back: that Max was good-for-nothing, a stain to the Drake family name and the worst of scoundrels. Sitting on this solitary side of things, he had no idea what kind of damage the last words he'd said to Max could've done.

The shameful memory pierced Ben like buckshot, shredding his already shaky confidence. In the past six months his assurance in his work as a doctor, and his trust in God, had been dealt some rough blows.

First, he'd been unable to help his brother Joseph after an accident that left him blind. Ben had doctored him to the point that Joseph demanded to be left alone. The sleepless nights Ben had spent worrying, praying, and reading anything that might be a key to Joseph regaining his sight had been to no end.

He swallowed a thick knot of guilt. The inability to produce a winning outcome did something to a man who was supposed to be an instrument of healing in God's hands.

Then his brother Aaron had been dealt a double blow when his newborn baby and his wife died within a day of each other. Complications of childbirth. Ben had done everything he knew to change the course, but it hadn't been enough.

And now this.

Surely, had he done things differently with Max, spoken some sense into him, things would've turned out differently.

He blinked hard as he stared at Callie, asleep and burrowed in a thick cloud of blankets and pillows. The frown that had creased her brow had smoothed out to reveal a feminine softness. And the stern, unrelenting purse of her lips had relaxed to render a full pout that made his mouth tip in an unprovoked, tired grin.

For a petite little thing, no more than five feet, two inches tall, she'd put up quite a fight. The bold determination he'd seen in her eyes and stubborn set to her jaw belied her small stature.

She'd felt alarmingly thin in his arms when he'd cradled her limp body and settled her in bed last night. He'd removed her cold, damp dress, its tattered hem caked with snow, to make her more comfortable. But her lightweight undergarments did nothing to conceal the fact that this woman probably hadn't seen a decent meal in a very long time. And they did nothing to hide her undeniable, womanly curves.

Forcing his thoughts elsewhere, he snapped open his pocket watch, flicking a glance at the hour. It was already nine o'clock in the morning, and though he'd dozed a time or two in the chair beside her bed, Callie's ragged breathing and rattled cough had kept him on the alert.

While he switched out the warm oil of camphor–soaked compress at her chest, he realized that as much as he didn't trust her, he felt drawn to this young woman. Wanted to make sure she received the best care he could provide.

Bracing his forearms on his legs, he monitored her breathing, watching her chest rise and fall in small breaths. All the while wondering what he was going to do with her once she was well. If he didn't give her the job would she hightail it out of Boulder?

It was painfully apparent that she needed help.

And it was no secret that he desperately needed an assistant. But was he willing to hire a young woman he had a deep interwoven history with, yet, until a few hours ago, had never even met?

Ben quietly crossed to the bedroom's lace-draped window and peered outside through the cloudy panes. The snow had finally tapered off to a light dusting of flurries that glistened like tiny diamond chips in the morning sun. He squinted against the stark brightness, his eyelids drooping over his eyes, weighted by fatigue and by the bright glare spilling into the room.

Kneading his forehead, his thoughts strayed to the past seven years. They'd tracked Max down several times, finding him in saloons, slouched at gaming tables like some permanent fixture. Though Ben had never met Callie—didn't even know her name—Max had lamented about how he'd needed to play the tables to keep his demanding little woman clothed in finery and frills.

Turning to glimpse the bleak condition of her ragged dress and threadbare cloak, he couldn't imagine that anything of the sort had been true.

Remorse regarding Max hovered over him like a coffin lid suspended, just inches from closing. He'd done his best to set Max's feet on the straight and narrow, but Max had given the term *maverick* a whole new meaning, dodging responsibility at every turn, thumbing his nose at right living and common sense, and bucking hard against anyone who tried to bridle him. He was nothing like the rest of the Drake boys, and for that Ben felt a guilt-laden weight of responsibility.

Ben had promised his folks before they passed on that he'd see to his brothers. Make sure they turned out to be the fine, upstanding men his parents had intended.

Moving over to the bed, he refreshed the compress at Callie's chest, praying that it would ease her deep cough.

When she stirred then dragged in a ragged breath in her sleep, he was grateful to see that it didn't catch on another cough. With attentive medical care, she might just be all right. The idea of any other outcome made his throat go instantly tight. There was something vulnerable hidden behind the inflexible front she'd worn that begged for release, and he couldn't ignore the strange desire he felt to be her liberator.

"You're going to do what?" Aaron protested, his voice likely cutting through the closed door to where he'd just peeked in at Callie.

"Keep your voice down." Ben shot his brother a glower of warning then tugged him farther into the waiting area. "I said, I'm thinking about giving her a job as a cook and housekeeper."

He glanced at the second-oldest brother, Joseph, whose brow creased in an unmistakable, disagreeing frown over his sightless eyes.

His brothers' forthright responses contrasted dramatically with the quiet, solemn grief they'd shown an hour ago when'd he'd broken the news of Max's death. There were plenty of regrets to be had regarding Max. The tension-filled years preceding his disappearance. The betrayal prompting his leaving. And the futile times when Ben and Joseph had tried to coax Max home.

All the years growing up hadn't been that way, however. There'd been good times, when all five of them had roamed the backyard on stick horses, as though the ground yawned like some wide-open range. When they'd worked together with their father to build houses for the steady stream of settlers moving West. When they'd hunkered down in eager anticipation of Christmas morning.

Those fond memories made it almost impossible to imagine Max dead. With nothing of his brother's life left to redeem, Ben was left feeling helpless.

"A cook and housekeeper?" Aaron's eyes widened.

"You want me to throw her out?" Ben queried, irritated.

Aaron splayed his hands in an it's-not-my-problem kind of gesture. "It's your call, but the whole thing sounds fishy to me. I mean, her showing up here in the middle of the worst October snowstorm I can remember, and then asking for a job? There's gotta be a good reason for that kind of behavior. If that's not fishy, I don't know what is."

"What other information did you get out of her, anyway?" Joseph inquired.

"Not much. She isn't very talkative." Ben's admission rankled a little, especially as he remembered how stubborn and evasive she'd been. "She's pretty sick. In fact, we need to make this brief so I can get back in there to see to her."

"If it were me, I wouldn't trust her as far as I could throw her." Aaron's sure look altered to an instant frown. "Well, maybe not, seeing as how she's such a tiny thing." He nudged Joseph's arm and whispered conspiratorially. "As small as she is, Joe-boy, a fella could fit her into his coat pocket."

Relishing descriptions, however lame, Joseph grinned at Aaron's remark.

"You're all talk, Aaron," Ben dismissed. "You couldn't turn your back on her either, and you know it."

"So, what if you're wrong about her?" Aaron folded his arms at his chest. "If I were you, I'd get that locket from her before she takes off with it."

"She already tried to give it back to me."

"Well, then…" Aaron held out his hand. "Why don't you have it?"

Ben met his disbelieving gaze. "I didn't have the heart."

"Oh, for the love of—"

"Go easy, Aaron," Joseph cautioned. "You never know how hard something is until you walk it yourself."

"I'm not arguing that. It's just that Max pulled the wool over Ben's eyes more than once," Aaron responded then turned to Ben. "And I think we all know that he left because of this woman."

With a tentative shake of his head, Ben raked a hand through his hair. "That might be what he said, but how do we know it's true? How can you judge her, if you haven't met her?"

"Facts are facts, Ben. And it was as clear as a mountain stream that Max got in with the wrong crowd," Aaron bit off, his jaw tensing. "He always was wild on the vine. I just never thought he'd go so far as to steal from his own kin then walk away without ever looking back. If you ask me, I'd say that little lady in there had to have played a part."

Ben peered down at the box Callie had brought. He hadn't wanted to take it from her room, and sure wasn't about to look inside at the contents, but he had to know if it was the box Joseph had made for Max years ago. That would be just another point of proof in her favor. "I know it doesn't make sense. And I can't say as I trust her, but—"

"I'd be disappointed if you did." Aaron snorted. "I wouldn't put it past some young, sickly thing sent by Max, to try and con you out of money."

Joseph shifted his long cane from one hand to the other. "Knowing how hard it was for you to come to grips with the way Max took advantage of you, I'm not sure why you'd want to take that risk again."

"I'll admit, I've been wrong a time or two." Aaron took the box from Ben. "But the lady came here with this one box and the locket. Lord knows she could be lying through her teeth about being married to Max— even about him dying."

"Why would she lie about something like that?" Ben asked.

"I don't know. Why would Max steal from his own brothers? And, when he was sloppy drunk and barely able to stand, kiss my girl?" Aaron's jaw ticked. "People with no conscience do the unthinkable."

"Just take some time to think this over." Joseph grasped Ben's shoulder. "Don't make any rash decisions."

"Why you'd want her workin' for you, I'll never know." Aaron scuffed over to a rounded-back chair and plopped down.

"Believe me, I wondered the same thing, too—when I saw the locket, anyway." Ben sank into a chair next to Aaron. "I don't have a single, solid reason why I'd say this, but I think she's telling the truth."

"And *I* think you're gettin' all thick in the head."

Aaron placed the box in Joseph's hand after Joseph sat down.

"You're a bleeding heart, Ben. Always have been." Securing his cane on the floor next to the chair, Joseph traced his fingertips over the walnut box. "It's been ten years since I made this for Max, and it's just as I remember."

"It's beautiful," Ben commented, impressed by his brother's talent. Even now, with his sight gone, he did flawless work. "You were good back then, and you're even better now."

"Taught him everything he knows." Aaron gave a self-satisfied wink.

Half grinning, Joseph shook his head and sighed. "That joke is getting old, Aaron. We've heard it…I don't know…what would you say, Ben, *hundreds* of times?"

"At least," he answered with a chuckle.

"Maybe try it out on someone new next time." Joseph's eyes grew wide with exasperation.

"You know I only say it to convince myself."

"That's better. Best to remember your place." With a wink, Joseph took in the detailed carving with his fingertips.

"It looks to be in good condition." Ben angled his head to examine the box again.

Aaron rose and scuffed over to the doorway leading from the front waiting area. He peered down the hallway to where Callie slept. "You better make sure you keep a close eye on her. You never know what she might steal."

The words stuck like a prickly burr, and had Ben narrowing his gaze at his brother, yet again. No matter that the callous comment could be true, it didn't diminish the sudden, unexplained need to come to Callie's defense.

Joseph set the box on the end table. "You're compassionate to a fault. Whether it's a stray animal or someone down on their luck, you'll take most anything in and not think a thing about it if you get bit in the process."

Ben couldn't deny Joseph's words. Puffing out his cheeks on a sigh, he pictured the most recent strays that now shared his home.

"Yeah," Aaron agreed. "Take those two starving kittens that showed up in your barn last summer. I sure wouldn't have wanted to get my hands close to them when they ate. The way they protected their food with those little, needlelike claws..." He demonstrated with an amusing amount of drama that had Ben chuckling. "And remember those pathetic, warning growls they'd make even while they chewed?"

"How could I forget? But now they're a good, healthy weight." With gleaming black and white fur, full bellies and a lackadaisical demeanor that made Ben wonder if he'd spoiled them to the point of incompetence.

"I realize I'm taking a chance here, but I'm not going to take the locket from Callie. I just can't do that to her." Somewhere deep inside his heart, his words rang true. "And, as far as the job goes, she's not going to take no for an answer. She obviously needs the money."

Goaded by the lackluster vote of confidence in the stoic expressions on their faces, he raked his fingers through his hair, trying to see their side of things. They'd all four been betrayed by Max. Even so, there'd been a hope that existed among Joseph, Aaron, Zach and Ben that Max would come to his senses someday. That he'd return home to the family.

The idea that Max lay cold in some unmarked grave made Ben's chest tighten with ready sorrow. How had he failed so miserably? It should've been different. He should've been able to turn Max around and get him to see reason.

When he thought of his brother's widow lying in the other room, her weakened body racked with fever and sickness, his heart wobbled off-beat. There had to be more to her than met the eye. And he wanted to be the one to uncover it.

"I think if you had the opportunity to talk to Callie, you'd see why I couldn't just turn her out in the storm."

"Maybe," Aaron conceded. "But why you feel like you have to go and give her a job, room and board, when it's pretty obvious she's trying to pull a fast one, is beyond me."

"Keep your voice down." Ben sliced another reproving look to Aaron and moved to stand next to him. "She won't take a handout. She insists on paying me back for her care, and I'm inclined to believe that she means it. You both know that I could use help around here. One good look at this place proves that."

"I don't know...it all looks fine to me." Joseph quipped good-naturedly, stepping toward them. He turned his head as though taking in the full measure of the place.

"This from a blind man." Aaron rolled his eyes, clapping Joseph's arm. "Inspect things with those sensitive fingertips of yours, and I think you will change your tune."

Ben chuckled softly. "I'm not arguing. We all know that I didn't inherit the 'neat and tidy' ways in the family like you, Joseph."

"At least you're right on that account." Aaron quirked an eyebrow.

"Listen, I know how much guilt you carry over Max

leaving the way he did." Joseph sighed, setting his focus dead center on Ben. "We all feel responsible in one way or the other, but we tried to get him to come back. Even doled out more money for him when it was obvious he'd been a fool and spent all of his inheritance."

Aaron slid his hands into his pockets. "Pulling this little lady into things when we don't know her from a stranger could be barkin' up the wrong tree."

Ben glanced over to the front window where the town slowly dug out from the foot and a half of snow that had fallen last night. In spite of the impeding snow that made movement outside difficult, at best, his brothers had been on his doorstep at ten o'clock this morning, checking to make sure he'd returned safely from his calls last night. The youngest, Zach, likely would've been here, too, but he was probably buried knee-deep in chores on the cattle ranch where he worked as foreman.

Ben valued the close relationship he had with his brothers. They looked out for each other, picked up slack when one was down. And they all felt a profound hole where Max had been.

His jaw ticked with edginess. "Max aside, Callie is obviously in need of a little help, and I'm going to do what I can for her."

He remembered, with a sense of shame, the panic in her eyes last night when he had as much as accused her of stealing the locket. "You're right, though. She could easily be some fast-talking thief who knows an easy target when she sees one. And if that's the case, I'll do my best not to get taken, but until I find out more, she's staying right here."

Chapter Four

"That is the *longest* uninterrupted stretch of sleep I've ever seen," came the soothing, cellolike timbre of Ben Drake's voice.

"What time is it, anyway?" Indulging herself in the heady, restful feeling, she stretched beneath the warm covers. She edged a sleep-fuzzed gaze over to see him leaning against the wall, one booted foot draped over the other and his arms crossed in a relaxed fashion at his chest.

The merest whisper of awareness quivered down her spine.

"Eight o'clock."

When he moved over to the bed, she focused on the way the sunlight danced about the room. "Hmm...the way I feel, I would've thought—"

"Friday. You've been asleep for over a day, straight."

Horrified, Callie slammed her eyes shut.

"Catching up, are you?"

She'd had no intention of languishing for so long. This would only delay her in getting the job. Ben could've hired someone else, for all she knew. She had to have this job so she could pay off the rest of Max's debt—before Whiteside came looking for her.

She glanced up at Ben, trying not to notice his fresh-shaven, squared jaw and the half grin tipping his lips.

And the rebellious trip of her heart.

She gave her head a hearty shake. "I apologize that I've taken up—"

"No apologies are necessary." He settled a warm hand against her brow. "How are you feeling? You look much improved from the night before last when you showed up here."

"I feel fine." Folding back the covers, she hauled her legs over the edge of the bed and sat up.

"Hold on, there. Not so fast." He braced a hand at her back and hunkered down, eye level. "You may feel better, but you're probably weaker than a newborn colt."

"I'm just fine. And I don't need your help." The sound of her own pulse surged like breaking waves through her head. Dizzy, she clutched the quilt to her chest and feebly pushed herself up to standing. She teetered, struggling for balance. "Better than ever."

Her knees buckled and she started to fall, but his strong arms caught behind her with disarming comfort.

"Well, I'll give you this much, your stubbornness hasn't weakened one bit." He lifted her into bed, his muscle-roped arms searing straight through her thin undergarments like a warm, mesmerizing flame.

She drew in a slow, pulse-calming breath.

"You must've grown up with a passel of brothers to stand your ground with, right?"

"Wrong."

"Then what?" His eyes sparkled. "Let me guess, the middle child in a houseful of girls?"

"Wrong again," she shot back, noticing, for the first time, a picture hanging on the wall next to the bed. Her gaze moved slowly over the photograph.

The image captured five boys, all neatly tucked in and trimmed for a moment in time. She stared at the hopeful faces. She recognized Ben, standing like some sturdy pillar, his dark hair dangling over his brow even as it did now.

"That's a picture of me and my brothers. I was thirteen, there." He pointed to the middle boy in the frame, his long arms draped around his brothers.

She shifted her gaze from the image to Ben then back again, remembering how Max used to say that Ben had been so controlling. That he'd been harsh and demanding, squashing fun and taking his role as the oldest way too seriously.

"And this is Joseph, Aaron, Zach…" He pointed to each face then stopped at the boy to the far right. "And here's Max. He was nine at the time."

She swallowed hard, seeing a much younger and far more innocent Max. "That spark of adventure was in his eyes even at that age."

"That's for sure. He was always off doing something or other. It was hard to keep tabs on him," he said, his voice low and tight.

She found it hard to disagree. Max would often be gone for days at a time, never disclosing his whereabouts when he left or returned.

Studying his image again, she noted the way he stood straight and tall, almost out of Ben's reach. He leaned away from his brothers, his arms folded stubbornly at his chest, while the other boys seemed to take comfort in Ben's arms.

Tucking the covers under her chin, Ben sat down on the chair next to the bed and sighed. "So, did you have siblings?"

She picked at an errant thread on the quilt. "I was the only child born to my parents."

"Spoiled, then, huh?"

She met his lighthearted gaze. "My upbringing was one of privilege, but little freedom to enjoy it. My mother died when I was five, and after that my father changed. Dramatically so," she admitted, even still missing the happy, carefree way of life before Mama had died and her father exacted a strict existence for her.

Ben gave a slight nod. "I'm sorry to hear that, Callie. That must've been difficult."

Swallowing back the familiar grief, she remembered just how difficult it'd been. To once delight in her father's love and care, only to have it replaced with a gruff demeanor and emotional distance. Her father's heart had been broken, of that she was certain. She'd often wondered if he'd been so fearful of losing her, too, that he'd hemmed her in so tight with his principles and rules that nothing ill could befall her.

Only she'd been desperate to escape the confines of her father's grief and frustration, and found ways around his stringent demands.

That's when she'd met Max and had fallen in love.

The man had fairly swept her off her feet from the moment their gazes connected. He was handsome, witty and—glancing at the picture again—had a spirit of adventure that had been like honey to a bee for her. With the elegant brushstroke of words, Max had painted pictures of places that had her yearning to break free from the colorless canvas defining her life.

The moment her father had discovered she'd been stealing away to be with Max, he forbade her to see Max, drawing a hard, dark line of demarcation.

She'd dared to cross it.

It didn't take long after they'd married for her to learn that Max's charm and wit went as far as the door to their house. Inside their private life there had lived a man who seemed as different as night was to day.

The guilt she carried from the way she'd left home had been nearly unbearable at times. It was as if her choices had set into motion a lifetime of sorrow.

Ben cupped her chin and urged her focus toward him with a tenderness that loosed a shiver of comfort straight through her. "Do you think you feel up to a hot meal?"

Her stomach growled as if on cue.

"Say no more." On a pulse-skittering wink, he crossed to a small table where he poured a glass of water. "You need to get your strength back so you'll be ready for what's ahead."

She frowned in confusion. "What do you mean?"

"The job…" He stood over her.

She gave an almost imperceptible nod, her heart thudding against her ribs. He was giving her the job? As thrilled as she felt, she masked the excitement. "So you finally came to your senses?"

His low chuckle warmed the room. "Let's see…that wasn't exactly how I was looking at it, but yes. I finally came to my senses."

Callie eyed him as he leaned down next to her. He supported her shoulders with one arm as he helped her to drink. When he gently laid her against the pillow again, she savored the residue of cool moisture by licking her lips.

His gaze fell to her mouth and lingered for a long, tenuous moment before he turned away as though embarrassed.

She barely noticed, though, since she was already calculating how long she'd have to work to pay him back for her care. "I'll work off my bill first. For the doctor services you've rendered."

"Consider it a benefit that comes with the job."

"Absolutely not. I told you before that I wouldn't take charity. And I mean it."

"Hmm…I don't remember saying anything about charity. I need a cook and a housekeeper, if you haven't already noticed." He swiped his index finger over the glass window panes, leaving a telltale mark. "Maybe even help with some medical calls. So, when you're well, I'll be expecting you to work for me. That is, if you think you can handle that kind of labor." He pivoted to face her, his challenging yet enticing gaze advancing on her.

She tried not to fidget at the sight of him, but it was nearly impossible. The honest expression he wore and the hopefulness in his gaze seeped into the very pores of her skin.

She fingered the edge of the quilt. "I— Of course I can *handle* this. It should pose no problem at all."

"You *can* cook, can't you?" He arched one dark eyebrow.

Callie stuck him with a prickly look.

"Apparently so." His mouth tipped in a distinctly male, self-satisfied grin. "Then it's settled. For now, I just want you to relax and take it easy. As badly as I need help, I can't have you sick, can I?"

She shook her head in outward agreement. But inside, doubt filled her mind. Why was he being so kind? So unlike Max's description? It just didn't make sense.

Callie's heart twisted with bitter irony, remembering the last words that had passed through Max's lips before he died.

Find my brothers. Find Ben. He'll see to your needs.

Max had died then, leaving Callie confused, angry and laden with sorrow.

Certain that his words must've been delirium-driven, she'd ignored his dying sentiment. She'd grieved for her husband, for the life he could've had and for the unfulfilled dreams she'd never know with him. She'd grieved his untimely death.

And that of their newborn baby girl he'd buried almost nine months to the day they'd married.

But instead of wallowing in the insurmountable grief that permeated every thought and every breath, she'd had to begin working immediately, to make right on his debt.

She wouldn't be here now, except that she'd had nowhere else to turn. At the moment she felt too weak to even drag herself out of bed. *And* she was in debt to a man Max had said was controlling, a cheat and a liar.

Just as soon as she could, she was going to make right on what she owed Ben by cooking mouthwatering meals and cleaning till his office and house gleamed. Once she'd paid back Whiteside, she'd leave, thereby ridding herself of the confusion of it all.

"I'll bring over something for you to eat while we wait for Katie to arrive."

At the mere thought of food, Callie's mouth began watering like a leaky pail. "Who's Katie?"

"She's my brother's wife. I thought maybe I'd have her help you with a bath. As long as you don't spike a fever before then, you can soak in hot, soapy water to your heart's content."

She gave a contented sigh. "It's been so long—" She cut her words off. Ben certainly wasn't interested in the details of her bleak, almost nonexistent, bathing schedule.

"It'll probably go a long way to making you feel better," he added with a brisk nod.

She barely hid her profound delight, finding it impossible to recall the last time she'd taken a full-fledged bath with hot water. Most of the time she'd made do with the invigorating yet harsh cold of a mountain stream or sponging herself from a pail of used dishwater. Twice, at the saloon, she'd managed an early morning soak after the customers had all gone home to their poor, unsuspecting wives and children. Even though she'd hated utilizing Lyle Whiteside's *girls'* amenities, it had been a memorable bit of pure luxury.

"That is, if you want to?"

"Oh, yes." She touched her matted hair. "That would be wonderful."

"Katie will help you. You'll like her."

Instant humiliation ricocheted through her veins as she lowered her hand to her side. Her stomach clenched. She fingered the rough seam of a haphazard, angry-looking scar that blazed like a streak of lightning around to her back, a result of one of Max's liquor-induced tirades and a lasting symbol of betrayal that had embedded deep into their marriage.

Oh, he'd been somewhat remorseful for the way he'd treated her, but not enough to get her proper medical attention. Drunk, he'd awkwardly stitched the gaping wound then stormed out the door, leaving for days while she struggled to fight off a wicked infection, alone. That had been a year ago, and though the gash had finally healed, the pain inflicted by his total disregard for her well-being stung, still.

"Callie?" Ben's voice cut through the dismal memory.

She jerked her attention back to the present. "I—I'm sure I can bathe myself."

His eyes shrouded with doctorly concern. "Tell you what, when you're stronger and well out of the woods, I won't argue."

"There's no need to bother her," she shot back. "I can manage just fine on my own."

"I'll rest easier if you have a little help." Moving toward the doorway, he turned to her as he cleared his throat. "And by the way, room and board is part of the job. That is, if this bedroom here suits you well enough." He gestured to her surroundings almost apologetically. "You can take your meals with me next door. Or bring them here and eat alone, if you'd rather," he added as he stepped out of the room.

Callie gulped against the thick emotion clogging her throat. She hadn't slept in a bed so comfortable, had a room so cheery, or had the delicious promise of consistent meals for seven years. The accommodations were modest by her father's standards. But to a woman who'd spent the past years moving from shack to shack, sharing a bed with rodents and contenting herself with whatever food she managed to purchase, this was a castle. And for a short while, anyway, she was the queen.

Ben peered down at where he'd absentmindedly heaped a plate full of shepherd's pie for Callie. The way her stomach had audibly growled at the mention of food, he felt confident that she finally had an appetite—just probably not enough to eat half a roasting pan of the tasty dish.

He dropped the wooden spoon in the pan and braced his hands against the counter, attempting yet again to convince himself that he was merely concerned for her as a patient.

Hauling in a deep, stabilizing breath, he glanced down as Molly and Smudge meowed sweetly at his feet, curling their thick tails in feline affection around his legs.

Who was he trying to kid?

He felt an unrelenting draw to her that plagued his every thought, making him wonder if he might well be getting himself in too deep.

The empty sadness he'd seen waft like some dark wraith across her face when she'd spoken of her upbringing tugged at his heart. What secrets did her past hold?

She'd grown up with privilege. And she was clearly uncomfortable with any action that could be viewed as charity. He couldn't miss the way she'd flinched at his touch. Nor had he missed the way her eyes had lit with awe then instant shame when he'd mentioned both the meal and bath. It was as if she didn't want to make herself vulnerable enough to receive help—so much like the strays he'd taken in. Often times he'd have to coax them to eat, even when their ribs protruded in glaring proof of starvation.

Ben recalled the way he'd found Callie that first night. In spite of her tangled hair, tattered appearance and puzzling background, he'd felt pulled by some unseen force to help her.

To save her.

Just like the scrawny kittens that had shown up.

He gave a short laugh and loosened his fists, reflecting on how this little lady had loosened his ordered world a few notches, turning his life upside down in less than two days.

Maybe he was the one who needed saving.

When he peered down at his feline companions, Smudge gave him one of those I'm-as-cute-as-a-button squinty-eyed looks while Molly stared wide-eyed up at him, as though he owned a pond full of tasty fish for the eating. He hunkered down and stroked their fur, tracing the ragged scar on Molly's neck that had been a festering wound when she'd come to him. He looked at the irregular kink crooking Smudge's front leg, saddened to think of what these two had suffered.

He couldn't help but open his heart to them when they'd shown up. And they seemed to know it, too, because like most all the animals that came his way, these kittens had somehow known they could trust him.

He peered through the kitchen window toward his office, and his chest tightened. Was Callie one of those strays? Had she scraped her way through life and, by providential design, landed on his doorstep?

Callie's pride prickled from head to toe. "I could never take these garments from you, Katie."

Katie sat on the bed behind her, gliding a brush through Callie's freshly washed hair. "Sure you can. Besides, I really want you to have them."

She ran a hand over the sturdy, attractive fabrics. "They're far too nice to give away."

"Ben said something about you being stubborn,"

Katie remarked, threading her fingers through Callie's hair. "He just didn't say *how* stubborn."

Having figured out long ago that her existence hinged on a firm resolve to keep moving forward, no matter what, she'd gladly embraced stubbornness like some lifeline.

When she slid her gaze from the lavender day dress to the emerald-green dress and then to the soft, white eyelet undergarments, she knew each item would be perfect. She hadn't seen clothing like this for seven years. And she sure hadn't felt cared for like this in almost as long.

But she already owed Ben—even though he'd said it was part of the job. She didn't want to take charity. Didn't want to be in debt to someone else. Not for a single cent. Not even for a single stitch of much needed clothing.

"Barring some unforeseen fortune splashing at my feet, it'd be a month's worth of paydays before I could afford a new dress, let alone nice undergarments," she admitted reluctantly. Even when she'd paid off Max's gambling debt, she wasn't about to spend her earnings frivolously on new garments. She had her future to think of.

Katie smiled. "Then you can look at this as a timely provision. But with the way you swim in this nightdress," she responded, plucking at the cream-colored flannel material, "I'm worried if the other items will even fit, you're so slight."

The simple nightdress whispered against Callie's skin like luxurious silk. "This is very comfortable, Katie, and I'm sure the other items will be absolutely fine. But I—"

"I've already shortened things a few inches since Ben

said you weren't much over five feet. If they're still too big, then I'll help you alter them."

Her chest grew tight and her eyes stung with ready shame. In all the years of living on the edge of destitution with Max, she'd avoided charity, while Max would seek it out.

"I want to tell you something." Katie drew the covers back, gesturing for Callie to lie down. "I don't know how long you'll be here working for Ben—"

"I'm not sure either," Callie noted with a sniff as she scooted down into the fresh linens.

"Well, however long it is, the Drake family is first in line when it comes to helping others. Believe me…I'm blessed to have married into such a wonderful family. And you are fortunate to be employed by such a fine man as Ben Drake."

Everything she'd ever heard from Max would lead her to suppose the exact opposite. She'd already made one severe, life-altering error in judgment regarding Max's character. She wasn't about to be fooled like that ever again.

But three days with Ben, and already she had inarguable reservations as to Max's sordid opinion.

Not just because of the tender way Ben had cared for her or the gesture of kindness he'd shown by not taking the locket, but it was the unsettling look of gentleness she'd seen deep in his eyes that stood in direct contrast to what she'd believed.

She sighed. She couldn't deny Ben's sincerity. And certainly couldn't seem to escape his earnest gestures of compassion and care, though she'd tried.

Maybe she could enjoy just a few days of refreshing. Time to collect herself, heal and firm up her determination to make the best of what lay ahead. To find out who

Callie Drake really was after years of being first under her father's strict hand, then Max's harsh one.

Though until she left Boulder, she'd just have to stay alert, keep a watchful eye. If she let her guard down completely, she could well walk out of this town with nothing, not even the scrap of dignity she clung to like some shredded lifeline.

"I guess what I'm trying to say is…" Katie's voice slipped through Callie's thoughts. "That if for some reason you oppose the idea of others looking out for you and treating you well, you might as well let that go right now, because it's bound to happen more often than not with the Drake family."

Callie nibbled at her lower lip, unsettled by how emotionally raw she'd felt the last couple of days.

"Believe me when I say that Ben has needed help around here for quite a while. He's talked about hiring someone for months, but has never gotten around to it." Katie moved to the knotty pine chest at the foot of the bed then began laying the garments she'd brought inside it. When she closed the chest with a quiet click, Callie felt utterly helpless to summon an argument. "That man keeps so busy that it would take an enormous weight off him to know that things here and at his home are being tended to as they should."

At those words, an instant swell of compassion-driven duty rose within Callie. After all, she owed Ben. Not just because he'd cared for her while she was sick, but also because he'd taken her in. A total stranger. And he'd tended her with a gentleness that had her broaching tears more than once. If the truth be told, he'd probably even saved her life.

Pulling her damp hair to the side to dry across her pillow, she decided that just as soon as she was the slightest bit stronger, she'd get to work cleaning and cooking. She'd steer clear of him. Fade into the background, as she had the past six months at the brothel. Hopefully he'd forget that she was even here. No one would give her a second thought.

"You know, Callie," Katie began, perching her hands on her hips. A wistful smile stole across her face as she eyed Callie in a way that had her squirming. "I think that you may have arrived just in time for Ben."

Chapter Five

"**I** was about to send the cavalry after you." Ben left Joseph in his wake, meeting Katie as she entered the front door of his house. "What happened? Did you lose Callie in the tub?"

She gave an innocent smile and edged around him. "She's a slight thing, but no, I didn't lose her. You know how girls can be." Waving a slender hand in the air, she moved toward Joseph. "Talk, talk, talk."

Ben pivoted, peering out a side window to his doctor's office next door where Callie was now. He turned and followed Katie to the dining table. "I was beginning to worry."

"Beginning?" Joseph focused his sightless gaze at his wife then arched an eyebrow Ben's way. "You started worrying the minute you left her side and came over here to wait. You're a dead giveaway when you're nervous, you know. Pacing and clearing your throat the way you do."

Ben produced a half-hearted frown. "And *you* are too observant for your own good."

With a self-satisfied grin, Joseph lifted Katie's cloak from her shoulders and draped it over the chair. "I can't help it that my other senses are so sharp. I come by it naturally."

Ben sighed. "Katie, maybe you ought to give him a lesson in humility. Seems like he's a little weak in that area."

"Believe me, I don't need her to do that. All I have to do is make an embarrassing mess of things, like last Sunday at church, and my feet are firmly planted on the ground." Joseph raked a hand through his chestnut hair.

"What happened this time?"

"Do you really want to know?"

"Well, sure I do."

On a heavy sigh, Joseph shook his head. "I was introducing myself to a newcomer and I reached out to shake her hand, but it wasn't her hand I touched."

Ben grimaced. "You didn't."

"I did." Joseph pinched the bridge of his nose. "I touched her—her bosom," he ground out. "That's not even polite to say in mixed company. Sorry, darlin'," he added with absolute sincerity to Katie.

The way she looked up at Joseph with undeniable adoration was something to see. And snagged at Ben's own yearning for the same.

At twenty-nine, he could've married several times over, but after a difficult end to a relationship while he was away at school, he'd decided to bypass that aisle. And with as much as his practice had grown, he could easily distract himself from the loneliness he felt at times, by throwing himself into his work and his patients.

Unfortunately a certain five-foot-two-inch, auburn-haired, blue-eyed patient residing in the living quarters of his office next door presented a bit of a problem. He was distracted completely by Callie's presence.

"I could've crawled out of the church," Joseph finished.

Grabbing the two empty mugs from the table, Ben couldn't help chuckling. "So, what did you do?"

"Apologized. What do you think? Then held my head high and made some small talk as if nothing had happened."

"If it's any consolation, I don't think she realized you were blind until…well, until that," Katie offered, stacking the plates and bowls and setting them in the basin, too. "She looked as shocked as you did."

"There's the silver lining." Ben clapped his brother on the arm. "You've been working hard at gauging where to aim your focus. Sounds like you're doing a great job—at least where your eyes are concerned, anyway."

"Very funny." Shoving his hands in his pockets, Joseph shook his head. "Next time I'll remember to hold my hand out and let the other person do the grabbing."

Inwardly, Ben was thankful to see the ease with which Joseph was handling his blindness. He was adjusting well. Though he could see some dim shadows, he was pretty much dependent on his other senses. And with the help of his wife, who'd come to him as a teacher of the blind, he'd made huge strides toward independence.

"So, Callie is back in bed, right?" He swung his focus back to the conversation.

"I gave her a fresh glass of water and tucked her in. Satisfied, Doctor Drake?" Katie teased.

Ben gave one swift nod. "As weak as she is, I want to make sure she doesn't overdo it."

"She didn't. We were just getting to know each other, that's all. She seems very nice, but you were right. She's a proud young woman." Katie tucked strands of blond waves into where she'd swept it up at the back of her head. "She almost refused to take the clothes I brought over. And she's determined to pay you for everything. Once she's on her feet again, I'm guessing she'll be a tough one to corner long enough to get her to open up."

He frowned. "That's what has me worried."

"I thought so," Joseph gibed with one raised brow. "You're taken by her, aren't you?"

Ben shrugged off the brotherly taunt. "Well, something about her has snagged my attention, that's for sure."

"Like I've said before," Joseph measured out, patting his chest. "You're a bleeding heart."

Ben dropped his gaze to the floor. "I'm just worried about her, that's all. It's obvious she doesn't have anywhere to go from here. As much as this area has been built up with the railroad coming through and all, a young woman trying to find her way alone is as good as a death sentence. It's clear that she needs a leg up in life."

"You're right to be concerned." Katie threaded her arm through Joseph's.

"What do you mean?" Ben's pulse prickled through him at the way her features pinched with concern.

"I have a feeling that if you want her to stay safe, then you're going to have to find enough things to keep her busy right here. But most importantly, you need to treat her with great care." Her voice grew suddenly soft and strained as Joseph wrapped her protectively in the crook of his arm. "Even though she tried to hide them, the awful scars I glimpsed on her body are a horrid indication that her past is something she'd like to forget."

The thought of Callie enduring a cruel beating, even once, touched every part of his mind and heart, stirring up anger so hot his blood still thrummed with furious force through his veins. Images of her being mistreated thundered through his mind, unearthing fierce rage and the innate need to protect her.

"Callie? Are you awake?" Ben spoke low as he gently knocked on the bedroom door and awaited her reply.

After several silent moments, alarm barged into his head, dominating all reasonable thought. He opened the door, peeking inside.

He hoped he hadn't seemed rude when just moments ago, he'd eagerly ushered Joseph and Katie out of his house. But from the second Katie had returned from helping Callie with her bath, he'd been chomping at the bit to get back over here to his patient.

Especially after Katie had mentioned the scars.

A few old scars. Some newer ones. The bold signs of chronic abuse that had been hidden beneath her tattered undergarments. He'd been fortunate enough to get her out of her wet and dirty dress after she'd arrived. But since then, every time he'd attempt to examine her, she'd flat-out refused, wrapping the covers so tightly around her, he thought she might cocoon herself in them permanently.

Completely missing the glorious opportunity to break free as a beautiful butterfly.

He gulped hard, sliding a trembling hand over his mouth. That thought had come out of nowhere. The delicate image of Callie emerging and spreading her wings to fly had his insides drawing up taut.

Every step from his house to his office, he'd kept telling himself that his was just a doctorly kind of concern, making sure she hadn't taxed herself too much or spiked another fever. But the way his heart thudded inside his chest as he quietly slipped into her room, he knew he was fool—

He stopped cold in his tracks when he glimpsed her nestled safe in a fluff of quilts and pillows. His throat constricted. His pulse skidded to a halt, staring at her as though he'd never seen her before. He was so taken by her innocent beauty that he couldn't seem to tear his gaze away, even if he tried.

He advanced one step closer, growing increasingly uncomfortable at the way his thoughts were so caught up with this patient and the intense need he felt to protect her.

And wholly compelled by the way her auburn hair fanned across her pillow like rich strands of fine satin, gleaming in the sunlight. The late-afternoon glow poured through the windows in warm, comforting streams, lighting on her face to reveal a freshly scrubbed, pink tint there. Revealing also a small, ragged scar at her hairline. He'd missed it before with her matted hair, but now in the soft glow, he could see it. And the sight fixed a tight cinch around his stomach.

He gritted his teeth. Fisted his hands as images of this delicate woman being mistreated whipped through his mind once again. Any man who'd do that to a woman wasn't worth his weight in gold, and must've been raised by the devil's minions. Had it been an employer? Her father?

An appalling suspicion brought him up short.

Surely not Max. Max may have come by lying and cheating and drinking and gambling easily enough, but surely he couldn't have found it so easy to physically harm his own wife.

Or could he?

Ben seethed with fury that Callie had been treated with such abject disregard.

When she stirred slightly and gave a small, distressed moan, he stepped nearer, instantly troubled by the way her brows creased in a frown. The way her mouth turned down at the corners in a distinctive look of fear.

Hunkering down next to the bed, he gently braced a hand on her shoulder. Instead of easing her distress, she jerked hard. Gasped in fear as her eyes flew open. She scrambled to the other side of the bed. Heaved a pillow over her head as if she meant to defend herself.

"Callie?" he spoke low, noticing how the covers quivered with the force of her heartrending trepidation. "Callie, it's me. Ben."

Her fingers blanched white with force. Her breath came now in short pants as she inched the pillow down. She slid a terror-filled gaze to him and blinked hard, once, then again as if bringing him into focus. He saw the light of awareness dawn in her eyes.

"What's wrong?" he asked as she swung her gaze aside, fastening it to the wall as though holding the structure in place. "Are you all right?"

"What are you doing sneaking up on me like that?" Heaving a big sigh, she shot up to her elbows and glared at him. "Do you always do that to your patients?"

"I didn't sneak up on you." He kept his voice low and even. If she'd suffered abuse, then it would certainly account for her skittishness around him. He'd have to tread lightly when it came to touching her. "I came in to check on you. Just like I would any other patient. You've been sick, remember?"

The way she studied him out of the corner of her eyes as he raised his hand to her forehead to feel for a fever, one would think he had a gleaming scalpel poised, ready to make a deep incision. But the way she jutted her chin out in obstinate refusal to show weakness pierced his heart straight through.

"Well, next time knock, if you would, please." She summoned her rose-colored lips into a headstrong pucker that brought to mind dainty rosebuds.

"I did knock." He wrangled up his patience and his good sense, even as unsolicited images of those perfect lips touching against his drifted through his mind. He was pretty sure she hadn't meant to convey that, but darn if his thoughts didn't find their way there. "You must've been having a bad dream."

"I was not," she retorted.

He tried to hide his dismay at her stubbornness. "You feel cool to the touch. I'm glad for that."

When he withdrew his hand, silky strands of hair whispered against his fingertips, kicking his pulse up a notch. He busied himself, pouring her a fresh glass of water as he forced himself to focus on her needs as a patient.

"I hope you didn't overdo it with the bath." He offered her the glass, his errant gaze locking on her lips as she took several generous sips. "I probably should've waited to make that suggestion."

"Don't worry about me. I'm just fine." She fell back to the pillow. "In fact, I can't believe how much better I feel. I'll be up and working probably by tomor—" Her proclamation was interrupted by an unceremonious, lingering yawn.

"No, ma'am. Not tomorrow, you won't." Ben shook his head, trying hard not to grin at her strength of will, and the small glimpse of innocence he saw right then in her cute frown. "Not the next day either. I'll let you know when you're well enough to begin work."

When she knit her brows together even tighter, he had the distinct feeling that he'd probably just stepped on her pride. He'd do it again, since he was a stickler for enforcing ample recovery time. And in her case, much needed rest.

"Thank you all the same, but I am fully capable of judging that for myself." She crossed her arms at her chest. "And I feel *more* than ready to tackle the tasks that need to be done."

"You are stubborn enough that you would, too." He gently grasped her wrist to feel her pulse. "But I'm a doctor. And, honestly, I question whether you're in the habit of making sound decisions regarding your health."

With a protesting huff, she jerked her hand back.

"And before you go thinking that I just insulted you, let me assure you that it wasn't meant as such," he cut in, distracted by the way her soft skin remained imprinted on his. "Given the way you showed up here, I'd say mine is a fair assessment, don't you think? No one in their right mind would have braved that kind of weather in the condition you were in at the time."

Crossing to the dresser, he eyed the locket lying atop her worn garment. "Nothing is worth that."

An uncomfortable silence filled the space between them and since he'd given her his back, he could only guess what her reaction was. But the one thing he'd learned about Callie, thus far, was that even though she'd make gallant efforts to hide her emotions, the uncertainty that churned inside her pretty little head was evident on her face.

"Your brother told me to find you." The words fell from her lips, stiff and measured and loaded with things unsaid.

He faced her. "What do you mean? Max sent you here?"

Suspicion, thick as mud, overpowered the compassion that had just moments ago pervaded his mind. Joseph's and Aaron's strong words of caution echoed through his mind. Maybe they were right—that he was too trusting at times. That he was too much of a soft heart. That he opened himself up to get taken.

But when he peered into Callie's distressed gaze, he couldn't bring himself to make that kind of outright conclusion. Not without direct proof, unshaded by doubt.

"That was his last sentiment." The words sounded as if forced from her lips.

"His last words were about me?" Rubbing his temples, he dragged in a deep breath.

The nod she gave was slow and painfully measured. And seemed meant to sever any further inquiry he might have, promptly pricking his irritation.

"Tell me what this is all about, Callie. Why are you here, anyway?" His voice had raised a good notch. "Because, had I not come along when I did, you likely would've frozen to death on my doorstep. Why would you put your life at risk like that?"

Hauling her chin up a notch, she glared at him as he advanced on her. Flinched as if he might haul out to strike her. Then gave him a hollow kind of look.

And that had him inwardly kicking himself.

When she slowly rolled away from him, he knew he'd pushed too far, too fast.

"Listen, I didn't mean to sound so—" He braced a hand at the back of his neck, feeling every bit worthy to play the evil part of the nightmare he'd found her in when he'd entered the room just minutes ago. He gently adjusted the quilt at her back, tucking it in so that she wouldn't catch a draft. "I'm sorry. I'm just glad that you turned to me."

When he pivoted to leave the room, he could've sworn he heard her whisper, "You were my last resort."

Chapter Six

For the past hours those words, *You were my last resort,* had marched through Callie's mind like dark shadows marking out her future. She'd hoped to eliminate Ben and the disturbing effects of his concern from her thoughts, but his subtle, piney and masculine scent lingering in the room infused her every sense with his memory.

She'd lost track of time as she'd crawled out of bed and slowly made her way around the room. She grasped the satin-smooth furniture to steady herself, studying the few other framed photographs hanging about the room. Raw emotion squeezed her heart seeing the way a much younger Max seemed bent on puffing his chest out in some kind of stubborn refusal. As she inched her gaze over a picture of Max, looking close to the age she'd first met him, she trailed a fingertip over his charming yet devilish grin. That smile had once drawn her, like some forbidden fruit.

But one taste of his empty promises confirmed the grave mistake she'd made in succumbing to his tempting charm.

The image of Ben's half-cocked grin and earnest

gaze barged into her mind as she made her way back to bed. This job was her only hope to earn the money she needed, but the way Ben seemed focused on probing into her life and her heart...well, she was walking in very dangerous territory.

Ben was nowhere near safe.

His caring touch, the tender way he looked at her, the kindness in his gentle ministrations, all of those things worked against her, wearing down a very hard-won safeguard she'd erected. His thoughtfulness threatened to destroy her resolve. Threatened to uncover the vulnerability she'd vowed to protect. She'd never again find herself stuck in a defenseless and vulnerable relationship.

Especially with a man like Ben Drake.

The heavy weight of her desperation pressed in hard, making her feel horribly frail and even weak as she crawled under the covers.

Max had always hated it when she'd cried. Rarely would she weaken, seeing as how he'd grow instantly angry. Out of mere survival she'd learned how to stop up the sorrow, though sometimes there was no helping it. Like an overgrown vine in dire need of tending, grief would smother the light of hope.

Especially after she'd lost her newborn baby girl at birth, six agonizing years ago.

Setting her trembling fingers to her lips, Callie tried to ward off the memory's bitter sting. But Max hadn't allowed her even the opportunity to see her little girl, kiss her, hold her. Callie had been left with an aching emptiness that hurt, even today. And sometimes, out of nowhere, that familiar, painful lump would swell in her throat, her stomach would grow queasy, and hot, unshed tears would threaten.

Would the anguish ever go away? Would she ever

rise above regret's relentless storm, enough to see the possible hope of what lay ahead?

Or maybe, for Callie, hope was dead.

"No," she whispered, thrusting the miserable thought away. If she didn't, she'd fall into the hands of a fate worse than death. A fate that threatened to crush her spirit.

Determined to remain strong, she dragged in a steadying breath. She'd need to be firm with Ben, especially after he'd decided that it was his place to tell her what was best for her.

Ha! As if he knew.

He had no idea.

She clenched her teeth, riled in an instant at the memory of his pushy, self-important ways. Twisting a corner of the quilt between her fingers, she remembered how her father had played that role. He'd been like one large, prickling burr to her side at social functions, scaring off any and all suitors with his gruff, unfriendly exterior.

Max had been much the same in his control, only he'd used force when she tried to exert her will. A hard backhand to her face, a rough shove into the wall, or his hands clasped like iron shackles around her wrists.

But his cutting words…they'd been the worst.

Apart from a few short seasons of seeming sanity, he'd remained the antithesis of the man she'd married.

Trembling now, she tried to shut out the bitter memories. Having seen her father take up residence in a stronghold of bitterness and resentment after her mama had died, Callie knew she could never stomach herself if she grew to be the same.

There had to be hope. Even if she couldn't see it, and

everything around her looked hopeless, there had to be hope.

There were times throughout the past years when she'd felt a quiet wooing, a gentle calling, to pray. To climb above the darkness that seemed to surround her.

But then the clear and dismal message she'd gotten about God, growing up, would haul her back down with ruthless force. Her father had jammed Scriptures down her throat and demanded she quote them to ensure her standing with God. The minister at their church had beaten his meaty fist against the thick, wooden pulpit weekly, decrying God's fiery wrath and judgment. And then Max, he'd barely given God a second thought unless he'd lost his shirt in a poker game, then he'd railed at God to the point that Callie would cover her ears and hide, fearing retribution.

Was God fickle? Was He liable to punish her at the hint of wrongdoing, as the minister back home often said? Had God sent all the heartache she'd gone through the past seven years as payment for her mistakes?

The very thought made Callie's heart pitch with deep sorrow. Just as she began to feel nearly overwhelmed by it all, she heard a rustling sound behind her back.

Rolling over, she rose to an elbow and found a boy staring back at her. Blinking hard, she took him in.

He was probably eleven years old or so. His dirt-smudged face and thick mop of dusty blond hair that hung almost to his eyes made her think of a sheepdog pup. The image lifted her heavy heart a bit.

"How did you get in here?" she asked when he made no move. She swiped at the moisture rimming her eyes.

His hazel gaze grew wide as he took a step toward the door.

"Is there something you need?"

"I—I was jest—" His focus cut from one thing to another in the room, finally landing on her face. "Lookin'. That's all. Who are you?" He gave an audible swallow then anchored his lips off to the side.

Pushing up to sitting, she leaned against the walnut headboard. "My name is Callie. And you are…"

"Luke. Luke Ortmeier."

"It's a pleasure to meet you, Luke Ortmeier." Nodding, she smiled, hoping to coax one from him, as well.

Instead, his eyebrows crept like small golden caterpillars into a suspicious scowl as he settled his fists on his waist. "Does Ben—Doc Drake know you're here?"

"Yes, he does. Does he know *you're* here?"

"Doc Drake's my friend." He folded his arms at his chest, revealing threadbare holes in the elbows of his muslin shirt. "Fact is…we're best friends, him and me. He lets me come to his office here and have a look at his things. All the time."

For some reason, that bit of knowledge settled on her like a soothing touch. That Ben had entrusted this young boy in that way cut off a few suspicions regarding the doctor's character.

"Oh. I see," she finally said.

"Yep," he confirmed with a single nod. Threading his fingers together, he turned them outward and cracked his knuckles in slow succession, making her wince. "I'm gonna be a doctor jest like him someday. Gonna git me a black bag and some of those whatnots he carries 'round with him."

"Really now?" Callie pulled her legs beneath her

as she turned to face him. "Will you attend school somewhere?"

"You betcha. I figure it won't be for long, though, seein' as how I'm learnin' so much already." Snuffling, he wiped his nose with the sleeve of his shirt. The innocent determination that cloaked Luke's unwavering gaze prompted a smile she struggled to bridle. He jutted his chin out and moved closer. "Right now I go to the schoolhouse down the way, but only sometimes, cuz my ma don' like it when I'm gone all day long."

"She doesn't? Why not?"

"She needs me to work," he responded in an offhand sort of way as he eyed the chair next to the bed.

"Here, have a seat." She patted the edge of the bed, wondering if he lived on a large ranch that needed many hands to turn a profit. "So, you must live on a farm?"

Luke edged over to the bed and sat down with hesitant care. And when he trailed his fingers almost reverently over the stitches on the quilt, she felt certain he wasn't used to a well-built, hand-carved bed or lovely quilt.

"Naw…we don' farm. Ma's mostly busy at nights. That's why she needs me 'round durin' the day to do the cookin' and such." Luke peered at her, his gaze drifting to her hair. "I leave now and again when Ma's sleepin' to visit Ben. Make sure he don' need my help or nothin' with his calls."

She smiled, her heart squeezing at his earnest loyalty. For some reason, she found herself easily imagining Ben taking this boy under his wing. Treating him like a son, even.

"I found me some kittens the other day," Luke offered.

"You did? Where did you find them?"

"In the alley behind Gold-Digger's."

"Gold-Digger's?" she queried.

"You know, the saloon. Anyways, the kittens musta' been 'bandoned by their ma cuz they was real hungry."

"Aww...the poor things." She felt equally sad thinking about this young boy scouting around in an alley behind a saloon.

"Don' you worry none." He gave his head an adamant shake. "I'm raisin' 'em now. Ben's helpin' me."

Turning toward her, Luke's face was alight as he looped his left knee up on the bed. "Did Ben ever tell you 'bout me goin' with him that one time?"

"Umm, no. He hasn't mentioned that."

"Well, I did. It was flat-out nasty, too." His hazel eyes transformed from round orbs to narrow slits.

"What happened?"

"A broke leg pinned under a wagon." He pointed to his midthigh with fingers that bore the red and raw signs of a recent blister that had her wondering what had happened. "We got 'im out jest in time. And Ben, he got the wound all patched up good as new. Took a spell for the feller to walk right again, but he did, jest like Ben said he would."

"That's wonderful. I'm sure the man is grateful."

"Yep. Lucky we was both there seein' to him." He shoved his thick hair out of his eyes then pulled in an exaggerated breath. "Otherwise, no tellin' what would'a happened."

Pride beamed like the noonday sun from Luke—Callie could feel it. "Well, I'm sure your parents had to be very proud of you that day, Luke. Very proud indeed."

He gave a quick shrug. "Don' know my pa. And Ma...

well, she don' take kindly to me bein' 'round here none. Says that I'm a big ol' bother. I asked Ben, though, and he said my bein' here is fine by him."

Ready compassion welled up inside her. She set her hand on his arm and gave a light squeeze.

"You're welcome anytime. You know that, Luke." Ben's low voice startled her, sending a tiny shiver of pleasure straight down her spine.

She glanced up to see him leaning against the doorjamb, his arms draped in casual ease at his chest, his legs crossed at the ankles. His steady, discerning gaze seemed to peer straight through to her soul.

She scrambled to cover the bitter scars grooved in her heart from years of regret and shame, but felt like her attempts fell short and that he could see everything.

"Were you sleeping, Callie?" He pushed away from the doorway, his intense gaze shifting not one inch from hers. A tender, thawing kind of smile tipped his lips, warming her from the inside out, even though she wasn't the least bit cold.

"No, no. I was wide-awake." She fumbled with the quilt.

"Cross my heart," Luke added, shooting up from the bed as he drew an invisible X over his heart. "I didn't wake her. She kinda looked like she'd been gushin' some, but she wasn't mad or nothin' when I came in here."

Without even touching her, Ben grabbed her attention, compelling her to look into his eyes. "I didn't think she'd be mad, Luke," he finally said. "I just don't want her rest being disturbed, that's all."

Callie glanced up to see Luke hook his thumbs in his pockets then gesture back at her with his head. "She yer girl? I figured she was, seein' as how she was layin' here and all."

When Callie's cheeks grew hot with an instant blush, she berated herself for acting like a ridiculous schoolgirl. This man had taken her in as his patient, then as an employee. He was her deceased husband's brother. And a low-down thief, spending Max's inheritance before Max could even get his hands on it—by all Max had ever said.

Or was he so bad?

The less-than-exemplary titles she'd tacked on Ben were beginning to hang on threads.

"No. She's not my girl." His crystal-blue gaze sent her heart fluttering inside her rib cage. "Right now, Miss… Callie is a patient here. Someday when you're a doctor, you'll need to make sure that your patients get plenty of rest, too—so that they recover fully. That's why Callie is here."

Luke angled a perplexed look her way. "She looks fine to me."

Smiling, she glanced from the boy to Ben. "You're a very smart young man, Luke. Very perceptive, indeed."

"Appearances can be deceiving," Ben argued. "She may look better and feel better, but if she gets up and resumes activity too quickly it could cause her to relapse."

"Relapse?" Luke's brow creased.

"It means that she'd get sick all over again." Ben peered down at the boy with steady patience. "We don't want that, now, do we?"

"No, sirree." Luke stuck his face in Callie's line of vision. "Miss Callie, I think you should be lyin' down.

When yer sick, ya gotta make sure you get rest. Jest like Ben said."

"You're going to make a good doctor someday," Ben remarked with a satisfied grin.

"Ya got any stitchin' that needs to be done on 'er, cuz I can hold 'er down for ya. T'ain't nothin' for me to do seein' as how small she is," he noted, pointing at Callie as though she wasn't even in the room.

"I'm sure you'd do a fine job, but I don't need to perform any stitch work today." Ben passed an all-innocence glance her way, prompting an unavoidable grin.

"It's a comfort to know that you would help me, Luke," Callie added, despite being ganged up on. "Really. Thank you for the offer."

"It's almost suppertime, so if you're hungry, Callie, I'll bring you a plate of food." Ben raised his brows in question.

She nodded, suddenly famished.

"You're welcome to stay for supper, too, Luke."

"Awww! I gotta git home 'fore Ma wakes and finds that I ain't made supper yet. She'll wring my neck."

"I'm glad you stopped by. Don't forget your coat and the sweater I fished out of my drawer for you. You might need it. It's cold out there."

"I won't. Thanks for the food. It was real good."

"Come again just as soon as you can. Promise?" Ben held out his hand.

"Promise." Luke clasped Ben's hand in an exuberant handshake then headed toward the door. "Good meetin' ya, Miss Callie."

"Nice to meet you, too, Luke." Callie smiled and waved.

Luke came to a sliding halt then suddenly backtracked.

He stood on his toes and crooked a finger, motioning Ben down, ear level. "She's a perty lady," the boy whispered, his words reaching her ears as Ben slowly stood, sliding his pulse-pounding gaze and heart-seizing half smile to Callie. "Real perty."

Chapter Seven

Ben had barely gotten a wink of sleep. His thoughts had been consumed with Callie. Her health. The way she'd been so kindhearted and engaging with Luke. The quick, intelligent responses she'd given. The delicate, lovely features etched with artistic perfection on her face.

In three short days, she'd acquired his attention, and he was pretty sure she hadn't the foggiest idea she'd done so, either. He'd been nothing but professional in his care of her, but it had taken uncommon restraint.

When he'd happened upon her conversation with Luke yesterday, he'd stood mesmerized by her tender ways and warm smile—he'd never seen her smile. It had forced his heart all the way up to his throat, and he'd been thankful they hadn't seen him standing there, if for no other reason than that he'd had time enough to find his voice again.

He stepped up to the porch, waving to Sven Olsson, the lumber mill owner, as the man drove his wagon through the sloppy streets. The foot and a half of snow that had covered Boulder in a thick white blanket the night Callie had arrived was now a sludgy mess of mud and slush. With the mild temperature that bathed the valley this morning, the snow would probably be a memory by tomorrow.

He unlocked the door to his office, his mind settled, as it had nearly every waking moment for the past three days, on Callie. This whole thing was as complicated as it could possibly be. When he stopped to consider the tangled mess, his head spun in outright confusion, leaving him feeling strangely out of sorts.

Striding into the front room with the basket containing her breakfast, he caught sight of the *Help Wanted* sign that was still propped against the window. He grabbed it, reminding himself as he shoved it under a pile of papers that there were several reasons why he should rethink his decision to hire her. And at least a dozen reasons why he should tug his heart away from the direction it seemed committed to traveling in.

He'd been silently naming those reasons off all morning long.

Callie had been married to Max. He sighed—that was a huge reason. And Max had betrayed Ben and his brothers, storming out of their lives with their money and anything else of value—another big reason. Also, Callie seemed set on remaining closed off, and as far as Ben was concerned, openness and honesty were nonnegotiable elements in any relationship.

And both Joseph and Aaron had expressed reservations about her presence here. Most often he trusted their judgment, but he wasn't so sure this time. This morning when Aaron had swung by for a cup of coffee before work, he'd urged Ben again to reconsider his dealings with Callie. Although Ben had come to her defense, he couldn't ignore the tiny niggling of doubt eating at him.

Walking down the hallway to her bedroom, he started when he glimpsed Callie dressed and sitting on the edge of her freshly made bed. He instantly furrowed his brow and gave his head a frustrated shake.

"What do you think you're doing?" He came to a sudden stop just inside the doorway. "It's way too soon to be up, Callie. You're not ready yet."

"I'm fit as a fiddle," she responded with honey-dripping innocence. Clearly avoiding his admonishing gaze, she painstakingly smoothed a hand over her dress.

Though she was still pale, she looked beautiful. The soft lavender print got along so well with her fair complexion and the auburn hair she'd plaited loosely down her back. The color gave her still-too-pale skin some semblance of life—though the pink tint coloring her cheeks made him instantly suspicious that she'd been pinching them for effect.

"I brought your breakfast." He placed the heavily laden basket on the table, bracing his hands at his hips as he tried his best to look stern. "And yes. I absolutely think you're up too soon."

"Nonsense." Callie stood then quickly grasped the bedpost with a trembling hand. The forced look of confidence etched in her features didn't fool him one bit. "If I spend one more hour in bed—I'll be impossible to be around."

Crossing his arms at his chest, he moved a step closer. Then another. "Hmmm…that would be interesting."

She flicked her attention to him. "Believe me, you wouldn't want to see it."

"It'd be nothing new, seeing as how you're being impossible right this very minute." He snapped open the basket and unloaded the contents, the unmistakable look of awe as she peered at the food tugging at his heart.

When she hugged her arms around her middle, it accentuated how thin she was, a small detail which he was determined to remedy. Starting now. She needed to put on weight, and if he had to sit with her at every meal and make sure that she ate, then he would. Gladly.

"Have a seat." He gestured to one chair as he pulled another one up to the table.

He watched her closely, and though his hands itched to steady her, he willed them to remain fixed at his side. He was fully prepared to catch Callie again if she weakened—which was highly likely given the way perspiration beaded her lip.

Once seated, she unwrapped the large hunk of cheese as he poured her a glass of milk. "So, what task would you like me to start with this morning?"

"I'd like you to start by crawling back in bed after you've finished eating," he urged. "That would be the best and *only* start as far as I'm concerned."

She broke off a piece of cheese and popped it in her mouth. "That's not likely to happen, so unless you make another suggestion, I'll find things to do myself." She slid her gaze around the room before she lifted the lid off the four eggs, three biscuits, generous portion of gravy and five thick slices of smoked bacon. "Oh my, this smells delicious. Did you make all of this?"

"Wish I could take the credit, but this morning Katie brought over enough to feed a small army," he answered, watching as she dug in to the cast-iron crock.

Almost as an afterthought, she pulled a napkin out of the basket and laid it over her lap, one-handed, since she kept her other hand clamped tightly around the fork. The way she closed her eyes as she chewed and savored each bite pierced his heart. She was so much like the strays he'd taken in, eating their food as though they might not live to see another meal.

"Taste good?" he asked, smiling.

Nodding vigorously, Callie covered her mouth with her napkin. After she swallowed she said, "This is wonderful. Just wonderful."

"I'm glad you like it."

"Oh, I love breakfast." She speared another chunk of gravy-covered biscuit then shot him an after-thought kind of gaze. "Would you like some?"

"No, thanks. I already ate." He couldn't help but grin at the way she seemed almost relieved.

Bite after bite after bite, she made quick work of the large meal. And he decided, somewhat unexpectedly, that he rather enjoyed a woman with a healthy appetite, instead of the usual picking at food and moving it around on a plate.

She chased down a mouthful of eggs with several swallows of milk. "Can't you think of a task you'd like me to do? Surely there's plenty of work to be done."

"First day up and you're already complaining about the living conditions?" he asked, grinning.

"I'm terribly sorry, but have you looked at these windows?" She nodded toward the glass panes directly in front of her as she bit down on the last hunk of cheese.

He glanced at the windows. "I know, it's a hazy view, isn't it? I like to think that it creates a sort of blissful mood with the sun shining in."

When she ignored his sarcasm, forking the last of the scrambled eggs into her mouth, he added, "I've never claimed to be a stellar housekeeper."

With a light elegance that contrasted sharply with

the hearty way she'd just eaten, she dabbed her napkin to her mouth. "*Stellar* would undoubtedly stretch the truth."

Sliding a fingertip down a glass pane, he affirmed her claim as he shifted his gaze back to her. "*Stubborn* for you, however, wouldn't stretch the truth one bit."

When she turned to look at him, he couldn't tear his gaze from the lovely blue of her eyes, like an early spring sky. He looked deep, but found it disconcerting when he couldn't seem to see past the protective barrier she'd erected. It was as if she'd firmly locked away any deep emotion or poignant memory, and the empty look he found there made his heart ache for Callie.

"I believe you've made note of my stubbornness more than once," she breathed, laying her fork down into the empty cast-iron crock. She dabbed at her mouth again. "Please, tell Katie thank you. That was—it was delicious."

"I will."

Her hand drifted to her neck as she fingered the locket with the lightest touch, peering out the window for a long while.

Ben lifted the crock back into the basket then rested his arms on the table, watching the way her face shadowed ever so slightly, as though some memory haunted her. "You must've been quite a match for Max, seeing as how he had a willful streak in him a mile wide and equally deep."

Callie clutched the napkin on the tabletop, her knuckles whitening with force. "My life with Max is not your concern."

Ben furrowed his brow. "Really?"

"Really."

He tapped the table with one solitary finger. "Callie… if you were married to Max then you're my concern."

"I've done fine on my own, this far. I don't want to be your concern."

"You're his widow." He crooked a finger under her chin and gently turned her head to face him. "Of course you're my concern. You don't have a choice."

The fleeting look of distress that passed over her fine features made him want to sweep her off her feet and carry her through every difficult thing she faced.

"I want to help, Callie. God knows I've been praying for you, but unless you're willing to open up, I can only take care of the outward things you need." He held her gaze. "I can make sure you have a warm comfortable dwelling, good food and a decent wage. And I can protect you from the elements. But I can't protect you from whatever it is that makes you so wary and guarded with me."

Callie pushed up from the table and walked slowly toward the doorway. When she sidestepped then grabbed the thick wood trim as if to steady herself, Ben trained an eye on her every move, her every breath.

She had undeniably captured his attention. She was beautiful, delightfully stubborn, and she was his only connection to Max.

The times he'd tracked Max down with Joseph, they'd found him at a gambling table. There'd been no warm greeting or farewell hug. The last time, Max had barely spared them a glance for a good ten minutes then he'd followed them outside, carrying on about how broke he was, how he needed their help. After he'd lamented about how hard he had it, they'd handed over a fistful of money, and he'd proceeded to thank them with a series of sarcastic, scathing remarks.

The whole thing had finally gotten to Ben. He'd been used one too many times. Infuriated by Max's total disregard for family and the way he was raised, something in Ben finally snapped. The quiet patience that usually was his guiding force was long gone and instead, years of frustration and anger he didn't even know existed had boiled to the surface. To this day he couldn't believe the words that had spewed from his mouth. At the time it had felt like a huge relief, a weight off his soul.

It hadn't taken more than a few hours for him to realize that his remarks were nothing but vengeful and caustic.

And as it turned out, they were the last words he'd ever said to his brother.

The blatant reality of that stung with burning, debilitating force.

Max had died.

And Ben couldn't make amends.

He felt himself slipping further and further into regret. Guilt ate at him, even more so now that he couldn't take back the last, awful words he'd said to his own flesh and blood.

When he heard Callie's feet shift on the hardwood floor, he was instantly jerked from his haunting thoughts. He watched to see if she was steady as he crossed to her.

"I don't know the first thing about what happened with Max," he finally said, stopping just behind her. "But I can imagine there was plenty. And if ever you want to talk about it, I want you to know that I'm a good listener."

On a muffled cough, she hugged her arms to her chest.

"You were married to my brother. Do you know what that means?"

"Apparently not," she breathed. Then did a slow turn to face him, sliding her arms down to her sides and pulling her shoulders back. The look she gave him—as if she were facing a firing squad—well, that nearly broke his heart. "But it appears you're going to tell me, Doctor Drake. So go ahead."

Ben gently grasped her thin shoulders and looked deep into her eyes. "It means that we're family. I don't know what that means in your book, but in mine it means that we take care of one another."

She barely breathed, confusion momentarily flitting across her face, leaving behind a very empty gaze that pierced his heart.

"My brother Joseph and I came after him a few times," he continued, gauging her response as he slid his hands from her shoulders. "Did you know that?"

Her brow furrowed. "You did?"

He nodded.

"I wonder why he never told me that."

"Maybe it wasn't memorable for him. I don't know," Ben offered with a frustrated shrug. "It was memorable enough for me. That's for sure."

A faint tremble stirred her rosebud lips. "Why wouldn't he tell me about that?"

"I'm sure he didn't just forget to tell you. It doesn't surprise me that he'd leave out information like that." Seeing the desperate edge to her gaze, he braced a hand against the doorway and leaned in a little closer, wishing he could just fold her into a comforting embrace. But like the strays he'd taken in, she'd probably run off, or at the very least, close herself up even tighter.

"We found him each time at a saloon," he measured out. "I wish I could say that he was glad to see us."

Her gaze drifted to the floor as if she were looking for some kind of answer there. "Were you trying to get something from him?" she almost accused, as if trying to convince herself even as she asked the question. "Is that why you tracked him down?"

Ben's ire-tainted chuckle died on a sobering sigh. "Not exactly. We were there because we wanted him to know that we still cared. That he was part of the family. And that no matter what had happened in the past we wanted him to come home."

The long moment of silence that followed had Ben wondering what exactly Max had shared with her about his family. She'd been married to him for seven years. The fact that she was so mistrusting didn't surprise him in the least if Max had filled her head with his bitter, blame-others-for-your-mistakes view on life.

She blinked hard as if forcing back tears. "He never said anything. And—and I wish I had known."

"I wish you had known, too." He threaded his hands together at the back of his neck in an effort to keep himself from reaching out to her.

"Listen, Callie…it has to be hard on you, this whole thing. Since you arrived a little over three days ago, you've made some difficult discoveries. You'd have to be dead not to have it affect you." And Ben was sure that she had too much fight in her for that. "It would've been helpful to meet you at that time. Instead of this way."

Ben recalled the stories Max had told about his wife. That she was demanding. Insisted on having the finest, most up-to-date clothing. Turned her nose up at anything less than the best… Having never met this high-need wife, they could only assume there must be some truth woven in amongst the words.

Looking at Callie now, and remembering the way she'd shown up in such overt need, his heart clenched with painful regret. Max had lied. About his own wife. Of that Ben was certain. She may have been tight-lipped about her past, but he could tell she'd suffered.

For that reason, Ben didn't know whether to grieve for the loss of his brother—or be glad for the fact that he was dead.

Chapter Eight

Water-wrinkled, red and chapped hands were a small price to pay if having them meant avoiding Ben Drake for the day.

He was a dangerous, dangerous man.

Oh, he seemed nice, all right. Probably was everybody's best friend. The town confidant. And though Callie couldn't imagine him lifting a hand to harm another living soul, he was an enemy to her resolve, and definitely a threat to her vow to never make herself vulnerable to another man again.

She'd gladly work her hands raw every day if that meant diverting her attention from him.

Heaving a bucket of cleaning water up to the sink, she dumped the filthy contents out, determined to just as easily get rid of her unruly thoughts regarding that man.

His face suddenly jumped into her mind and she could've sworn she heard his deep, mellow voice right along with it, saying, *"Callie, it's me again and I'm not leaving."*

She hissed a breath through gritted teeth, nearly

losing her grip on the bucket handle as she forced the image from her thoughts.

Getting him out of her mind wasn't going to be as easy as she thought. Not when he had such a—a *way* about him.

He was disarming. Charming. And downright pushy, too. The way he looked at her, with that silvery-blue gaze of his that seemed to travel deep inside her heart. His smile…well, that was another risk altogether. The effect of his half-cocked grin wriggled inside her like a sneaky snake, wrapping around her determination and nearly constricting the strength right out of it.

And the way he showed such concern… She'd tried to convince herself that the compassion was all just a wonderfully crafted act. A show. But she was horribly, horribly afraid that that wasn't the case.

Every time he'd get close to her, she'd feel her will-power crumbling like a poorly constructed barricade. She'd catch herself staring at his arms, wondering what it would be like to be swallowed in his steady and comforting embrace. She'd find her focus riveted to his eyes, craving one of his deep, hopeful glances that made her want to believe in 'good' again.

Callie picked up a towel and swiped at the perspiration beading her forehead. She felt near to collapsing, she was so worn-out, but she'd made it through the entire day. And if she put her mind to it, she could last a little longer, before she dropped, half-dead, into bed.

After the conversation she'd had with Ben this morning, she wasn't so sure she'd be any use at all. To find out that Max had never said a thing to her about their visits had stirred instant anger. He'd always—*always* made her believe that when he'd left home, they'd gladly pushed him out into the world and slammed the proverbial door.

Callie sank into a chair, resting her elbows on her knees. Betrayal had cut deep, lancing all the way to her heart. It'd been her stubborn pride that had seen her through without letting loose the deep cry that begged for release.

She couldn't take Ben's words at face value if she wished to remain exempt from getting *taken* again. The fact that he was Max's flesh-and-blood brother should give her pause, for sure. No matter what she felt when he'd do all of those…well, *nice* things, she had to keep him at arm's length.

Just thinking about warding off his niceness made her weary, though. How long could she keep this up?

Drawing in a deep breath, she wiped her face with her apron, determined not to give in to the raw emotion waiting in the shadows. No man was worth that.

"Callie? Have you seen my stethoscope?" From down the hall came that rich warm voice she couldn't seem to exterminate from her mind.

She raised her head just in time to see Ben walk in the room, his long legs eating up the space between them. The starched, ecru shirt he wore had been rolled up to reveal muscle-roped strength.

"Your stethoscope?" She rubbed a hand over her eyes as she made to stand.

"No. Please, stay seated." He hunkered down next to her, setting the back of his hand to her forehead. "You overdid it, didn't you?"

"Not at all."

"I don't believe you." Quirking his mouth to one side, he moved his hand down to her arm. "You look completely worn-out. You're pale and your eyes are red and watery again."

She gave a weak, sardonic chuckle. "Oh, Doctor Drake, you do have quite a way with words, don't you? Do you say that to all of the ladies?"

"Only the ones that don't listen to good, common sense." He brushed a tendril of hair from her forehead, sending a quiver through her.

"I listened. I just didn't line up and salute."

When he set his fingers to her neck, palpating her glands, she tried not to squirm under his warm, gentle, spine-tingling ministrations. Scrutinizing him out of the corner of her eye, she wished he'd just keep his doctoring hands to himself.

But something in the way his fingers felt against her skin awakened a hunger that rumbled deep inside her for a comforting touch   *his* comforting touch. It'd been years since she'd really felt cared for.

"Your glands aren't as swollen. That's good news." Standing, he braced his hands on his hips. "By the way, do you mind calling me Ben? Most everyone does, apart from an occasional few, and since we'll be working together it'd make things a little more relaxed."

She nodded, having silently referred to him as such from day one. "Yes, if that's what you want."

"That's definitely what I want. Would you prefer Miss Callie, Mrs. Drake, or…*just* Callie," he said on a wink.

Oh, she hated it when he winked. Who'd guess that a simple little gesture like that could inflict such massive damage to her resolve?

Averting her gaze to the dainty lilac flowers splashed across her dress, she touched her fingers to the locket at her neck. "Callie is fine," she finally said, pushing herself up from the chair.

"Good, that's settled. Now, about the stethoscope," he continued, clapping his hands together as he walked toward the examination room. "I'm sure I left it in here. Have you seen it?"

She slowly followed him, trying to recall. "I don't remember seeing it and I've cleaned that room from top to bottom."

"I noticed. You've been busy." He scanned the room, a satisfied smile growing on his lips. The day's growth of his dark beard shadowing his face gave him a rugged look that kicked up her pulse a notch. "I'll say it again… I wish you'd take it easy for a few more days, but I do appreciate your hard work. The room looks better than it has since I built the place five years ago." He turned to her, his ice-melting gaze making her stomach turn to mush. "Thank you."

She swallowed hard. "You're welcome."

While Ben began searching around the room, Callie inwardly berated herself for falling so easily for his charm. How in the world was she going to be able to continue working for him? If she had another choice, *any other choice,* she'd jump at it. But she had to have this job.

As it was, with every passing day, she risked having Whiteside find her and drag her back to his nest to settle up. Having spent months walking down the hallways, cleaning his girls' rooms and getting to know them in the process, she'd much rather be here in Ben's care.

For the most part, Whiteside's girls didn't seem to be much different than herself. Harder maybe, but then, she'd gradually seen the same hardness start to develop in herself, too. Though their backgrounds were varied, one thing had seemed a common thread among them: they'd all been down on their luck and had grabbed at the promise of food, clothing and shelter.

But surely they'd never been loved in a place like that. They'd sold their souls for basic needs. Callie would rather go hungry and wear rags under the shelter of a pine bough than do that.

She noticed the perplexed look on Ben's face as he searched in vain. "Maybe you weren't thinking and stuck the stethoscope somewhere else."

He angled his head in challenge.

"What?" Callie said with a defensive shrug. "You might have forgotten what you did with it." She sank to her hands and knees to peer under the examination table again. "I moved every last piece of furniture in this room and scrubbed the floor, so I seriously doubt it's here. Are you sure you didn't put it in your bag?"

When she reached to pull herself up, a warm rush traveled straight through her as he gently grasped her arm to help her. His touch did something to her. It had an effect that was destabilizing, yet completely alluring.

When Max had touched her, it had always been to take. But when Ben touched her...well, his touch just seemed so different, as if he meant not to take, but to give.

"I suppose anything's possible." Ben's jaw tensed. "But I usually leave it in this room since this is where I see to my patients. Wouldn't that make sense to you?"

"I'll keep looking." Callie moved out of his grasp in an effort to calm her pulse. "It must be around here somewhere."

He gave a resigned sigh. "I'm sure it'll show up. But if you happen to remember where it is, I'd be much obliged."

She walked over to the medicine cabinet in the corner of the room and knelt down, ducking her head to look under the large cupboard.

A rattling knock sounded at the door. "Doc, ya in?" A thin, male voice straggled into the room.

"In here," Ben poked his head into the hallway. "What can I do for you, Pete? Is that leg giving you trouble again?"

Out of the corner of her eye, Callie caught sight of a lanky man trailing Ben into the room. "I been tryin' to do what you told me with that salve and them bandages, but—"

"But maybe you missed a time or two?"

Pete hung his head. "Well, maybe."

"You're becoming a regular fixture here, Pete—not that I mind your company, but I'm sure you have better things to do."

When she glanced up to see the man's reaction, she found herself under his close scrutiny.

"I'd like to introduce my assistant, Miss Callie." Ben stepped over to lend her a hand up. "This is her first day working with me."

Callie gained her feet then adjusted the bodice of her dress.

"Ma'am." The man tipped his wide, dusty Stetson to her.

"Callie, this is Pete O'Leary."

"It's nice to meet you, Mr. O'Leary." She held out her hand to the man, trying to hide her surprise when his slender, sweaty hand shook hers so vigorously that she had to tug her hand free. She made her best attempt to smile.

"Ben's gonna be mighty glad fer yer help, to be sure, ma'am. He's been needin' it for a while now."

"When my patients make comments like that, I guess you know that the *Help Wanted* sign was long overdue," Ben commented.

She had to smile at that. If he was half as glad to have the position filled as she was to have this job, then hopefully it'd benefit both of them.

"You look mighty familiar, ma'am." Pete tugged at his collar, but even buttoned clear to the top, it gaped open, revealing his razor-sharp Adam's apple bobbing with a swallow. "Do I know you from somewhere's?"

"I don't think so." Uncomfortable with his direct perusal, Callie dodged his gaze. "I can't imagine where you might have seen me."

"I jest swear I seen ya before. Not too long ago, neither." He took a step closer, narrowing his already small eyes as if to bring her into better focus. "You from around here?"

Callie swallowed hard. She didn't want to cause any embarrassment for Ben and his family, and therefore didn't plan on going into detail.

"No," she finally responded. "No, I'm not."

"Hmm…it's bound to come to me. I'd never forget a perty face like yours."

"So what seems to be the problem today, Pete?" Ben cut in, stepping between her and Mr. O'Leary.

She squeezed her eyes shut, knowing that she would have to field questions. She just didn't want to divulge any more information than necessary, and Ben had obviously been astute enough, good enough to rescue her at the moment.

She tried to counter the warmhearted feeling that little fact gave her with the reasons why he was not safe. But for the life of her, she had a hard time scrounging up even one.

"That shifty little good-for-nuthin' ferret I bought off that travelin' salesman is gonna be the death'a me. I swear to ya, Conroy went and drug that tin'a salve off somewhere and now I can't find it. That varmint steals pert near everything—specially if'n it shines."

"You haven't seen a stethoscope lying around your place, have you?" Turning, he slid a wink to Callie then faced his patient again.

There it was. That wink again.

She buoyed herself against the effects.

"Huh?" Pete pulled his head back.

"Oh, I just can't find my stethoscope. Wish I could blame Conroy, but that wouldn't be very fair to him since he's not stepped his little paws in here."

"I'm near ready to throw that varmint's wily be-hind out the door. He's a rascal, I tell ya." The man sliced a breath through gritted teeth. "But sure as shootin', I'd probably miss the little feller."

Ben chuckled, the low, comforting sound like gentle, lapping waves against her soul. He patted his hand on the exam table. "Why don't you take a seat up on the table, Pete, and we'll take a look at your leg."

Jamming his cowboy hat down on his head, the man lifted his chin a notch. "No need fer that, Doc."

"Now, Pete, you know me better than that. I'm just going to check you over, and if the wound looks decent then I'll send you on your way with a new tin of salve."

The lanky man managed an inordinate display of grumbling under his breath while he scuffed over to the table.

She could barely hold back her grin. It was clear as the sun shining through the sparkling clean windows that Mr. O'Leary knew what he was in for when he'd stepped into this office.

She had a feeling that Ben probably always conducted things in that way—making sure his patients were well cared for. He'd done the same for her.

"Get on up there." Ben laughed as he made his way to the doorway. "I've got to run next door for the new shipment of gauze I just picked up. Don't you go any-where." Turning to Callie, he added, "Would you mind fetching me a fresh basin of water?"

"Not at all," she answered before the front door shut.

Retrieving the basin off the small table, she carried it into the kitchen, cleaned and rinsed it well then filled it with fresh water. She tried to ignore the weary fatigue in her arms as she carried it back to the exam room and set it down.

"I know where I seen ya." Mr. O'Leary gave a thin chuckle. "Denver."

Her stomach did a slow churn as she turned to face him. The smug smile he wore did nothing to calm her as she tried to place him.

She forced her feet to stay planted right where they were even though she wanted to run from the room. Tucking a wayward strand of hair behind her ear, she comforted herself with the idea that he might well have her mixed up with some other woman. How could he remember someone like her, anyway? She'd certainly never tried to draw attention to herself. And the jobs she'd worked most often kept her busy behind the scenes.

"Yep." He nodded slowly. "Took me a while, but I finally figured it out."

"Really?" she asked, silently scolding herself for the strangled sound in her voice.

"Must say, it threw me, with you bein' here, workin'

fer Doc Drake. He's a good man, Ben is." He slid his suddenly not-so-friendly, leering gaze up the length of her in a slow, rude manner. "He don' strike me as the kind, but then—"

"The kind?" Callie backed up a step. She wished Ben would return. "The kind to what?"

"Oh, now don't you start with that. You take me fer a fool, missy?" Pulling his hat from a slicked-down mat of bright red hair, he gave it a hearty slap against his leg, sending a cloud of dust into the freshly cleaned room.

Refusing to be intimidated, she braced her hands at her waist as she watched the dust settle. "I'm sorry, sir, I have no idea what you're talking about."

He turned his hat in his hands, a poor showing of teeth centered in his unsettling grin. "That sly dog, Ben. He must be gittin' his money's worth outa ya, huh?"

The coarse chuckle that erupted from his mouth made her cringe. She didn't want to cower like a rabbit frozen in fear, but the way he looked at her… She'd been stared at with that greedy, predatory look before, when she'd been cleaning the saloon and brothel, and it had made her feel dirty.

Then it dawned on her…his meaning. She drew her hands into balls. Tried to still her quaking knees. Fought to calm her raging pulse as he gave her a slow nod.

"You for hire by others, too?" He quirked his eyebrows at odd angles over his beady little eyes. "'Cause it's been too long since I had me a good-lookin' woman like you."

If what Ben had always believed was true, that children and animals were a good judge of character, then Callie surely passed with flying colors.

He watched as Luke angled a buoyant glance at Callie from beneath a mop of sandy hair, seemingly oblivious to the fact that Ben sat with them in front of the woodstove.

Ben braced his elbows on his knees, watching as Callie met Luke's admiring gaze. The way she smiled at the boy, giving him her undivided, honest attention, made Ben's throat grow thick. Luke might've been ten feet tall for the look of sheer pride on the boy's dirt-smudged face.

It was good to see Callie smile. For the past two days she'd been more withdrawn. When Pete O'Leary had visited two days ago, he remembered walking into the room, finding her eyes wide and wary and her flushed, as if she'd just run a mile.

She'd shrugged off his show of concern afterward, chalking it up to being tired, though that did nothing to minimize the reservations tumbling through his mind and heart. If somehow he'd pushed too fast, and in doing so shoved her away, then he wanted to make things right.

Seeing her now, looking so relaxed and at ease, he dismissed the lingering uncertainty.

The boy had lugged his heavy crate of six-week-old kittens all the way over here—the third time this week—just to show them to Callie since she'd not met the little felines yet. The look of pride on the boy's face as he slowly scooped up a slumbering kitten from the box was enough to make a grown man cry. And the sensitive way Callie responded to Luke made his heart surge with admiration. She was a natural with children.

Taking extreme care, Luke held up the black-and-white short-haired kitten. "I named this one here Mittens."

"Oh, that's a perfect name for her," she cooed, trailing a fingertip down to the kitten's tiny paws. "The white markings on her feet look just like mittens."

"Yeah. She'll be ready this winter." With an endearing giggle, he carefully laid the kitten down into the bed of straw Ben had replenished just moments ago.

"How did you come up with the names for your kittens?" she asked.

"Easy." He fluffed some of the straw around the sleeping kittens. "I 'membered hearin' Ben prayin' once for one'a his animals, and I got ta' thinkin'...if'n God answered his prayers 'bout that, maybe He'd answer me if'n I asked Him 'bout names."

Ben squeezed his eyes shut for a moment, sobered by the simple and complete trust Luke placed in him. Even when he felt like his faith in God was challenged, this young boy found enough faith to grab on to, to spur him toward believing.

"And this one's named Fluffy." Luke reached down into the crate and carefully lifted out a puff of gray fur as he glanced up hesitantly at Ben. "I know it sounds kinda girly and all, but with how puffy he is, that's what fits 'im. Don'cha think?"

"Absolutely." Ben gave a brisk nod. "You couldn't have chosen a better name."

"It's a perfect name." Callie cradled the ball of fur then nuzzled the downy softness. "He's so soft, isn't he?"

Wide-eyed, Luke observed Callie as if he'd never seen a woman fawn over an animal before. It didn't surprise Ben one bit that Callie would be kindhearted toward animals. Watching her now with the kittens, the way she quietly cooed to them and gently pet them, he could see that she was likely as much of a soft heart as himself when it came to animals.

"I had a cat named Fluffy once." Ben omitted the small fact that the cat had been a female.

"Really?" Luke's eyes widened further.

"I sure did." Ben slid one finger gently down the kitten's head, inspecting his eyes and nose as he did. "This little guy's eye infection seems to be healing up just fine. What do you think?"

Luke instantly scrambled to his knees, leaning over and peering at the kitten. "Yeah. I'm thinkin' so, too. There ain't no more stuff in his eyes."

"You're doing a good job caring for them, Luke." Callie smiled at the boy then briefly swung her gaze up to Ben, making his mouth go suddenly dry.

When she looked away, he focused his attention down at the crate of felines again and drew out the biggest kitten in the box. "What about this little guy? His fur is almost like a panther, but with how fat his little belly is, he reminds me more of a black bear cub. What's his name?"

Luke pulled his mouth to the side, staring at the kitten in Ben's hands with a look of pure affection and pride. "That's Benjamin."

Ben's heart tightened in his chest. A lump formed in his throat. When he stroked the tubby little guy, he realized that for some reason, Luke naming this kitten after him meant more than if an entire state had been named in his honor.

"And why did you call him that?" Callie asked softly.

Luke hitched his shoulders up. "Oh, I don' know. I just wanted to, that's all. Seemed like a good name for a little cat like him."

The boy's bashful response had Ben swallowing hard.

"Well, Benjamin's certainly a nice-looking kitten." Callie touched the kitten's thick paws.

"You must be feeding them plenty. This little guy is as round as he can be." Ben handed the kitten back to Luke.

"Yeah. I feed 'em four times a day, jest like ya said." He lowered his head and touched his nose to the kitten's. Then he shot his bright gaze up to Callie. "Ya know what?"

"What?"

"He's really strong. He can almost climb out'a this here box already."

"That's quite an accomplishment for such a little one."

With an adamant nod, Luke pulled the kitten to his chest, cradling it in a most tender way. "He's prolly gonna be a real good hunter, too. And the way he's always snugglin' with the other kittens, I'll jest bet he's gonna make a good daddy cat. Don'cha think?"

"Yes, I'm sure he will." Callie slid her gaze to Ben, the subtle look of appreciation he saw there taking him aback. "What about this little girl?" she finally asked, averting her attention to the last kitten.

"Oh, I named 'er Beauty." Luke lifted the long-haired black-and-white kitten out of the crate and delicately handed her to Callie. "After you, Miss Callie."

She gave an almost inaudible gasp as she cradled the kitten in the crook of her arm. "Aww…that's so sweet, Luke." She blinked hard, giving Luke's hand a squeeze. "So very sweet."

"Thanks." He cracked his knuckles, emitting tiny popping sounds into the quiet room.

The tender warmth that stole over Ben as he stared

down at Luke and Callie took him by surprise. Never had he felt quite this way. It was almost as if he could picture himself as a father and a husband.

He'd been hard-pressed to get this young woman out of his mind. Found himself daydreaming about her when he had several reasons not to.

He couldn't help himself. She unknowingly commanded his thoughts, even when she'd made a habit of avoiding his presence.

The tender gleam in her eye gave him pause.

"She's the prettiest one in the bunch," Ben agreed quietly.

Silently, he hoped that he could keep his head enough to notice if she decided to turn on him. But seeing her now, the genuine way she had with Luke, he couldn't imagine her being so callous.

Chapter Nine

Callie…

The sight of her stole the breath from Ben's lungs.

Securing the reins, he stepped up to his office porch, all the while reminding himself to breathe. He had to will his pulse to stop pounding through his veins as he took her in.

The color of her dress was so perfect for her that Ben was pretty sure God must've had Callie in mind when He created the emerald-green shade.

He gave a long, approving sigh. "You look very nice."

"Thank you." She met his gaze with a wobbly smile. Then fastened the last button of the heavy wool cloak he'd purchased for her yesterday. "And thank you again for the cloak. It's very warm and more than suitable. I'll pay—"

"Shh…" Ben gave his head a slow, steady shake. "You agreed you wouldn't argue with me about this. Remember?"

She dropped her focus to the small reticule she held—compliments of Katie. "I must've been delirious."

"I don't think so." Ben chuckled low. "You seemed perfectly in control of your actions and speech."

When he prepared to help her up into the wagon, she pulled away. "I can make it just fine by myself."

"I know you can, but you're a lady and I'd like to help. All right?" He circled her waist with his hands and lifted, noticing that she didn't feel quite as fragile as she had the night she'd come to him, almost a week ago. Once she was settled on the seat, he spread a thick wool blanket over her lap, silently thanking God for the progress she'd made.

It had been a whirlwind six days. Since she'd been up, she'd been as diligent and hardworking as anyone he'd ever known. And though he was getting her to open up a little, he had a feeling it'd be a long time before she'd trust him.

He'd promised himself that he'd not push her to open up too hard too fast, but the more time that ticked by, the harder it was to live up to his promise.

Situating himself next to her, he clucked his tongue to urge his horse along, waving to the bundle of folks in a passing wagon.

"I'm glad you decided to come with me today," he said, glancing down at her. "It'll mean a great deal to Katie to have you join us for dinner after church."

"Are you sure it'll be all right if I attend with you?" Her knuckles grew white as she clutched her reticule.

"Of course."

She avoided his questioning gaze, her throat visibly contracting.

"Are you worried that you won't be welcomed? Is that it?"

She traced a fingertip the length of the braided, drawstring cord closing her bag. "Not exactly."

"Then what?"

She turned those beautiful eyes of hers on him. The depths of which made him seriously question his long-ago decision to remain a bachelor.

"It's just that, well, a while ago I inquired after a job at an orphanage that was run by a church. They made it clear that they didn't want me working with the children." The faintest of winces contorted her delicate features.

"Why would they say something like that?" He swept his gaze over each of her lovely, sweet features. "I can't imagine anyone turning you down."

He hadn't been able to turn her down. She had that certain look about her that pierced the heart. It wasn't a piteous look, but he imagined it was a David-against-Goliath sort of look. He'd seen it in her from the get-go… a certain strength and courage to face the unknown.

"Did Max have anything to do with the minister's perception of you?"

Her focus shifted downward. "He wasn't looked upon very favorably. Wherever we ended up living," she added discreetly.

"And being his wife, neither were you, right?"

Determined silence was his answer. The way she'd skirted the truth, as if she'd somehow dishonor Max, made Ben's heart ache. He wondered if she felt like she had to protect Max's memory by protecting his name.

"Ahh, Callie. I'm sorry." Knowing how hard it must've been to be shunned because of Max, his heart broke for her. "I've seen the patient and loving way you interact with Luke. You would've been their best and brightest asset."

He had to battle back the instant irritation that her words had triggered inside him. He was furious at Max, yet again, for not taking into account how his actions might affect others.

And he was furious at the way some people, in the name of God, could set up ridiculous standards that had nothing to do with God, and everything to do with their selfish desire to have a respectable club of sorts, instead of a family.

He struggled to tamp down his ire as he reined his horse to a halt in the wagon-packed churchyard.

"I didn't tell you that for your sympathy. The last thing I want is your sympathy." Brushing a hand over the wool blanket's thick weave, her fingers trembled. "I just don't want to cause any embarrassment for you or your family. That's all. If you'd rather that I not attend with you, I'll completely understand."

Ben set the brake and faced her. Draping an arm on the seat behind her, he gave a brief nod to a lone straggler entering the church building.

"Listen to me, Callie…" He covered her hand with his, pleased that for once, she didn't startle or pull away at his touch. "First of all, no one here knows that you were Max's wife. They'll find out sooner or later, but even if the whole town was privy to the information, it wouldn't matter."

At the faint strain of some hymn seeping through the thick, tall doors, Callie moved to get down from the wagon, but he pulled her back to the seat.

"You'll be late." A slight quaver undermined her usual calm reserve.

"It's all right. I'm sure that God is every bit as much here with us as He is inside with the other folks." He gave her hand a gentle squeeze and continued. "I'm sorry about what happened in the past, Callie. It was wrong, plain and simple. I can assure you that you'll be welcomed here." He nodded toward the church building.

Staring down at where his large hand covered hers, he felt an overwhelming desire to protect her like this and more. He wanted to help her trust again. To break through her protective barrier, allow her to spread her wings and fly.

But what if she refused his help?

And what if the niggling suspicion that had taken up residence in his mind was warranted? In the past two days he'd discovered that both his stethoscope and then some tweezers had come up missing. In five years of doctoring, he'd never, ever misplaced those things. He might lack for administrative and housekeeping skills, but he'd never been careless about the tools of his trade.

Though she might be tight-lipped about her past, there was nothing about her demeanor that would point to her being a thief. She was caring, patient and hardworking, just to name a few noteworthy attributes.

So what was he thinking?

He fought back the doubts and suspicions, ashamed that he could've made such judgments. He'd thought himself to be above such actions, but this whole situation with Callie had so far served to reveal a side of himself he didn't much like to see.

"You have to know that when that kind of judging and blame-casting happens, it has nothing to do with God." At the faraway look in her eyes, he crooked a finger under her chin. Drew her half-shuttered gaze to his. "People can be cruel. But God…He's never cruel."

"I want to believe that," she whispered, nibbling her bottom lip.

He wanted to believe it again, too. At one time he'd

never questioned that. In spite of his mounting failings and regrets, he wanted to trust God. But could he ever forgive himself for the way he'd made a mess of things with Max? For the way he'd let his brothers down in their greatest time of need?

Had God brought Callie into his life as a way to make up for his failings with Max? Something about that idea didn't quite sit right, deep down, but he couldn't deny that the thought had crossed his mind more than once.

After a long moment, he instinctively reached out to pull a fallen leaf from where it had floated down to land in her hair. The backs of his fingers touched feather-light and ever so briefly against her cheek.

She slid an expectant gaze to him, the whisper of space between them resonating and humming from the simple touch.

When he held the bright yellow aspen leaf out to her, she took it from his hands, staring down at it and tracing the brown spots marring the brilliant yellow hue. "It's always so sad, isn't it? That things have to die?"

"It is. But if they didn't, new life could never come forth." Trailing a finger over the edge of the half-dried leaf, he smoothed his hand over hers. "It's God's way," he said as much to himself as to her.

He relished the feel of her silky-smooth skin. Cherished the tender glimpse of vulnerability. It was small, but real.

The heated, searing sensations, as true and as warm as if he sat before a blazing fire, seeped from her fingers all the way up to his heart, belying the freezing temperature outside.

Its power affected him in ways that undermined his common sense. Tugged at his self-restraint. And upended his moral convictions.

Pulling his hand back, he hauled in a thick, steadying breath. Willed his heart to slow to a normal beat. It took every bit of summoned restraint to resist the urge to pull her into an embrace. His arms ached to hold her and drive away the shadows of her past. But she wasn't ready for that.

He didn't know if he was ready for that, either.

While she tucked the leaf into her reticule, Ben jumped down from the wagon and crossed to her side, lifting her down. "It's only fair to warn you…"

"Warn me about what?" She burrowed a hand in the pocket of her cloak.

"Some of the busybodies in the congregation will probably beeline for you just as soon as the pastor says his last *Amen*." Winking, he crooked an arm and held it out for her then led her up the steps of the white clapboard church. "Don't mind them if it happens, though. They're fairly harmless. Besides, they'll love you."

Upon opening the door, he stepped into the harmonious sound of his favorite hymn. He wasn't sure he'd ever felt as proud as he did now, walking into church with a lovely young woman beside him.

He had to remind himself that Callie was Max's widow.

And his employee.

But he sure did have a hard time remembering that.

While the congregation sang the last strain, he noticed heads turning, staring at him as though he'd brought the Queen of England into their midst. Ben was certain that his appearance here with Callie would be an all-out shock. Over the years, the townsfolk had finally gathered that he wasn't in the market for a wife and, for the most part, had ceased trying to set him up with every eligible young woman this side of the Rocky Mountains.

That had been a relief of epic proportions.

He wasn't sure he was in the market now, but he couldn't deny the attraction and growing feelings he felt for Callie. And he sure couldn't ignore them since they seemed to consume his every thought.

With a hand placed lightly at her back, he ushered her into a pew toward the back where Joseph and Katie stood singing. The eager way Katie greeted Callie, and the way Callie seemed to glow from that warm acceptance, made his heart swell with an odd sense of satisfaction.

When the song ended and the people turned in the pews to greet each other, Joseph leaned toward Ben. "You're putting the fear of God into some of these women." He shot Ben a playful grin.

"What?" Ben asked, confused.

"Katie tells me that Callie's liable to make a stir among the single men, with how pretty she looks." He leaned back in the pew then, all casual and carefree, as if he'd just made some benign comment on the weather.

Katie answered with a shake of her head and bridled grin.

Out of the corner of his eye, Ben could see a pink blush touching Callie's cheeks.

Throughout the service, he found himself inarguably distracted. First…by the simple fact that Callie, beautiful and extraordinarily resilient, was seated here beside him. And second…by the guarded reactions he witnessed from her. Her tightly balled fists. The rigid posture she'd maintained throughout the service. She closed her eyes and tensed several times, as if bracing herself for a regular old fire-and-brimstone, pulpit-pounding message. Hugged her arms in unyielding protection of herself—a stark contrast to the single-minded strength she normally displayed.

But it was the visible sigh she gave at the benediction that made his heart fall hard. It was as if she was inordinately grateful to have made it through the church service without some scathing rebuke aimed her way.

The image still weighed him down when they arrived at Joseph and Katie's house to join his family for dinner. The way she seemed to trudge on in the face of her apparent fears made him want to pry away all of the demons of her past.

Though right now it seemed she was facing a new demon.

Aaron.

From the moment they'd stepped foot in the house, Ben could see and feel the heated stare coming from his brother. For some reason, Aaron's mistrust and dislike of Callie had swelled like some infected wound in the past two days. Though he had no intention of making a scene about it, Ben was bound and determined to wrangle Aaron aside and pin him with a few pointed questions.

"Callie, I want you to meet my family. Of course, you already know Katie," he said.

Katie threw her arms around Callie in a huge hug. "This is my husband, Joseph," she said, stepping back. "He's the second Drake brother."

When Callie reached for Joseph's hand, Ben noted that the usual awkwardness that new folks felt with Joseph's blindness didn't seem to be present. At all. "It's nice to meet you."

"Good to meet you, too," Joseph greeted congenially. "Sorry if I embarrassed you with the comment in church."

Her carefree chuckle made Ben proud. "That's all right."

"Katie's told me a lot about you."

Callie shifted a surprised look to Katie.

"All good, Callie," Katie affirmed.

"This is Zach," Ben continued. "He's the baby of the bunch."

The past months that Zach had spent working on a cattle ranch just north of town had done him a world of good. At twenty-two, he seemed comfortable in his own skin. Even sported a manner of contentment about him that had been refreshing to see. And he looked healthy, had packed on hard work-induced muscle. Though he was a good three inches shorter than Ben's six feet three inches, Zach made up for it in his sturdy build and quick speed.

Zach held out his hand to Callie. "It's nice to meet you, Callie. Good to have you join us today."

"I'm glad to be here."

"I hear you've been spending time reading classic literature," Ben aimed at Zach, chuckling when his brother rolled his eyes in mock annoyance. "Shakespeare and the like... Maybe you can do a little recitation for us today?"

"Yeah, what do you say?" Joseph added.

"What is this? Pick on your little brother day?" Sighing, Zach angled an exasperated gaze down at Callie. "They love to do that to me. They think it makes them all big and powerful. Honestly, I doubt they could even understand the stuff."

"Really," she braved, sliding a hand to her mouth.

"Well, that's insulting enough," Ben parried.

Zach stuck Ben with a good-natured glare. "Ya know, you'll rue the day you decided to pick on me."

"You're all talk," Ben retorted in dismissal. "Powerful as a charging bull, but harmless as a nursing pup."

"Rue the day?" Joseph cracked with an ire-provoking smirk. "You've definitely had your nose in Shakespeare again, haven't you?"

"So what if I had?"

"Nothing." Joseph crossed his arms at his chest, shaking his head in innocence. "Not a thing."

Zach sighed. "Don't think that just because you can't see, Joseph, I won't take you."

Joseph pulled his shoulders back, his deep amber eyes sparkling as he rubbed his hands together. "I'll be waiting for you. Listening for your every move."

"And this is Aaron," he said, gesturing to where Aaron leaned into the corner of the room.

Callie stepped forward and held her hand out to Aaron.

When Aaron merely looked from her hand to her face as if determining whether he could stand touching her, Ben almost decked him. Right then. Right there. Scene or no scene. No matter what bias Aaron had against her because of Max, it didn't warrant that kind of rude behavior.

At Ben's scathing, dart-throwing gaze, Aaron finally came to his senses and stepped up to shake her hand, but the look in his eyes bordered on sheer malice as he peered down at Callie.

"Callie, would you be so kind as to help me in the kitchen?" said Katie in a rescuing request.

"Of course." Callie slid her hand from Aaron's grasp. When she turned to follow Katie, she avoided Ben's searching gaze and whisked right past him.

Not a second later, Ben jerked a thumb toward the door, fully expecting Aaron to follow, and if he didn't… well, then Ben would drag him out. When the door closed, Aaron, Joseph and Zach were all standing on the porch with Ben.

"*What* was that all about?" He balled his fists at his sides. Glared at Aaron.

Aaron managed a disbelieving snort. "What are you doin' bringing her to church? And then here?"

"We invited her for dinner, Aaron." Joseph raked a hand through his hair. "Katie wouldn't have it any other way. Neither would I."

With a rough shake of his head, Aaron narrowed his eyes. "I don't care if the president of the United States invited her. She has no business being here."

Ben jammed his hands to his waist, his blood nearing the boiling point. "She has just as much business being here or at church as you or I do."

"Well, if she's fooled you that bad, then you're twice as blind as Joseph here," he spat out, slapping the back of his hand against Joseph's broad chest.

"Keep my eyes out of this." Joseph raised his hands.

"Sorry."

"What is the matter with you, Aaron?" Ben challenged.

The loathing that had cloaked Aaron's words hung in such an awkward fashion for him—as if wearing an overcoat four sizes too big. He'd gone through a difficult time in the past months, but even that didn't account for the bitter edge with which he spoke.

Ben attempted to tamp down his ire. "I mean, I know that you and Max weren't exactly on the best of terms when he left, but why do you have to hold that over Callie's head?"

Aaron's jaw muscle visibly pulsed. "It's not right that Max could plant an unwanted kiss on Ellie-girl without so much as a thought. He did it just to spite me, even though he knew good and well that her lips were for me, and me alone."

"I'm sorr—" Ben began.

"Then he added insult to injury and blistered me in a fight," Aaron added, his jaw so tense, Ben thought his tendons might snap. "It's something I'll never forget."

Ben remembered well how enraged Aaron had been that night. Drunk, Max had stumbled in one evening shortly before he took off for good, and had helped himself to a kiss with poor unsuspecting Ellie. She'd tried to push him away and wriggle from his grasp, but he was too strong and too drunk.

Settling his hands at his waist, Ben commanded Aaron's attention. "It was wrong what he did to Ellie and to you."

"It was wrong what he did to me. To Ellie. To you. To all of us," Aaron hissed, throwing his hands up. "But for some reason, you had to go after him to try to make amends. Not once, but several times."

"I'd hoped to reason with him." Ben felt the old, familiar clamping in his gut at the memory of each failed endeavor. "To talk some sense into him."

"He was weak. Weak willed." Aaron pulled his mouth into a rigid line and gave his head a stiff shake. "And it seems to me that if you have to talk someone into doing what's right, then it'd be just as easy for them to be talked out of it. They've gotta *want* to do what's right. And Max, he never did."

Ben's whole body tensed, ready to retaliate with some

kind of excuse, but Aaron made sense. "You're probably right. As many times as we'd try to convince Max that he was heading down the wrong path, he never would turn around for good."

Aaron jammed a finger into Ben's chest. "Exactly. And if he did it for a short season, then it wouldn't take more than a gentle breeze to blow him into the wrong path again."

"I had to try," he finally said. "I promised Ma I'd raise him to walk the right path." And he'd failed. Miserably.

"I don't think Ma or Pa, either one, expected you to raise the dead." Aaron jammed his hands into his pockets. "And as far as I'm concerned, that would've been an easier task."

Joseph gave a frustrated sigh. "Ben carried more responsibility with Max than you may realize, Aaron. It wasn't easy being the oldest and having to look after all of us."

"I'm not questioning that. What I am questioning is why, with the way Max betrayed us time and again, he feels the need to look after that girl in there." Aaron cast a glance over his shoulder to the front door. "She just can't be trusted. Max said himself that he'd shacked up with some harlot."

"You watch your mouth," Ben warned, his voice low as he glared at his brother.

Aaron met his icy, angry stare. "That woman in there helping Katie is one-and-the-same. Do you know that?"

"You know how easily Max lied." Joseph's jaw pulsed.

"I just met her, but I sure can't imagine Callie playing

the harlot." Zach's eyes grew wide. "Come on, Aaron… lighten up. Does she look like one to you?"

Aaron narrowed his scorn-filled gaze.

Ben stood firm, the ready contempt Aaron exhibited raining down upon him. Images of the dress Callie had shown up in flashed like streaks of lightning through his mind, the tattered and worn ruby-red dress, cut so low in front that the word *decent* would come nowhere near describing the garment.

But nothing about her—not her actions, the way she walked, the way she handled herself around other men—would come close to measuring up to her being a harlot.

"She just doesn't have it in her," he finally said.

Aaron raised his eyebrows in a way that had Ben ready to haul off and hit him. "She's a harlot, Ben, and she's going to rob you blind, just like Max did. Mark my words. Even from the grave Max is trying to tear us apart. And he's using his widow—his *harlot*—to do it."

Ben jammed his brother against the side of the house, doing everything in his power to contain the fierce anger rushing through his veins. "I'm warning you now, if you don't shut your mouth about this, I'll shut it for you," Ben ground out. But even as the words crossed his lips he wondered why he felt the need to so vehemently defend Callie. Something about this sprightly young woman had snagged every single protective bone in his body. Maybe his heart, too.

Chapter Ten

Callie had never felt quite so wanted. Or unwanted, where Ben's brother Aaron was concerned.

She glanced around the kitchen in the doctor's office, searching for the thick pad she needed to lift the steaming teakettle of water from the stove.

Aaron was nothing if not surly. Proud. Arrogant, really. She hadn't shrunk back from his unfriendly, cold greeting that—she recalled with a generous amount of indignation—had come as hard as tack from him. If not for dear Katie saving the day and suggesting Callie keep her company in the kitchen, Callie might still be standing there, five days later, toe-to-toe and nose to chest with Aaron.

His reaction only confirmed Max's descriptions of his brothers, and had irritated her almost as bad as a rock in her shoe. As far as she was concerned, she'd spent far too much time and mental energy trying to reason his response. Maybe he harbored more ill will toward Max than could be overcome. Or maybe he simply had a strong aversion to auburn hair.

With a dismissive shrug and sigh, she headed toward the exam room where Ben waited with a twitchy Mrs.

Duncan. Whatever had caused him to be so aloof, she wasn't about to let it waylay her.

Things were finally starting to look up.

Callie hadn't ever felt so useful. Between cooking hearty meals for Ben, cleaning his office and home, and assisting him with patients, her days were full. And very rewarding.

On the way home from knitting with Katie one day, she'd even gotten an offhand chance to talk with one of the girls from down at the Golden Slipper. Callie had beelined to strike up a conversation with the woman.

Someday, after she had the debt paid off and a little nest egg for herself, she wanted to maybe try to help some of the ladies. Where others looked on them with a derisive snort, Callie had seen another side to the women in her months of cleaning for Whiteside. She had to believe that those women yearned for something more than what they had settled for. That somewhere hidden beneath their hard exteriors were vulnerable young women in need of a friend and a fresh start. And Callie wanted to be that for them.

She entered the exam room, feeling bolstered by the fact that she was making a difference. The wages she'd received so far had been generous. In fact, if things continued as they had been the past ten days, she could well deliver the remainder of the balance to Lyle Whiteside by Christmas. Though this would be her first Christmas without Max and she was sure to feel that loss, being freed from his gambling debt, and from a mean-spirited bully who stood for everything she detested, would be an enormous weight off her shoulders.

Feeling a wonderfully foreign sense of control over the direction of her life, she set the kettle next to the basin and smiled. "Here's the hot water you asked for."

"Thank you." Ben glanced her way as he stood in front of Mrs. Duncan.

Callie turned and took in the plump woman who sat perched on the examination table, her full skirts draped around her in a fluff of light gray-and-peach print fabric. Like a hen refusing to leave her nest, she folded her hands in her lap all prim and proper, while fiery-red wisps of hair frayed from her chignon in an unruly contrast.

"So, you're Miss Callie..." A sedate, almost deflated smile contorted Mrs. Duncan's thin lips.

"Just Callie," she responded, unable to miss Ben's quick wink. "How do you do?"

"I saw you at church a few days back. But land's sakes, I can't seem to go far without some soul or t'other stopping to speak at me," she muttered, somewhat self-importantly. The way the woman worked her hands and leaned forward slightly conjured up unpleasant images of a spindly spider preparing to cocoon its prey.

Callie bit back an amused grin. At least it was glaringly apparent what this lady was here for. Information.

Callie hated to disappoint her.

"By the time I'd made my way clear to the back of the church, why, you were up and gone already." Her haphazard eyebrows rose in awkward arches over her eyes. "Seems that you made an awful fast escape."

"Actually, I lingered for several minutes." Callie stepped over to the cupboard and retrieved a tray of clean and readied medical tools for Ben. She took shamefully morbid satisfaction in lifting a sharp, gleaming scalpel from the metal tray, as though inspecting it. "I had the pleasure of meeting some of the church members. Very nice people you have here in Boulder."

"Course, the welcome wagon sets the tone there. If a body makes folks feel welcome as they join our town, those folks'll turn around and do the same." She gave a swift, confident nod then added, "At least that's what I'm always preachin', bein' the Chairwoman of the Boulder Welcome Wagon, as I am."

"You must be making quite an impact." Callie nibbled her lower lip.

"My friends certainly tell me I do." Mrs. Duncan's full face creased in a pleased-with-herself kind of grin. "So, what brings you to Boulder?"

Ben cleared his throat as he took the tray from Callie's hands. "Callie's my assistant. She's here working for me."

As if struck by a sudden case of dropsy, the woman's face fell. "Well, now, I can see that just as clear as a church bell, Ben Drake," she scolded, her beady-eyed gaze not leaving Callie for an instant. "What I'm meanin' is—"

"Mrs. Duncan, I believe you came here about your toe. Am I right?" He gently tapped the lady's brown-booted feet poking out from under her skirts.

"My toe?"

"You said that it'd been giving you some trouble. You thought you might have an infection?" he added as if to jog her memory.

"I did?" The woman's face pinched in squeamish distaste. Peering down her nose, she stared at her feet as if unsure whether they belonged to her.

When Ben turned and gave Callie another wink, her stomach launched into a flurry of activity. His playfulness, and the ready, warm smile he always seemed to have for her, constantly caught her off guard.

"We would hate for you to go walking around town with an infection." Pushing his sleeves up, he scanned the display of medical instruments. "That wouldn't do at all. Would it, Callie?"

"Not at all. In fact—"

"So, girl…do you have a husband? Family?" Mrs. Duncan's loud voice interrupted. "Setting a good example as Boulder's welcoming committee, I surely wouldn't want to miss them on my rounds. I make it my *personal* business to get to know the new folks in town."

Callie ventured a guess that there was more to her work than met the eye. Mrs. Duncan struck her as a woman who definitely made it her business to not only meet folks, but to get to know every little thing about them, as well.

"No family," she answered carefully.

"She's part of our family," Ben added.

"Well, now, that's not unusual for you Drakes," she dismissed. "Especially you, Ben Drake. You'd take in most any wretched thing."

Callie clamped her jaw tight, wondering if she'd actually heard the woman say something so tactless.

"I hear tell from Mr. Peter O'Leary that he's seen you before?" A distinct element of accusation threaded through the woman's words, sending dread snaking through Callie's veins.

Swallowing hard, she suddenly craved fresh, cool air. Maybe from some mountain over on the next range. A heated blush crept slowly up her neck. She'd do most anything to keep it from advancing all the way to her cheeks, but it was no use. Her cheeks started burning even as the thought popped into her head.

She chided herself for responding as if she'd been caught red-handed in a crime. She had nothing to hide. Sure, she'd not been forthcoming with Ben about the details of her life with Max, or about some of Max's activities, or about the fact that she'd carried Max's baby. But knowing how difficult it must be for Ben and his brothers to learn of their estranged brother's death, she hadn't wanted to add to their misery and grief. If his brothers had composed their own pile of bad memories with Max, then she wouldn't want to add to it with her own unpleasant recollections.

In the strange, misplaced sort of way that had ruled her actions for seven years, she felt as if she had to protect Max. Or at least Max's memory.

"I have no idea where Mr. O'Leary would've seen me, ma'am," Callie finally said, her voice steady.

With a dirty sense of shame, she remembered the way the man had looked her up and down as though she was one of Whiteside's 'girls.' The leering gaze he'd given her had made her stomach convulse with instant dread.

"Really, now?" the woman uttered slowly. "No idea?"

Ben cleared his throat, the muscle at his cheek pulsing. "Could you slip your boot off for me, Mrs. Duncan? More than likely, you've got one of those sore spots again, and I'll probably want to do some cutting around the nail. What do you say? We might as well get at it." He picked up the same scalpel Callie had held. "Callie, could you please get me a clean towel. Maybe some thread for stitching while you're at it."

Mrs. Duncan shoved her thick frame off the table, landing with a heavy thud on the floor. "Actually, my toe is feeling better already." She stomped her foot. "You see. It don't give me a lick of pain. I'm sorry to take up your time like this, Doctor, but I do believe I'm feeling much improved."

"Callie? Are you awake?" Ben's voice sounded from across the room, followed by a knock on the door.

"Ben?" She turned over in bed, forcing her heavy, sleep-laden eyes open.

"I'm sorry to wake you at such an hour." Urgency permeated his words. "May I come in?"

She tugged the blanket up to her chin. "Yes, of course." Blinking against the dim lantern light penetrating the dark room, she brought him into focus. "What time is it, anyway?"

"Just past two o'clock."

Callie rose to her elbows. "Is everything all right?"

"That's why I'm here." He knelt down next to her. His nearness, the warmth of it and the way his breath fanned feather-light over her skin, sent every nerve ending humming to life. "I was hoping that you could help me with a delivery. Mrs. Nolte's oldest boy, Travis, showed up at my place a few minutes ago. His mama's laboring."

"She's having a baby?"

"Yes. And I'd feel better if I had extra help on this one since her husband's out on the range. She had a hard time with the last baby."

Sitting up, Callie rubbed her eyes and stared at Ben's whisker-shadowed features. The flickering lantern light played across the strong, masculine angles of his face, knocking her heartbeat off-kilter. Had the night's nipping chill not sent a quiver of reality down her spine, she might've thought she was in some wonderful, breathtaking dream.

She gathered her wits about her. "Yes, of course. Just give me a couple of minutes. I—I'll be right there."

Callie made fast work of getting ready. But with each inch the wagon traveled from town, her stomach knotted tighter and tighter. She'd never attended a birth except when she'd been an active participant in the delivery of her very own baby girl. The wee hours of that night had been a blur of pain and suffering. One that had left a deep chasm in her heart she feared might never heal.

She'd barely spoken of the baby girl in the past six years. Max hadn't tolerated her tears or any of her nostalgic musings. Not even when anguish and sorrow threatened to consume her. She'd had to pull herself up from the trauma and move on. But, silently, she'd grieved plenty.

There were no guarantees with pregnancy. But never in a million years would she understand why it had been her baby girl who had been taken.

Had God punished her for defying her father? Had He made the past seven years one continuous, humiliating consequence born from one hasty decision? If so, there might never be a second chance for Callie. A second, life-changing chance to find the peace she longed for.

Perhaps Mrs. Nolte also had done something that was grounds for punishment. Would this woman lose her baby, too?

Hoping to allay her growing fears, she grasped her cloak tight around her and asked Ben for a detailed description of what she could expect. She found great comfort in the methodical, calm way he explained the process. His knowledge of the situation went a long way to quelling the insecurity and apprehension creeping around her heart.

Ben pulled the buggy into a small ranch yard where

the full moon's gentle, pearly light illuminated a generous-size house that sat amidst two large barns.

He set the brake. "If you can gather the items we'll need, I'll check her over to see how close she is to delivering."

"All right," she responded, mentally going over the list of things he'd told her to prepare.

"Travis should've made it back by now, and Dillon will be here," he said, grabbing his bag from the floorboards and helping her down. "But since they're just eight and four, it'd be best if you could coax them back to bed."

Callie agreed, her heart going out to the little boys. Before they were even at the door of the clapboard house, she could already hear a woman's anguished cry coming from inside.

Her heart sank rock hard and fast. Her stomach lurched while brisk, northerly winds whipped mercilessly across the front yard.

When the door opened, a young boy, his eyes wide with fear, stood before them. "Ma's hurtin' real bad, Doc."

"It's a good thing you came for me, then, Travis," Ben answered, hunkering down to eye level with the youngster. "Your pa will be proud of you."

"I sent our ranch hand out lookin' for him."

"Good thinking." Ben gave the lad's shoulder a squeeze.

"Thee'th thith way," came a soft voice from the shadows. The younger of the two boys stepped forward in his nightclothes, his chest stuck out proudly even as he clutched a blanket in his chubby little hand.

"Thank you, Dillon." Ben gave the boy a gentle pat

on the head then passed a sobering glance Callie's way before he disappeared behind the door.

"Why don't you boys come with me?" She bent over to catch their attention. "My name's Callie."

Almost in unison, the two boys turned and peered at the door behind them. The staid and brave way they held their ground, like two little soldiers guarding a sacred monument or a beloved patriot, had her struggling to keep her composure.

From the bedroom their mother cried out in pain once again. Callie motioned for the boys to follow her as she made her way to the kitchen to boil water. While she located clean rags and other linens Ben had requested, she tried to distract the boys by asking questions. She also found herself praying for the woman as pain-filled moans filled the dwelling.

After she tucked the children into bed, she loaded up her arms and carried the hot kettle and rags into the bedroom, closing the door behind her.

"Just pour the water into the basin there, Callie," Ben instructed, his hand bracing the pale woman's shoulder as she toiled for each short panting breath. Perspiration had plastered the poor woman's light brown hair against her head. Tiny rivulets streamed down her face. "I'll need your help on the other side."

Willing her heart to slow its frantic pace, Callie did as she was told, each step toward the bed a silent victory.

"Mrs. Nolte, this is Callie, my new assistant." Ben felt the woman's pulse at her wrist. "She's going to be helping us tonight."

"Hello," Callie offered.

The woman's eyes fluttered open and she braved a smile. But her face almost instantly contorted with the arresting pain of another contraction. She stared up at Ben, pleading with a fearful gaze for him to help.

"It's all right. Just take deep breaths," he uttered, his voice like a gentle, calming touch.

Callie sat on the bed opposite Ben, patting the woman's face and neck with a cool, damp cloth.

"Good, Callie." He nodded her way. "Just keep her as comfortable as you can."

As the moments ticked by she felt her control slipping from her desperate grasp. She silently berated herself. If she couldn't maintain her composure in this situation, she could well risk losing her job. Ben needed her to keep her head.

And this poor woman…she needed her, too. Callie had only to focus on the pleading, fear-filled look etched in Mrs. Nolte's kind face to testify to that.

Ben glanced up at Callie every now and then, offering her an encouraging look. She found that if she kept her eyes on him, watching the way he worked with quiet direction and confidence, she was able to maintain her focus.

Just seeing how tender Ben was with the poor woman as she battled through each contraction made Callie's heart swell with gratitude. He handled Mrs. Nolte with a gentle strength and wisdom, challenging every last, lingering question as to Ben's character.

The tenderness she witnessed called up a heartbreaking contrast of bad memories. When her own nightmare barged into her mind, Callie's tender world jerked off its axis.

Six years ago this had been her. She'd labored for a day and a half. There'd been no doctor, not even a midwife. Max had refused. And she'd struggled alone through every pain and contraction. She'd been exhausted at the end, much like this woman. And it had been with the final push that she'd lost consciousness.

The woman gasped, jerking Callie from the agonizing memories. "Oh, dear… Please. Help me. I can't—" Mrs. Nolte clutched Callie's arm with such force, as if a pack of ravenous wolves were nipping at her flesh. She cried out in pain, but this time it merged into an almost animal-like grunt as she bore down, pushing.

"Lift her shoulders, Callie. Prop another pillow behind her." Ben moved to the foot of the bed.

"You're doing fine, Mrs. Nolte," he spoke above another gasping cry. "Just make the most of each contraction, all right? You're almost there."

Callie looked up and found herself pinned by Ben's concerned look. In spite of her best attempt to keep every emotion shuttered deep inside, he must have sensed her unease and raw emotion. He was like that, and where it had strongly irritated her just a few days ago, now it almost gave her a strange sense of comfort.

"Are you all right?" he mouthed while Mrs. Nolte sank with relief, albeit brief, into the feather bed as that contraction subsided.

Callie nodded, probably a little too vigorously since Ben cocked his head as if to say *Are you sure?*

She had to be all right.

Ben needed her.

Mrs. Nolte needed her.

When the woman began growing restless again, Ben braced a hand at one of her knees. She clawed at then gripped the bedsheets, her perspiration-beaded brow furrowed in pain and concentration with the onslaught of another labor pain.

"Garrett is going to be proud of you when he gets off

the range, ma'am. Just keep up the good work and the little one will be here before you know it."

Callie heard Ben's encouraging words to the woman, but all she could seem to see was her own worst nightmare playing out in her mind. The helpless moans. The intensity of each tormenting contraction. The fear that permeated the room. The evening was wrought with stark reminders of six years ago.

She could face anything. Blood. Gaping wounds. Protruding bones. She just didn't know if she could face the most natural and beautiful moment, when a newborn child entered the world.

It loomed as a horrifying reminder, a shameful testament to the fact that she'd been unable to last out the labor to see her child born safely. Maybe if she could've held on for a few more minutes—even seconds—she might've given birth to a healthy baby girl. Maybe if she'd taken matters into her own hands and insisted on help. Maybe if she'd never made the decision to marry Max in the first place…

But then—then she'd never have known the intimate honor of carrying her baby for nine blessed months.

With the wound still gaping in her heart, she had to wonder if nine months in the womb was better than nothing at all.

When she peered down and saw Mrs. Nolte sinking into the bed as though she was unable to last through another second of labor, Callie felt overcome with desperation.

"Mrs. Nolte… Don't—don't give up now, ma'am," she managed through clenched teeth and a thick throat. "We're right here with you. Just make it through this one. That's all you need to think about right now."

Ben's head snapped up. He stared at Callie for a

lengthy moment then gave her a single nod of appreciation. "That's right. Just this one contraction," he echoed.

The next minutes seemed to blur by for Callie. Mrs. Nolte made it through the last few pushes with one encouraging word after another from Ben and Callie. And when her newborn boy finally emerged, Callie felt a shared sense of enormous relief.

But the relief was swallowed whole in the next few moments. Her blood ran cold. Dread and raw fear pulled down all hope like a lead weight.

The baby was bluish in color. He wasn't moving. Wasn't breathing. Wasn't making a sound.

While Ben focused completely on tending to the newborn, Callie's hands trembled uncontrollably. She tried to calm Sarah Nolte's growing panic. Tried to stuff down her own seizing panic. But she couldn't seem to tear her gaze from the little baby, wondering if this was what it'd been like when her little girl had been born.

When the newborn finally let out a small whimper what seemed like minutes later, Callie's stomach surged. The cry of relief that came from Mrs. Nolte, and the quaver Callie heard in Ben's voice as he assured the woman that all was well, brought ready tears to Callie's eyes.

She might've cried a river then, but she couldn't. Wouldn't. If she let herself break down now, she might never, ever stop up the deep well of tears that capped off all of these long and anguished years.

Chapter Eleven

Ben was still shaken inside.

Though it'd been three hours since Sarah Nolte had given birth to her baby boy, and the little guy was doing just fine, the tenuous moments when it seemed the baby wasn't going to breathe still tromped over Ben's weakening confidence.

This baby, the third boy in the Nolte family, had been bigger than the first two. Probably close to nine pounds. And he'd come face up and with the cord wrapped around his chubby little neck. Sarah had been courageous throughout, and by the look on Garrett's face when he flew through the door an hour ago, he wholeheartedly agreed.

Ben remembered breathing a heartfelt prayer of thanks when the strapping newborn had finally taken his first breath, after a good minute outside of the womb. Within half an hour, the little one's coloring was nearing perfect, and his cry hearty. A very good sign, indeed. The baby was healthy. Doing well. And even suckling at his mama's breast as Ben ushered Callie out to the wagon to return home.

So why didn't those things comfort Ben deep down? It

seemed that one tragedy after another stacked up against him, challenging his ability and skill as a doctor. Ben had failed to turn Max around and bring him back into the fold. He'd failed to save Aaron's sweet baby and dear wife. And he'd failed to restore Joseph's vision.

Over the past hours, it'd been all he could manage to hide the lack of confidence that plagued him without mercy.

The look in Sarah's eyes—that pleading, unquestioning look that bequeathed Ben far too much faith in his expertise—troubled Ben to the core. And then the way Callie had peered at him, with a vulnerability and trust as tender and fragile as a tiny seedling. He swallowed hard, remembering the way it shook him deep—made him wish he could be found worthy.

But the fleeting look of terror he'd seen cross Callie's face had almost brought his heart to a sudden, sobering stop. Plain as day, he'd seen it. Her fear had tugged at his compassion with relentless force.

As the pale glow of morning's earliest light climbed over the horizon, Ben urged the horses down the frost-covered, grassy path. He contemplated the sense of helplessness he felt, finding an odd sense of quietude as he watched the way the horses' warm breath made rhythmic puffs of steam into the cool and crisp late October air.

When Ben glanced over at Callie hugging her arms to her chest, his uncertainty faded some. She was a mystery, just Callie. A deep and exquisite and beautiful mystery. A gift to him the last two weeks…tonight. Perhaps forever?

His nerve endings hummed to life. Grew louder as he saw the wisps of hair that had fallen in loose waves from her braid. He had to clench his fist tight to keep from touching the rich strands. The radiant, almost ethereal way her fair skin reflected the first inkling of breaking light entranced him completely.

"Are you cold?" he finally asked, his throat gone tight.

"A little." She breathed into her hands.

Ben grabbed the lap robe from behind the seat and settled the blanket over her shoulders. "Here, this should help."

The fact that she didn't flinch at his touch or his nearness was heartening. "Were you all right in there?" On a sigh, Ben threaded a hand through his hair. "Did I throw too much at you?"

He focused down the road, realizing that maybe he'd assumed too much from her. But for several days now, she'd been remarkably adept as she assisted him with patients. Never once had she balked or seemed uneasy. She'd handled situations as naturally as if she'd had training. In fact, he couldn't quite get over just how perfectly she complemented him.

"I guess I thought with how well you've handled other patients this past week, you'd do fine."

She turned toward him. "It's not that."

"Then what is it?" He met her gaze, and even in the pale light he could see the way her eyes took on that faraway, pain-filled shadowing. "The way you looked, I thought I was going to have another patient on my hands."

Callie lifted her chin in that familiar and stubborn I-don't-need-your-help kind of way. "It won't happen again."

Ben gave his head a slow shake. "Callie, I—"

"I promise," she added, laying a hand on his right forearm. "I won't let you down again, Ben. I don't know what came over me, but I promise I won't let it happen again."

He dropped his gaze to where she held his arm, saddened that she could think him so demanding and unforgiving.

And moved by the way her touch soaked right through his heavy sheepskin coat and wool shirt, to his skin. Then to his heart. Her touch, her lingering gaze, the way she seemed torn between maintaining her distance and reaching out to him, brought his breath up short.

He covered her hands with one of his. "You didn't let me down, Callie. You were wonderful back there." He gave her hands a gentle squeeze, hoping this glimpse of vulnerability heralded, even as the morning's first light, a new day. "The encouragement you gave Mrs. Nolte couldn't have been more perfect. It kept her with us."

She swallowed visibly. Sitting so close to her, he could feel her tense as she averted her attention to where the horses plodded steadily toward home. He hadn't really been privy to this fragile side of Callie before, and seeing it now made him wish that he could take her in his arms, sheltering her from her silent storm.

Right now it didn't seem to matter that she'd once been married to Max. Or that her past was still shady, at best. Or that a hint of suspicion hung over her.

"What matters to me isn't *that* it happened, but *why* it happened. You looked like you'd seen a ghost." Pulling on the reins, he brought the horses to a halt in the middle of the path. "Please. Tell me what's bothering you."

She pulled her hands into her lap. "I can't."

"Can't? Or won't?" Ben closed his eyes momentarily and sighed, wondering if he was pushing too much. But at the moment, it didn't really seem to matter. He opened his eyes and looked at her, pointedly. "Do you trust me, Callie? Have I ever given you a reason not to trust me?"

Callie studied him as though trying to dig deep into who he really was. It evoked a strange discomfort when she looked at him like that.

Was she seeing Max?

Or comparing him to Max?

The thought of being compared to his wayward, immoral brother stung deep.

"The way you're looking at me now, I'd think you were trying to find some reason to mistrust me," he choked out. "Some piece of evidence that would justify your determination to keep your distance. For whatever reason, you're committed to staying at arm's length."

"No. It's not like—"

"Do you think I'm like Max? Is that it?"

"I thought—I thought she was going to lose the baby," she finally said, her rosebud mouth drawn down at the corners as though she might cry. "She almost did."

"But she didn't." Toning down his ire, Ben cautiously reached up and smoothed wayward strands of hair from her face even as he battled back his own taunting failures and silent accusations.

"She was in such pain." Her voice quavered. "And having such a hard time."

He cupped his hand at the side of her head, struggling to remind himself that ultimately life wasn't his to give or take away. That ultimately, God was in charge of the outcome.

Seeing the remnant of torment in her eyes, he searched for words that would ease her. "It was a difficult labor, but she made it through—and you were part of that."

She almost leaned into his touch, but not quite. "I feared for her, Ben."

He swallowed past a lump that had been there since the time they'd arrived, three hours ago. "I did, too."

Her breath caught. "You did?"

"I did. It was touch-and-go. But we made it through. God saw us through," he added, remembering how desperate he'd been to find God's presence there guiding him.

Ready emotion seized his throat as he recalled the overwhelming expression of gratitude and relief he'd seen on Sarah's face when her baby gave his first, small cry.

And the look of trauma and fear he'd witnessed marring Callie's lovely features. There had to be something more to the unveiled look of horror. Yes, she'd feared for Sarah Nolte and her baby, but was there something beyond the sympathetic, compassionate concern? Some dark and daunting image from Callie's past that had come back to haunt her?

Callie might as well have aged ten years in four days.

With an unnerving sense of irony, she peered at her image in the mirror hanging above the bureau. The woman staring back at her, all done up and ready to attend Boulder's annual Harvest Dinner and Town Hall Dance, appeared far younger than the way she really felt.

Ever since Sarah's baby was born, Callie's struggle with the haunting memories of her own tragic delivery had been nearly insurmountable. The incident had dredged up the familiar pain and deep ache far more than she'd experienced in the past.

But comfort seemed out of her reach. Like the rippling cascade of a waterfall echoing through mountains, she was almost sure she could hear comfort's alluring, peaceful call, but she couldn't seem to find it.

She'd longed, yearned for someone to talk to these past days. Callie found herself craving a real peace to subdue her very real fears and hurts, but nothing she did seemed to satisfy. Not throwing herself into her job, helping Luke with the kittens, befriending one of the girls at the Golden Slipper, or even knitting mittens for the orphanage with Katie.

Perhaps she was missing something. Something bigger than herself. Bigger than the things she did to feel useful. Bigger than the stubborn strength she'd strapped on these past years. Bigger than even Ben Drake.

In a moment of utterly shameful weakness, she'd almost spilled everything to him. About her pregnancy, the labor, the delivery. But she just couldn't tell him about all of that. Doing so would only add to the shadows already cast over Max's memory. Besides, there was certainly no guarantee that he'd believe her.

With a heavy sigh and determination to climb above the grief, she adjusted the lace collar on her emerald-green dress as images of Sarah's chubby little boy flitted through her mind.

Jared Benjamin Nolte…

He was such a sweet baby, so content and peaceful. She'd gone along with Ben to check on the little one the day following the birth, and when Mr. Nolte had told Ben that they'd named their new boy after him, Ben had become disconcertingly quiet.

A heartwarming smile coaxed up the corner of Callie's mouth.

First a kitten. Now a baby.

Ben should be honored—at least that's what she thought. But for some reason he seemed agitated by the whole thing. As if he didn't think he deserved the tribute.

Callie hadn't met anyone who deserved such an honor more than Ben Drake. He was caring. Kind. Compassionate.

He was everything that Max was not.

For the past three weeks she'd seen Ben tend to one patient after another, his steady demeanor never altering from his usual calm and gentle way. Even in the face of one patient's rude behavior, he seemed to walk above the unseen realm of discourtesy, treating the person with respect and consideration and patience.

At times, he seemed almost larger than life.

That very attribute had been the quality that had drawn her to Max seven years ago. It was the trait that had dramatically changed after they'd married, too. But for some reason, with Ben things seemed different, as though the person she saw day in, day out was the real, genuine Ben.

When she heard the front door open, she felt her heart skip a beat. He was here. Ben had come for her.

And she was going to be attending the dinner and dance with him. It'd been a last-minute request on his part, and though she was fairly certain he was just making an attempt to include her in community happenings, she'd been glad for the invitation. For as long as she could remember, she'd wanted to attend a function like this. But first her father had deemed dancing a sin, and then after she'd married, Max hadn't wanted anything to do with an occasion like this.

He'd preferred a more raucous crowd to fulfill his desire for pleasure. And thankfully, he'd never once forced Callie to accompany him.

Regardless of the fact that she considered herself to

be fairly naive, it wasn't hard to guess what he did when he was out. He'd drag himself home in the wee hours of the morning with red lip paint on his neck and face. And the overwhelming smell of perfumed powder and booze wafting around him in a noxious cloud.

Having no intention of dwelling on those unpleasant memories, she swept her gaze down her dress one last time then emerged from her room.

She glanced up just in time to see Ben come to a sudden stop in the hallway. He stood there all still and straight, staring at her, almost as if he were seeing her for the first time. His gray-blue eyes darkened with an intensity that sent a quiver of contentment all the way down her spine to where her toes curled in her new, buttoned boots.

"You look lovely, Callie." His voice was low and husky as he advanced a step closer.

She slid a hand up and touched the locket at her neck, taking in his appearance, as well. Indulging herself—if truth be told—in his striking good looks. "You're looking very nice, yourself, Ben," she breathed, swallowing hard as she noticed how handsome he looked in his dark gray trousers, crisp white shirt and navy blue vest and coat.

Feeling a warm blush coloring her cheeks, she worked frantically to stuff those thoughts back down.

After Max had died, she'd vowed never to make herself vulnerable to a man again, and now here she was, practically throwing herself at Ben. As good as Ben Drake seemed, there had to be a flaw to him. And if she knew what was best for her, she'd figure out his weakness just as soon as possible.

If not for the fact that she felt her resolve fade away

whenever she was around him, she might be able to do just that.

Though a good three feet still remained between them, they may as well have been nose to nose. Her heart fluttered madly inside her chest. The distance between them seemed charged with a force she was sure she could touch, its command so real and powerful that she had a difficult time breathing.

A sudden shyness crept over her. She glanced down at her dress, fingering the fine fabric between her thumb and forefinger. "I've worn this before," she mumbled. If she'd been any more ridiculously inane right then, she might have won some kind of award for it.

"I know." He nodded, one side of his mouth curving up in one of those devastating sideways grins of his that made her knees all weak and stomach all aflutter. "You look beautiful."

Max had said that kind of thing to her early on in their relationship.

But never—*never* had his words matched the look in his eyes, like Ben's did now.

Pulling in a steadying breath, she grasped at her wilting resolve before it fell completely away from her. She made a mad dash, groping for a way out from the strangely consuming emotions he induced inside her.

"I must say, you're getting better with your compliments, Doctor Drake," she managed, her voice trembling. "From—how did you put it—'You look completely worn out, pale, and your eyes are red,' to this," she blurted, trying desperately to douse the mind-numbing, heated intensity that seemed to build whenever they were in close proximity.

"That's not fair." He slid one breathtaking step closer. "When I said those things, I was making a medical statement of fact. Trying to get through that stubborn head of yours that you had no business being up when you were so sick."

She willed her hands to grow still. "And I thank you for your concern. But I'm none the worse for the wear. Am I?"

He shook his head. "You give *stubborn* a whole new meaning." Dragging in a breath, he moved to grab her cloak and hold it out for her. The soft edge of a grin tugged at his mouth. "Are you ready to go?"

"Absolutely," she answered sweetly with a smile, as he covered her with the warm wool. "Will Katie be there?"

"Oh, yes. She loves to dance. So does Joseph."

Before she even knew it, he was securing the ties of her cloak at her neck, the errant, featherlight brush of his fingers against her skin sending heated sparks straight through her again.

She willed her mind to stay clear of the emotions she felt at the moment. "Really? Without his sight?"

He held the door open for her as he picked up the basket of food and followed her out. "Without his sight."

"Well, that's remarkable. The first time I met Joseph, it was a few moments before I even realized he was blind." Peering at Ben, she couldn't miss the sudden, far-off look that had half shuttered his gaze.

"He has a remarkable ability to look you in the eye, doesn't he?" His voice had grown tight and strained.

"Ben? Is there something wrong?"

"No." His quick retort was far from convincing.

Something had altered the fine mood he'd been in just moments ago, and Ben wasn't given to being moody.

"What's bothering you?" she tried again. "You can tell me."

"It's nothing," he ground out through tightly clenched teeth as he stepped down from the porch.

"Are you sure?"

"Yes. Let's get going." He turned around and gave her an are-you-coming kind of look.

Callie threaded her arms at her chest and planted her feet. She nailed him with the most serious look she could muster. "Is this how this works? You can pry and prod to try and get me to spill my heart, but the same rules don't apply to you?"

"It's not that, Callie. And I certainly haven't pried or prodded." He raked a hand through his dark hair. "I've been very *careful* with you."

"I'm choosing to ignore that you've been *careful* with me." Failing miserably, she stalked to the front of the porch. "I don't want to be treated as though I'm fragile."

His wide-eyed look made her cringe. "Can you honestly say that you wouldn't have taken off if I had been pushy?"

"Maybe," she forced through clenched teeth.

He tilted his head, quirking one dark eyebrow.

"All right. So I would have." She jammed her hands on her hips. "But what about you, Ben? Here you are, obviously bothered by something all of a sudden, and I… Well, I just wanted to help. That's all."

Ben unceremoniously set the basket down on the ground and clenched his fists. "You want to know?"

"I wouldn't have asked otherwise."

He gave a shuddering sigh. "Every single time I see Joseph, whether it's at church, in his home, in his wood shop, or out and about on the streets of Boulder," he added, fanning an arm in one giant, sweeping gesture toward the heart of town, "I feel responsible for the fact that he can't see more than the dull gray shadows he does."

"Responsible? Why?"

Ben dragged a hand over his squared jaw. "Isn't it obvious? There must've been *something* that I missed. *Something* I could've done for him that would've made a difference." Even in the fading light she could see his jaw clench, his hands fist at his sides. "If only I'd had more training. Or done something differently."

"Does he blame you?" she asked in stunned disbelief.

She didn't know Joseph Drake well at all, but she couldn't imagine him casting even the slightest bit of blame Ben's way.

"No. He's never said so." He shook his head slowly then added, "But, then, Joseph's a big enough man that he wouldn't admit to it even if he did feel that way."

An odd sense of anger built inside her. Not at Joseph. Not at Ben. But at the very idea that Ben had been on the losing end of a lie.

"Then why are you blaming yourself?" She stepped down and came to stand in front of him. Made bold by her resolve, she reached out and grasped his hand. "I've seen you work, Ben. You're so thorough and attentive with all of your patients. Boulder is lucky to have you around." Her chest tightened with emotion as she gave his hand a warm squeeze. "You're a wonderful physician. You have to believe that."

His mouth formed a harsh, unforgiving line as he stared down at where she held his hand. "But I couldn't save my own brother from a life of groping around in the darkness. I couldn't protect him from the life he now faces."

"But you did all you knew to do. And from what Katie's said, you brought her into Joseph's life," she added, desperate to ease his guilt. She swallowed hard. "You gave him a gift. Love. That's more than some people will ever hope to know."

Was it more than she could ever hope for?

Chapter Twelve

Ben had never told another soul about the guilt he carried. Not Aaron, not Zach, and certainly not Joseph. There wasn't an ounce of self-pity attached to his struggle, but with each additional failure he met, the sense of responsibility and regret he carried haunted him with greater ferocity.

No matter how successful he was at his profession, no matter what praise others had given him, he'd let his family down. He was desperate for a way out of the shame and regret that had him trapped.

He hadn't felt inclined to offer another word of explanation as they walked, side by side, to the town hall. But for the distance between them, he may as well have been on the other side of the Flatirons. When they'd arrived at the already crowded town hall, Ben had to force his bad mood aside. For Callie. He was pretty sure, from the excitement lighting her face when he'd first arrived to pick her up, that she'd been looking forward to this evening.

He'd been looking forward to this, as well. It'd been three weeks since Callie had first come into his life. And in that short amount of time he'd grown very fond of her. The spirited way she met a challenge, like when Mrs. Duncan had come to the office to steep information from her. The brave way she faced an uncomfortable circumstance, as she had with the birth of the Nolte baby. The deep, almost childlike need she had for friendship, yet refused to acknowledge.

And then there was the way her eyes, recently, had begun to light up whenever she caught sight of him. He could tell that she'd try to snuff out the telling glow. Had cleverly found ways to busy herself in order to avoid him. But he'd be willing to wager the house, the farm and the whole town of Boulder that she felt the same innate, powerful attraction as he did.

He remembered that first night she'd shown up, the way his heart had been pierced by one look in her blue eyes. For all the stubbornness, strength and willful tilt of her chin, she had gripped his heart and mind without even trying.

Ben had spent a good amount of time praying about what purpose God had for him in all of this. Would God defy all of Ben's reason and lead Max's widow straight into his arms? Could he trust God with the outcome of all of this? Ben was committed to finding a way through this and had to trust that God was committed to the very same thing.

Even last night when he'd prayed about his relationship with Callie, he'd felt like God reminded him of the Old Testament Scripture addressing the issue of widowhood. Where God charged the husband's brother to take the widow for his own wife. To see after her. To protect her.

Ben would never presume to know God's plan, but he couldn't help but wonder if he was living out that Scripture.

He didn't consider himself a hero. A martyr. Or even a strict religious man. Just a man who knew God. A man with compassion. And, as they entered the newly built structure, a man with a growing amount of love for a certain young woman who'd shown up on his doorstep like some lost and lonely stray.

If only he could put to rest the lingering question as to her honesty. He'd tried to ignore the missing stethoscope here, the vial of medicine there and the other things that had gone missing over the past three weeks, but he couldn't deny the uncanny, oddly coincidental timing of it all.

"I been wonderin' if you was comin'," Luke exclaimed, his booted feet clomping over the wood floor as he rushed up to meet them.

"You were, huh?" Ben smiled down at the boy.

Seeing Mrs. Duncan just ahead, he nodded in greeting as she stood gaping at him and Callie as if she were preparing to paint a portrait of them. In some ways, Ben figured with a wry grin, she probably was. It was common knowledge that the woman was the hub, self-proclaimed and generally recognized, for gossip in this town. With her colorful descriptions and deep-hued intrigue, she'd painted plenty a portrait. Most of which he didn't pay any attention to.

"How are those kittens coming along?" He reached down to give the boy's shoulder a squeeze, relieved to notice that the hearty meals Callie had set in front of the lad were starting to pay off.

"Jest fine. They're growin' up real fast. Had to get a bigger box to put 'em in and everything."

"Really?" Ben replied.

"Yep or they'd be jumpin' out everywhere. Then they'd prolly go and get theirselves lost."

"They're definitely growing fast," Callie remarked.

"I wonder jest how heavy they are…" When the boy grabbed his shapeless, threadbare hat from his head to scratch his blond mop, Ben made a silent note to purchase a warm hat, mittens and a scarf for Luke tomorrow. "You'd be real proud, Ben. I been doctorin' 'em some, and they're doin' jest fine."

"I am proud of you, Luke." Ben looked him in the eye, man-to-man, wishing that Luke's mother could see what a treasure she had in Luke. "Very proud."

"You want me to bring 'em by again so you can see 'em, Miss Callie?" he asked, stuffing his hands into his pockets.

"Of course."

"Bring them with you anytime," Ben added then slid a subtle glance around the room, hoping that maybe his ma had shown up for Luke's sake. "Is your ma here with you, Luke?"

His ma had never been one for attending church functions, town functions, or any other function Boulder might have. She kept late, active hours, mostly with men-folk from out of town. She was usually too hung over during the day to do much socializing. Or housekeeping. Or parenting.

Ben's jaw bunched at the thought. His pulse fired a rapid, ugly rhythm in his veins. He had a great deal of sympathy for the poor folks who struggled to provide enough food, yet still found plenty of love to go around. He'd just never understand how a mother could disregard her own child so thoughtlessly.

"Naw…she's sleepin'. Been sleepin' all day, so I decided to come down myself."

"Why don't you join us for dinner, then?" Ben suggested.

"Can we sit over there with Mr. Joseph and Miss Katie?" Luke pointed to the far end of a long line of tables, where Joseph and Katie were sitting. "He said he was gonna teach me to write my name usin' them funny dots he's gone and learnt."

"Sure we can." Ben felt a small tugging at his heart as he ushered Callie and Luke around the gathering crowd. After a chorus of greetings and hugs, they'd barely gotten seated when Luke shifted a shade closer to Joseph and tapped him on the shoulder.

"Hey there, partner." Joseph draped an arm on the bench behind Luke.

"I'm ready." Luke sat stock straight on the long bench, his hands fastened around the hole-riddled hat in his lap.

Ben glanced to his left to see Callie holding a hand over her mouth, her beautiful eyes dancing with amusement.

"Ready?" Joseph furrowed his brow and angled his head as if trying to gather Luke's meaning. "For what?"

Ben had to chuckle when Luke slid him a wide-eyed, what-do-I-do-now expression.

"Seems that Luke's eager to learn how to write his name in Braille," Ben explained, giving the lad a how'd-I-do nod.

"Well, sure. But you've got to promise not to show anyone." Joseph set his hand on Luke's mop of hair. "It'll be our secret little code."

When the first dance began after dinner, Ben turned to find Callie watching him, her eyes so full of hope and joy that he had to swallow hard. Had there been no lanterns, the unrestrained smile lighting her face could've illuminated the room.

With his gaze firmly locked on hers, he strode over to where she stood with Katie, wanting nothing more than to have the valid, acceptable excuse of a dance to hold Callie in his arms. "Would you care to dance?"

For a brief moment, as her attention drifted to the edge of the crowd where Aaron stood rock still and staring right at them, he thought she was going to refuse him. He wouldn't blame her if she had. Aaron was being as rude as he could be to her, and Ben was determined to put a swift end to the silent protest and discourteous behavior just as soon as he had a chance.

"Yes, thank you."

He led her onto the table-cleared dance floor, joining the others who'd already begun a lilting waltz.

"You dance very well, Ben." Her alluring glance was cloaked in a shyness she seemed completely unaware of. She displayed no coyness, no predictable batting of her eyelashes or demure side glances to tempt.

No. This beautiful woman in his arms was without pretense or pomp. She was just Callie.

"Thank you. As do you." Ben gave her a slow, easy grin, loving the way her mouth and cheeks suddenly went all tight. "Where did you learn how to dance so well?"

She focused on where he clasped her hand. "Max taught me."

He chuckled as long ago memories trickled into his thoughts. "Max always did enjoy going to town dances. As long as I can remember, he enjoyed them." He gave her hand a tender squeeze. "I suppose he dragged you to every dance there was to attend?"

She slowly met his gaze, the rosy color in her cheeks fading some. "Before we were married, yes. And we always had so much fun." Swallowing, she lifted her chin ever so slightly. "But once we married he wouldn't go anymore."

"I can't imagine Max passing up a dance." He furrowed his brow, grasping her hand a little tighter. "I'm sorry, Callie."

On a sigh, she smiled, though it didn't quite reach her eyes like it had only moments ago. "There's nothing for you to be sorry about. Max just found other things he thought were more enjoyable."

Ben gradually swept her to the fringe of dancers. He pulled her a shade closer, just on the edge of being considered inappropriate, though right now, he didn't much care. Not when all he wanted to do was to bring Callie a small bit of comfort.

"Callie, remember…we're talking about my brother here," he acknowledged, slowing to a stop. He settled his gaze firmly on hers so that she wouldn't look away. "If you wanted to go…well, then, Max should've whisked you off to every dance there was to be found. But he didn't—for some selfish reason—and for that I am very sorry."

"Thank you," she finally managed after a long and weighty silence. "But let's not talk about all of that tonight. It's too wonderful in here to darken it with those silly old memories," she added, the warm glow from the room flickering in her deep blue eyes.

His chest tightened at the way she was making such a valiant effort to dismiss history's sting.

How much had Callie missed out on over the years because of Max? Town dinners? Church functions? Special nights out? Romantic dances? Just how little had Max cherished Callie and seen to her desires and needs? Had he merely cloistered her within the four walls of their home, giving her no opportunity to socialize with others?

A life like that would be torment for a woman like Callie. She was strong and smart. Given the time to trust and the courage to spread her wings, she would pale other women with her ready wit, intelligent responses and her resourceful approach to life. And the simple yet striking beauty that indelibly marked her outward appearance would be hard to match. Anywhere.

Pulling in a breath, he cleared his throat of the thick wad of emotion. "All right. For you, Miss Callie, the night has just begun. And if you want to dance every single dance I will gladly oblige."

She blinked hard, a softness stealing over the remnant of bitter memories etched on her face. "It's a perfect evening, Ben. Thank you."

He slid his gaze down to her neck where her creamy white skin colored to a tempting shade of pink. Folding her hand in his, he felt the slightest, almost undetectable tremble there, and a lingering feeling of satisfaction stole completely over him.

He loved the way she responded to him. The tiny shudders. The trembling. The shy glances filled with longing.

He'd completely broken his own standard. Where he'd once decided that he rather liked being single, he now felt a strange sense of being unfulfilled—as if he needed Callie to be complete. He wasn't thinking with his head, but with his heart, and though he'd cheered both Joseph and Aaron on when they'd done the same and found their brides, he now wondered if it was a safe path to follow.

He peered down at Callie again as another song began, maneuvering her between the other couples. The slow and steady way she seemed to relax in his arms, as if she found a long-awaited security there as the night wore on, made his heart lurch. He wanted her to find security and trust in his arms. And love.

He—Ben Drake—wanted Callie to find love in the center of his embrace.

At that startling revelation, his mind spun. The music seemed to fade into the background, the other dancers and people, too.

Except for Aaron.

When Ben had turned Callie around in a graceful sweep just seconds ago, he'd come face-to-face with his brother. The pointed, unrelenting look on Aaron's face could've frozen spring's first sprigs of grass on the spot. It was all Ben could do not to react. For the remainder of the evening he avoided Aaron's attention, setting his focus completely on Callie. He wasn't about to let his brother's morose mood ruin her night.

When the last dance of the evening came to an end, he set his hand to the small of Callie's back and ushered her protectively over to where Katie and Joseph stood with Luke. Excusing himself, he stalked to where Aaron stood alone as some silent sentry.

"Who nominated you to head up the cheerful committee?" Ben forced through clenched teeth.

Aaron snorted, rolling his eyes in disgust.

Ben stood directly in front of him so as to block out the unpleasant view from curious others who milled about as if they wished the night had only just begun. "So, what's with the glowering mood tonight? Care to tell me? Or not? Either way, I'm not leaving you alone till you do."

Aaron narrowed his eyes. "I'm pretty sure it's nothin' you'd want to know about."

"Really?" Folding his arms at his chest, Ben was grateful that most everyone had taken to the dance floor as the musicians announced one more dance... the Virginia reel. "Maybe you should let me make that judgment."

"Do you know who you're dancing with?"

"Callie. My brother's widow. My very capable employee," he said, clipping off each word.

Glancing over his shoulder, his heart swelled at the sight of Callie and Luke walking out onto the dance floor. When the music began, he watched the way the two of them smiled and laughed as she instructed Luke in what to do. Ben's throat tightened with instant and very real emotion. And he knew...he *knew* that she was everything he'd ever wanted in a woman.

Turning back, he found Aaron's face contorting in disgust as he shifted a glance to Callie. "You're fallin' for this woman even though we all warned you not to."

Ben's hands formed fists. "Listen, I'm sorry for how you're hurting over Ellie," he said, figuring that Aaron was having a hard time dealing with his wife's death with all of the festivities around him to remind him of the empty loss he felt. "I know that it must be hard seeing other couples enjoying themselves. If there was a way I could go back and change—"

"Keep Ellie out of this," he hissed. "This isn't about her. It's about that woman out there."

Ben flexed his fingers. "Since you haven't taken the time to get to know Callie, what is so important that you feel it needs to be said?"

Aaron averted his gaze for a brief moment. "You know Pete O'Leary?"

Ben sighed. "Of course I know Pete. What about him?"

"He told me he recognized Callie."

"Yes, I know. He said so the day he came to the office about his leg and I introduced him to her. So, what about it?"

Aaron shifted his boots nervously on the wood floor, the stamping feet of dancers drowning out the scuffing noise. "I'm telling you this for your own good, Ben." Aaron raised his chin a notch. "Callie's fooling you and everyone else around her. Leading us to believe she's our poor, widowed sister-in-law."

"You doubt that she was married to Max?"

"I never said that."

Ben jammed his fists at his waist. "Well, she's sure not bemoaning her past circumstance. And from what Katie saw, Callie has the scars to prove that her situation was undesirable, at best."

"Oh, it was undesirable, all right."

He could've throttled his brother from here to tomorrow for the caustic way he referred to Callie. "You and I both know that life married to Max must've been horrible, yet she's never uttered one single, bitter word."

"Did you ever think that maybe life married to *her* had been horrible, too?" Aaron challenged, meeting Ben's severe gaze.

"Not only have I not thought that, I can't imagine it, either." He glanced over his shoulder at her again, the way she lit up the room as she danced with Luke, likely making the boy feel like a king. She brought immeasurable joy to Luke's life. And to Ben's.

"Pete saw her plain as day in Denver." Aaron's features creased in a frown. "She was walkin' the halls of a brothel, dressed in one of those low cut, silky get-ups that no decent woman would wear."

Ben's stomach clenched at those words. His pulse slammed steady and loud in his ears as he remembered the dress she'd shown up in. The tattered, ruby-red satin dress with a dangerously low neckline and a wilting flounce of gaudy ruffles. His blood ran cold as he recalled how sick he'd felt seeing the way his mother's locket had hung in the midst of all of that.

"Pete saw her talking to one of those harlots down at the Golden Slipper the other day, too." Aaron's voice was low, apologetic. "Callie…she's nothin' but a harlot."

The night hadn't ended soon enough for Ben. After Aaron's disturbing news, he'd walked her home, doing his best not to spoil her perfect evening.

With a groan, he sank down lower into the stuffed chair in front of his fireplace. Stretching his feet out on the ottoman, he tried to keep his head above the battering, heartbreaking accusation. Much as he didn't want to admit it, it all made sense. Her showing up here unannounced. In a harlot's dress. Desperate for a job. Unwilling to parcel out anything but the most general information about her past.

He swallowed hard, fisting his hands, wishing he could waylay something with his pent-up fury. But what good would that do? It wouldn't change a thing. Not her situation. Not his situation, either.

A strong northwestern wind howled outside, emitting an eerie, lonely whistle down the stone chimney, adding to his already dreary mood. He stared into the fireplace, watching the flames leap and flicker, and he wondered how Callie could do such a thing. How could she cheapen herself, selling an act that was designed as a God-given gift for a man and wife?

He'd tried to act as normal as he could around her when he'd walked her home, but it'd been next to impossible. And sadly, she had to know that something was amiss.

Until he could corroborate the claim, she wouldn't know, either. Pete O'Leary certainly wasn't a man given to gossip or to the telling of tales—he shot straight. Though the fact that he'd walked the halls of some brothel didn't exactly boost Ben's opinion of Pete's character. But regardless of all that, Ben wouldn't be able to sleep sound until he'd validated the information for himself. If he had to locate the brothel Pete had seen her at and make his own inquiry, then that's what he'd do.

He remembered the stories he'd heard told of women who'd been caught up in that lifestyle. When they'd tried to escape they'd been dragged back, beaten or worse, then thrown back into bed to pleasure the next patron as soon as the bruises faded some.

"What am I going to do?" he forced through a weighted sigh and thick throat.

He could find out the truth for himself, but would it change anything?

No.

Yes.

Maybe…

Tension ticked at his jaw. It might well change everything. It would raise all kinds of questions about her life with Max, and why he'd been driven to drink and gamble as he had.

When Smudge hopped up on his lap, turned a circle then plopped down, purring loudly, Ben smoothed his hand over the soft fur. The cat peered up and gave Ben one of those trusting kind of looks, and Ben couldn't help but remember how long it'd been before the cat had been this comfortable around him.

Trust hadn't come fast. And it hadn't come easy. In fact, it'd taken several weeks of proving that he was worthy before Smudge obliged. So why should it be different with Callie? He'd gone slow with her, working hard to get her to trust him. He'd opened his heart for the taking, and…he'd been taken.

"When will I learn?" he choked out.

His compassion was like some disease, at least sometimes. In spite of the red flags that had whipped around wildly for any sensible person to see, he'd forged on in his growing admiration of Callie.

Yet she'd omitted a very large and questionable detail of her past. One that challenged the very standards he lived by. And Ben didn't know if he could ever look past that omission. Or that she'd falsely represented herself.

Just Callie…

She'd been light in his day, humor in his evenings, and a decidedly uncomplicated outlook at the morning's first break.

Until now, he had discounted any thought of her as some harlot. Remembering how shy and hesitant she'd felt in his arms when they'd danced that first dance tonight, how she'd glowed when she'd taught Luke to dance, Ben didn't know if he could imagine her as a harlot now, either.

Bone weary and emotionally spent, he bunched down deeper in the chair and gave a slow, exhausted yawn. Closing his eyes, he leaned his head against the winged side of the chair. Just hours ago, he'd entertained thoughts of marrying this woman. And now? Now he had to admit that thinking with his heart had definitely not been safe at all. It'd set him up for a long, painful fall.

But if he was led by his own understanding, then he was bound to find himself lacking. And if he trusted enough to open his heart and follow God's leading, there were no guarantees. None.

Fatigued, he gave himself over to sleep's coaxing call. His last thought was, if he followed his heart, he would get hurt.

Again. And again. And again.

Chapter Thirteen

Ben woke with a start, his body protesting the awkward way he'd slept, slumped in the chair all night long. The flames had long since died in the fireplace, giving way to the invigorating chill of the morning. When he shoved himself out of the chair, both Smudge and Molly slid down his legs and plopped unceremoniously on the floor in a furry heap. They gave him one of those what'd-you-do-that-for kind of looks as he hunkered down to pet them.

"Sorry, little ones." Ben gave them both a scratch behind the ears. "I didn't realize you were still there," he said to Smudge then looked at Molly. "And you joined him sometime in the night, didn't you? You two kept me warm."

Standing, he rolled his head on his neck in a vain attempt to work the kinks out. It'd been a night of unrest. And in the midst of the flurry of dreams, and God-breathed truths that had floated through his mind as he'd slept, one thing had been made startlingly clear... when it came to Callie, he needed to listen to his heart, trust God with the outcome.

Problem was…he didn't know if he could. Could he just look the other way?

Raking his hands through his mussed hair, he noted that he'd never been one to let unresolved conflict fester long. If there was a way to bring resolution, then that's what he'd do…even though he felt a small reservation in his heart. There was nothing bad, and everything honorable in being open about the claim, getting the truth out on the table. Right? All he needed to do was talk to Callie.

After he washed up and pulled on clean clothes, he walked next door, grappling for the right words. Words that would bring life into the situation.

While he slowly moved down the hall to Callie's door, his heart slammed hard against his chest. His hands grew damp.

He wiped them down his britches as he peered in her room and saw her standing at the bureau, holding the wood box she'd brought with her—the one Joseph had made. Though she looked like the same Callie from last night, he couldn't seem to see past the startling image of her as some harlot. He fought to push away images of her flaunting herself in front of a man, a commodity for the purchasing.

He tried to remind himself of what God had spoken to his heart…that he needed to trust God and follow his heart.

He pulled in a slow breath and watched her as she stared intently at the contents inside the box, as if she were caught up in some faraway memory. Was it a good memory? Bad?

"Callie," he said, his voice low.

She started, dropping the box to the floor with a crash

and clatter. "Oh, I didn't see you there." She pressed a hand to her forehead.

It took one glimpse into her eyes to realize that the light he'd seen there recently had dimmed some, and that stirred up a sadness he really had no business feeling right now. Not if he was going to keep his head about this whole thing. She'd lied. She'd falsely represented herself. *And*...more than likely, she was guilty of stealing the medical things that had come up missing over the past three weeks.

He didn't know what she planned on doing with the items she'd taken. Maybe sell them. The money she might make from the objects certainly wouldn't be the equivalent of her ship coming in. Not even a small boat.

"I'm sorry. I didn't intend to sneak up on you." He moved into the room to help her gather the few paper items that were strewn about the floor. Then realized that the box had broken into several pieces.

"Oh, no." She crouched down and fingered the pieces.

"It's my fault," he breathed.

"No." She neatly tucked away any vulnerability. "I dropped it."

The sight of her tenderly gathering the few photographs, along with a small square of fabric apparently taken from some cherished garment or blanket, tugged at his heartstrings. This attempt to clear the air wasn't getting off to a very good start. Already, moments into seeing her, he was losing focus.

She began picking at the wood pieces, her breath catching as she fingered a folded paper. "What's this?" She picked up the yellowed and stained paper. "This wasn't in the box before. It must've been hidden."

He noticed how one wood piece was thin, square and made of a different kind of wood than the rest, as though it'd been added at another time. "Hmm…looks like there might have been a false bottom to the box."

He collected the remaining pieces and set them on the bureau in a neat pile then gave her a hand up.

Callie lent him a strained smile as she swept a trembling hand down her lavender print dress then carefully unfolded the paper.

She stared down at it. Her brow furrowed. Face contorted in a look of utter horror. Her hand shot to her mouth, but not before a small, unforgettable and haunting whimper escaped her quivering lips.

Dread rooted firmly in the core of his being. He rested a hand on her shoulder. "Callie?"

"Oh, dear," she cried, sagging to the point that he caught her against his chest. "No. It can't be. It can't be."

His heart surged to his throat as he wrapped her in his embrace. "What? What is it, Callie?"

It was several moments before she responded, and with each second that ticked away, the sense of dread building in Ben cut a path, deep and wide, straight through his heart. Since she'd never allowed herself to give over to emotion, he had no idea what the paper in her hand could say that would induce such a strong response. He braced for the worst.

She pushed away enough to slide the paper out. With hands that quivered almost unnaturally, she held it up to Ben, her tortured gaze locked on the yellowed parchment. He took it from her and folded her into the crook of one arm. Read the words to the heartrending backdrop of her anguished, muffled cries.

I, Maxwell Henry Drake, deed my infant daughter, born August 22, 1884, to Thomas Blanchard, as payment in full for the said amount of one hundred eighty dollars in gambling debt.

Maxwell Henry Drake

The hair at Ben's neck stood on end. His pulse pounded through his veins.

No. There was no way...

Surely he'd read it wrong.

He blinked hard, wondering if maybe his gaze was still sleep-fuzzed. Ben held the paper up, read the words again and examined the signature. Bile rose and burned in his throat as he peered at Max's unmistakable, looped scrawl that had been scratched across the bottom, sealing the deal.

His brother, his flesh and blood, had sold a child, a baby girl, to pay some gambling debt?

He swallowed hard, nauseated.

How?

What would cause Max to stoop so low?

His hands seemed to burn from holding the contract. He set the paper, a validating, sickening stamp of his brother's legacy, on the bureau.

Flexing his hand, he crooked a finger beneath Callie's chin. Lifted her focus to him. "Whose baby, Callie?"

His heart came to a grinding, arresting halt. His jaw bunched and his blood ran red hot with anger at Max for deeming a young life, an innocent baby, so invaluable.

"My baby," she squeaked through a muffled cry. Her whole body shook. "My baby girl."

He folded her in his arms. Held her. When she glanced up at him again, pasty-white with tears streaming down her face and pooling in her eyes, his concern grew tenfold.

As did the pure fury that was directed completely at a man who could no longer answer for his actions. A man who'd taken his pitiful reasons for doing such a heinous thing with him to his grave.

Ben held her for some time, stroking her silky hair, tightening his arms around her to give warmth to her quivering, shuddering form.

Through a pool of his own tears, he glanced at the window, to see the sun spilling inside in cheerful rays, a direct contrast to the grief-stricken pallor that filled the room. "I'm so sorry, Callie. So sorry."

She pulled in a fractured breath. "I thought my baby had died. Max told me she'd been stillborn."

He gave his head a slow shake. "Why would he…"

"He'd never want—never wanted the baby," she braved on a fractured breath. Even in the light of this kind of revelation it seemed she still felt the need to protect Max's honor.

"Callie, listen to me." He grasped her arms and set her back a few inches so she could see him. Dipped his head to catch her eerily blank gaze. "You don't need to protect him. Not from me or anyone else. I want you to tell me everything. Do you hear me?"

She finally gave a hesitant nod and slid her focus to the note on the bureau. Her face contorted in a pain that went way beyond the physical. "He didn't want the baby. Not from the time I'd gotten pregnant."

"Why?" Seeing her shuddering with such force, Ben pulled her into his arms again. "Why wouldn't he want the baby?"

Then Ben remembered the reason he'd come here this morning. To question Callie as to her past. If she'd sullied herself, if she'd become pregnant from some long-gone patron, then Ben might be able to half reason why Max would've had a hard time accepting the baby. But he'd never even begin to reason the fact that Max had sold off the baby.

The child wasn't at fault.

"I don't know. Once, when I was six months along," she continued, clasping her hands beneath her chin, "he pushed me down some stairs. He said it was an accident, and I wanted to believe him, but it had seemed so deliberate," she choked out, her entire body heaving on a sob.

If Ben had thought he was angered before, it was nothing like what he felt now. Whether or not the child was Max's was irrelevant. In Ben's book, any man who'd lay a hand on his own wife or child, born or unborn, to bring harm wasn't worth the air he breathed.

"Then when my time came, he—he didn't want to help." Her voice pinched off like the heartrending sound of a child, terrified and alone. "I asked him to bring someone to help if he couldn't, but he ignored me."

"No woman should have to go through that alone." He pressed a silent kiss to her head. "I'm sorry, Callie."

Callie's breathing came in short, labored gasps, as if she'd run the length of town and back. "I'd been laboring for over thirty-six hours. I was so tired, Ben," she whispered against his chest. She burrowed deeper into his arms, as if trying to hide from the memories. "So tired. I could barely hold my head up."

"I'm sure you were. Anyone would be tired."

"When it came time to push, I couldn't seem to get enough breath. I was so worried about my baby. Would the little one be all right? I hadn't felt any movement for some time."

She peered up at him; the frantic look in her eyes sent an alarming chill straight down his spine. He raised a hand, and with the pad of his thumb caught a tear that poised just above her lips. "He shouldn't have done that to you, Callie—or your baby. It wasn't right."

In a roundabout way he felt responsible for all of this. If he'd been able to turn Max around then the man wouldn't have turned out like some minion of darkness.

"It didn't seem like the labor should be so hard. And Max wouldn't help. I was scared, Ben." She gave a strangled cry.

After a few moments, she sniffed raggedly and raised her chin a notch, that same look of bravery she'd shown the night she'd arrived here right there on her face.

Ben thought he might break down himself, for the sight of it.

She wiped her eyes then pulled in a steadying breath. "I barely remember Max coming in at the end. And right before the baby came I lost consciousness. I ha-had no idea of anything until probably two hours later."

"You could've died," he breathed, his insides seething with anger so deep he could've killed Max in cold blood—if the hopeless excuse for a man wasn't already stiff in his grave.

He'd seen women go through far less and lose their lives because of it. But Callie was a fighter. She would have never made it through such an ordeal, otherwise.

"It might've been be-better if I'd died," she sobbed, her breath broken by uncontrollable emotion. "At least that's what I thought for a while, anyway."

Ben swallowed hard and hugged her close, aching to take away her pain and anguish.

At the moment it didn't matter what Pete O'Leary saw

in Denver. It could all be true, that she was a harlot. The stealing…that could all be true, too. But at this moment, it just didn't matter. Not when he held a woman who'd endured a cruel betrayal that had wounded so deep, he wondered if she'd ever trust again.

"Then he told me," she continued, struggling to hold her tears at bay. "He told me that the baby had been stillborn. And that he'd *done the right thing*."

She peered up at him, her chin quivering, her mouth all tight. "I wanted to hold my baby. I wanted to see her. Even if she wasn't alive, I wanted to kiss her tiny head. She was my baby, Ben. My little girl," she whispered, piercing him straight through with her frantic, imploring gaze.

"But Max wouldn't hear it. He refused to show me where he'd buried her, too." She swallowed hard, her throat convulsing. "Finally, he did. But apparently it wasn't a grave," she added, her voice the faintest of whispers. "I cried countless tears over an empty grave."

"I don't know what to say, Callie." Ben's voice was rough with emotion. "It was so wrong. Max did the unthinkable, and he let you believe it."

"All of these years I've grieved alone because he didn't want to hear it." She pulled away from Ben then, her hands fisted and her body quaking so that the floorboards shook beneath her small frame. Deep anger flitted across her face as she looked past him, her mouth pulled into a grim line. "It probably reminded him of how he'd betrayed me."

"He was a coward. He always was."

"It hurt so bad. He knew it wasn't true and never ever said one thing to lift my sorrow." Untold fury turned her pupils to deep, dark holes that took over her beautiful eyes. "He lied to me, in spite of my grief."

She hugged her arms to herself and shook, her shock-filled gaze planted on the floor as if seeing it all play out again. "And God…" she said, glancing up briefly. "He allowed all of it to happen."

Ben pulled her to himself, wishing that he could take the grief and pain barraging her body and heart, but only God could heal a wound that deep and that wide. Ben could say and do all the right things, but he'd miss the mark. He smoothed a hand down her back as she gave in to the overwhelming emotion again, her deep sobs coming harder and louder this time.

With her fists bunched and pressing into Ben's chest, she cried, "How could God allow my own husband to do that?"

Callie had been cleaning nearly nonstop since she'd learned the truth about her baby two days ago. Ben had insisted she take as much time off as she needed, but if she didn't keep her mind and hands occupied, she'd lose herself to the bitter rage that snapped at her mind and heart.

Having just finished reorganizing the vials of medicine for the third time today, wiping each glass bottle till it gleamed in the lantern's glow, she ceased cleaning for a moment. Reaching into her apron pocket, she withdrew the small square of flannel fabric she'd kept in the wood box all of these years. Brushing her fingers over the soft pile, she remembered how she'd cut the small snippet from the blanket she'd made for her baby, since Max refused to have the blanket lying around. She'd kept the flannel all of this time, every so often holding it while struggling to reconcile the loss of her baby.

Struggling to reconcile something that never happened.

Anger, hot and ready, boiled up inside her at the thought.

Had it ever touched the soft pink of her baby's skin? Or had Max just fled into the cool night with barely a stitch of clothing on their little one, delivering the baby as though she was some crude package?

"Was that from your little girl?" Ben's low voice broke into her helpless thoughts as he stepped up next to her.

She nodded, pulling in a quivering breath. "Do you think she's all right?"

"I don't know, Callie. But I have to believe that whoever received your baby could only love her." He turned her to face him, his comforting touch remaining on her shoulders. "Is there anything I can do to help?"

She paused, wishing she could release the heavy, dark burden weighing down her heart into his hands, but that wouldn't be fair to him. Her sorrow, grief and anger were hers alone. She'd been without help this far.

Slipping the flannel back into her pocket, she knew that she'd continue to stand and face this alone, just like the past seven years. "There's nothing."

He slid his hand down her arm and scooped her hand into his. "Are you sure you can't remember who Thomas Blanchard is?"

"The name sounds vaguely familiar, but I can't recall."

Warmth from his hands moved up her arm to her heart. She longed to make her way into his embrace again—like she had when she'd found the note. Had it not been for his arms holding her then, she surely would've collapsed under the horrific discovery. But if she did give in to her need for his comfort now, she'd question if he bestowed his compassion upon her because of guilt. Guilt for Max's sins.

She shook her head, hugging her arms to her chest. "It's been six years. Besides, I've thought about this, Ben. What if something happened to her?" Her hands trembled as she tucked wayward wisps of hair back into her chignon. "I don't know if I could bear the idea of learning that now."

He gave a heavy sigh. "I understand."

"And if she's with a loving family, then to try and get her back would be no better than Max taking her from me in the first place. It wouldn't be fair to her. It would be just as wrong," she admitted, her voice tight with emotion. "I'd give anything to know that she's safe, though. And healthy."

She would, too. But until she fulfilled her obligations here, she'd have no opportunity for searching. And no money.

Ben threaded his hands through hers. "Callie, I'll never understand how Max could do something so awful. I wish I could somehow make it up to you."

Exactly as she thought. He wanted to make up for Max's mistakes. Well, he couldn't. They weren't his to resolve.

Eager to turn the attention elsewhere, Callie gently tugged her hands from his grasp as she crossed to the exam table to wipe its already gleaming surface once again. "I forgot to tell you…I found this, too." She pulled a small piece of paper from her pocket and held it out to him. "I didn't see it at first when I found the other—the other paper. But apparently he'd hid this, too."

"What is it?" he asked, taking it from her.

"It's a wire from my father. The date is hard to decipher, but from what I can tell he'd sent it about eight months after I left home."

Ben stared down at the tattered paper as Callie silently recited the words while he read them.

Callie. Please come home. We'll work things out. I miss you. Dad.

He turned his focus to her again, a shadow of sorrow crossing his face. "You didn't leave on good terms, then?"

"No. He didn't think much of Max. He'd forbidden me to see Max after he found out we'd been meeting secretly." She took it from him and slipped it back into her apron beside the flannel and the contract. "Until two days ago, I had no idea he'd tried to contact me."

Ben shoved a hand through his hair. "Why would Max keep this from you?"

"I keep asking myself the same question." She fingered the two life-altering pieces of paper in her apron, wishing she could find a reasonable excuse, even a small one.

Ben came to stand across the exam table from her. "Are you going to contact your father?"

"Eventually, maybe," she answered, staring down at the small scars in the exam table, remembering how bad things had been when she'd left home. She'd never imagined her father could seethe with such rage and hatred. "But as much time as has gone by, he may have already burned the olive branch."

"Oh, I'm sure he'll still want to see you, Callie. More than likely, he'll gladly open his arms to you again." Bracing his hands on the table, he leaned heavily over it. "I know that if Max had come home, I would've opened up my arms. No matter how much water had streamed under the bridge."

That, she'd learned over the past three weeks, was the exact antithesis of what Max had ever told her. And now she knew enough to grasp how much Max had lied. About most everything. She should've never trusted him.

But could she put her trust in Ben?

And could she put her trust in God when it seemed He'd looked the other way?

Would all of this have been easier had she not discovered the notes? There were so many unanswered questions that swirled through her thoughts.

"Ben? Why do you suppose Max kept the notes?" Staring out the window to where the sun eased down to meet the horizon, she felt where she'd worn the edges of the papers down to a soft, buttery feel. "It seems like it would've been easier for him to just burn them."

With weighted steps, Ben moved over and parted the lace curtains to look outside. "Maybe he figured that someday he'd have the courage to admit his failures—though I can't imagine Max doing that. He never could seem to apologize for things. He was always bent on blaming someone or something else, instead of himself."

That much was true. He'd blamed Callie plenty…for everything bad that had happened. It'd taken a while for her to see it for herself, and from that point on she'd silently refused his blame when it wasn't hers to take.

Now, if only she could face her own blame.

Chapter Fourteen

Three days had never lasted so long. From the moment he'd learned about Callie's baby, he'd been compelled to do all he could. He'd had the sheriff working with him; even Aaron had lent a hand.

Though Ben had almost refused his offer, something kept him from doing so. Maybe Aaron was having a change of heart or maybe this was his way of getting back at Max…either way, Ben was grateful for the help.

Ben rode out as the break of day began a slow and steady creep over the eastern horizon. He prayed his trip would produce something hopeful. He had to allow God to work out the details. As much as Ben wanted to take matters into his own hands, he had to trust God. He couldn't jeopardize the life of Callie's daughter.

It was a long shot, and nothing short of a miracle that he'd managed to locate Thomas Blanchard. Six long years had passed since Callie's baby had been born, but with the sheriff's help, and the help of Brodie Lockhart, a U.S. marshal living in the area, they'd discovered the man's whereabouts to be in the Golden area, a few miles from where Callie had given birth.

That's exactly where Ben was headed now.

The trapper by trade was no stranger to the law, and no stranger to gambling tables around the area, either. He'd even spent some time in jail.

That small detail strummed a chord of urgency deep in Ben's heart.

He touched his hand to the wad of money in his heavy, deerskin coat pocket. Yesterday at the wide-eyed, disapproving inspection of Thurman Franklin, the bank teller, Ben had made the hefty withdrawal. He figured that maybe with a little coaxing, a man like Blanchard could be paid off and relinquish what he'd purchased six years ago.

Pulling his coat a little tighter to ward off the wind that stormed through the canyon, a small niggling of guilt ate at him thinking of Callie back home. He could've brought her along, but had chosen not to. He didn't want to get her hopes up only to have them crash down again if they arrived to find out that something had happened to the child. She'd said herself that she didn't think she could bear such news.

He wanted to protect her…any way he could.

Rounding a narrow bend a few miles south of Golden, his watchful gaze landed on a small, run down cabin with a rickety front porch hanging on the house like a frail old woman on her way to her grave. After leading the horse into the yard, he tethered the gentle, trusty mare to a post, giving her a pat before he strode up to the house.

Spotting a ruffle of hen feathers beside the house, he was surprised that a mangy dog or two wasn't skulking around the edge of the scrub brush like ravenous wolves circling their prey.

He scanned the property, his attentive gaze snagging

on a makeshift lean-to hidden in a thick grove of trees, where the sound of a few nickering horses met his ears. Brodie had mentioned that Blanchard was suspected of horse thieving.

With a shake of his head Ben decided that he'd gladly tip off the U.S. Marshals. But only if he had the girl in the safety of his arms and far from this place first.

"You got yerself exactly ten seconds to git yer hide off'a my property." The gruff voice came from the deeply shadowed porch.

This wasn't getting off to a good start.

Setting a hand to his brow, Ben shielded his eyes from the sun and peered straight ahead to see a grizzly mountain of a man prowling at the edge of the porch, his britches hooked low beneath a rounded belly. A shotgun lodged in the crook of his arm.

Ben ignored good sense and moved closer so that the sorry looking structure with its crumbling rooftop created a block for the sun. "I'm a doctor from up north. Are you Thomas Blanchard?"

He narrowed his black eyes on Ben. "I am. What're you wantin' with me?" The man's voice reverberated, thick and liquor-slurred.

Blanchard shifted his feet awkwardly against the decaying porch floor. Made several clumsy grabs at a suspender hanging down his back, invoking images of Joseph's Newfoundland, Boone, halfheartedly chasing his own tail. Finally he pulled it forward and hooked it to his pants.

He looked just as Ben had imagined…like a filthy, gambling drunk who'd heartlessly agree to forgive a debt with the procurement of an innocent baby.

"I'd like to talk with you about—"

The rickety front door creaked open and a small face

appeared. A little girl with lily-white skin, smudged with dirt, her clothes in need of a wash, and her thick, auburn hair awkwardly tied up in a tattered, pink bow, squeezed through the door. She stood there, timid as a church mouse yet brave as any orphaned kitten.

And he knew right then that this little girl, the spitting image of his stubborn, brave assistant back home, had to be Callie's little girl. She had the same courageous tilt to her chin.

It was all Ben could do to keep a steady front.

"Didja git yer chorin' done, girl?" The abrasive sound of the man's voice sent a whole flock of birds fluttering madly away, their wings beating the air as though their very lives depended on it.

She gave a quick nod, glancing longingly at the birds for a brief moment before she locked her wary gaze on Blanchard's hands. "Yes, sir. I did it all, just like you said." The slight quiver in her voice raised the hair at the back of Ben's neck.

"Then git yerself back in there." He gestured the little girl away with a brisk nod. "I got me some business out here."

With a certain dignity that defied her age, the girl slowly turned then scampered back inside. But not before she passed one last glance Ben's way, her large, innocent eyes sadly shuttered, just like Callie's had been.

Ben advanced to the bottom step, throwing off any plans of easing through this confrontation with diplomacy. "I'll not beat around the bush. Is the girl yours?"

Blanchard cocked the hammer on the shotgun, holding the gun with both hands now. "You insultin' me, son? Cuz iffin' you are, you better hope that horse'a yers can cut and run fast."

He held his ground, his jaw tensing. "Is she yours? Because I heard otherwise."

Blanchard spat a brown wad of tobacco, just missing Ben's boot by a few inches. "Course she's mine. I won 'er fair and square."

At that thick-skinned response, Ben could've knocked the drunk to kingdom come, if not for the fact that the life of Callie's child—his niece—was at stake.

"Won her?" He set his back teeth and stepped up to the porch. Resisted the urge to ball his fists. "How's that?"

"The wife never could seem to grow herself a young'un. She was always belly-achin' 'bout needin' a baby to put things right," he slurred, liquor's loose lips on Ben's side. "Yessiree, Lady Luck smiled on me when some fella over his head in a game'a cards made me an offer I couldn't refuse." He tapped his thick fingers against the gun's steel barrel. "Didn't have to listen to the wife's wailin' and carryin' on no more. No sirree, she shut right up, sure shootin', soon as she had the baby in her arms."

Setting his focus over the man's shoulder to the door, Ben's heart dropped a notch. Any woman who'd ache like that had to love this little girl. "Your wife…is she here?"

"She gone and died. Four months back."

Ben cleared his throat. "I'm sorry for the loss," he managed, not because Blanchard seemed overly wrought with grief, but because the little girl had been in this man's sole care for so long.

"That's the way of it," Blanchard dismissed as though referring to the loss of one of the poor laying hens Ben had spotted. "Bein' a doctor and all, you should know that."

"It must be hard…raising her on your own." Ben jammed his hands into his pockets. "Without a woman around."

"I'm doin' fine." He snorted. "Just don't know what I'm gonna do with 'er come winter."

"Hate to be the one to break the news to you, but winter is here," Ben added, rubbing his gloved hands together.

"That's what I mean," the man retorted, impatiently. "Trappin'. All over them hills." He peered with a half-lidded gaze at the mountains surrounding him, as if they were his very own pot of gold. Then with a sneer said, "Ain't no place for a sissy girl like her. The wife spoilt her somethin' awful."

Having seen the girl and the surroundings with his own two eyes, Ben found that impossible to believe. He didn't doubt the woman had loved her, he just didn't think Blanchard cared much about providing. And was repulsed by the fact that the man considered Callie's daughter so lightly.

"She ain't nothin' but a bow-decorated, ruffle-clad girl who don' like to get dirty. It's jest like I told the wife. Tess, I says, she gonna be nothin' but trouble."

Ben swallowed back the bile burning his throat. Perhaps Max had felt the same way…that this little girl was going to be too much trouble. The thought made his blood boil hot with rage and regret for how Max had gone so astray.

"I believe I told you that I'm a doctor…"

"What of it? I'm fit as a fiddle." He stood up a little straighter then sagged a moment later. "Don' need no doctor pokin' on me."

Ben pulled his shoulders back. "You're in a predicament, Mr. Blanchard," he stated boldly. "With the missus gone and winter setting in, you won't be doing much trapping with that young lady in there."

"I'm not stickin' round just cuz'a her. If'n I don' git my lines out in them hills, some other greedy son will," he guaranteed, confirming that his trapping territory was of more importance than a little girl.

"Well, you can't exactly leave her here to fend for herself. She's hardly old enough."

Blanchard aimed the gun at Ben and spat again. "T'ain't none of yer business. 'Sides, I got me some other prospects that'a way. She's nearin' the marryin' age."

"Well, it's my business now. Now that I know." He stared hard at the sorry excuse for a man. "And she's nowhere near the marrying age."

Decayed, yellowed teeth showed through Blanchard's sneer.

"The law will have to know, too," he added. The last thing Blanchard would want if he possessed stolen horses was the law sniffing around. "It's only right."

Blanchard's gaze slithered the length of Ben, as though sizing him up to see if he'd fit into a boiling pot. "The wife's the one who wanted her. I had nothin' to do with 'er till Tess up and died."

"Exactly." Grasping at his fading self-control, Ben bit back the vicious litany of names he could let fly at the man. "Tell you what…I know of a young woman who lost a baby girl some time back. She'd love this little girl as her own." With the most authoritative air he could muster, he added, "I'd be glad to take this young charge off your hands."

After tenuous moments of deliberation, where Blanchard's knuckles turned white around the barrel of the shotgun, Ben wondered if he'd gone about this all wrong. He'd tethered a small handgun to his saddle, but that would do him little good now. The man had done jail time for attempted murder. Ben didn't want to give him a reason to pour out his rage on an innocent little girl.

He nailed the man with a steady, unwavering stare.

Blanchard met his gaze with a hungry grin. "For a price."

Callie hugged her arms to her chest and grasped for some silvery thread of hope, her heart barely thudding inside her chest.

On her way down to Golden, her optimism had surged to new levels, thinking that she might be able to see her little girl—just once. But when she'd asked around town and finally located the Blanchard homestead just minutes ago, she'd made the agonizing discovery that Thomas Blanchard was gone.

The weathered door hung open, dangling by a single rusty hinge as it creaked with eerie sadness in the brisk wind. The run-down house had been ransacked, and every last item in the sparsely furnished dwelling had been turned upside down.

Much like her life.

For six years, she'd lived in turmoil, had thought that God had punished her for the way she'd disobeyed her father and run off with Max. That had been a horrific and shameful reality to come to terms with. Learning that her baby had been born alive, and that Max had given the little girl—*his little girl*—as payment for a gambling debt, had been devastating. How could God allow such a horribly unjust thing to occur?

And now this?

A chill worked down Callie's spine as she slid her

gaze over the small, two-room cabin. She could barely breathe. Had there been some kind of attack? Some kind of ambush that sent her little girl fleeing for her life?

Aided by the wide-open door and the daylight that streamed through cracks in the walls where chinking had long since fallen away, she gave the cramped cabin a thorough, bone-chilling perusal. There were no signs of blood—at least that much was good.

She pulled in a steadying breath, wishing that Ben was here with her. She'd feel safe then.

He'd been a refuge in those moments after the discovery. Her saving grace…the way he'd held her and listened as she'd spilled more information than she ever should have. At the time, she hadn't been able to stop herself. The words had tumbled out so hard and so fast that if she'd tried to put a lid on them she might well have exploded.

Her head and heart still swirled with unanswered questions. She longed for peace…any kind of peace she could find.

She wanted to find peace with God. It wasn't good standing on the other side of a powerful and wrath-filled God.

Before her mama had died, Callie remembered watching Mama sing the hymns at church. Where the other adults had seemed so stoic and somber as they'd sung, Callie had often wondered if her mama was singing the songs to God Himself. She'd looked so beautiful. Had sung beautifully, too.

But it was her father's fear-invoking, anger-filled words that had haunted her time and again, marking her steps. He'd always said that until she straightened herself up and lived by the Lord's word and commands, the Almighty wanted nothing to do with her.

Even now, knowing that he'd tried to contact her didn't seem to remove the rut his words had formed in her soul.

"I've been trying, God," she whispered, stepping over the trash littering the floor. It just seemed like every time she was getting her footing, feeling like maybe she could approach God without fear of punishment, something came in to knock her off her feet.

A shaky sigh escaped her lips. She cushioned the crumbling anticipation of seeing her daughter with the idea that maybe the place had been empty for some time and had fallen prey to passing thieves.

She could only hope, could only pray that her daughter was safe. But when she spotted a little girl's dress, tattered, filthy and heaped near a straw-filled mattress, dread crept like a whole host of spiders down her spine.

Ghastly images infiltrated her thoughts. When she spied a small rag doll in the corner, her hopes faded to a deathly pallor. She knelt and picked up the doll, held it to her chest, trembling with the thought that perhaps her daughter had held this very doll. She pulled it to her face. Breathed in the distinct scent woven in the fibers. The doll hung limp in her hands. It was worn, almost to shreds, really. Probably well-loved by her little girl.

Carefully, almost reverently, she tucked the doll inside her cloak, her heart quaking with ready emotion. But when she felt the makeshift contract in her pocket and recalled how Max had boldly signed his name, her heart churned with revulsion. The deep, cavernous hole those emotions created threatened to consume her.

If she allowed that to happen, she'd go to the grave knowing that she'd been no better than Max. Or her father, who'd become so bitter and angry after her mama had died.

Callie refused to let that happen.

She'd faced plenty of bad things before and she'd made it through. She could do it again.

It's just that she'd so wanted to see her daughter. Just one glimpse to ensure that her little girl was healthy and happy and content...then maybe that huge hole in Callie's heart would begin to heal.

At the distant pounding of horses' hooves, she hurried to the door, eager to leave before someone discovered her here and accused her of pilfering. On the way to the door she caught sight of a silver filigree frame lying on the floor, the glass broken, photograph torn, and the frame bent. She picked it up.

Her breath hitched as she peered at the image. A woman, her hair dark and her smile timid, cradled a baby, her arms wrapped around the little bundle in motherly protection. The woman looked happy, Callie decided, blinking back tears as she raised a hand to her mouth. Very happy.

While the pounding hooves grew closer, she glanced at the man in the photograph. A chill set her hair on end. Her heart came to a grinding halt.

She'd never, ever forget that face.

It was him.

The man who had shown up at their small home. Nearly breaking down the door to get at Max.

Being well into the ninth month of pregnancy, Callie had been hard-pressed to find a hiding place when the man barged in, drunk and mean as a cornered badger, insisting on Max paying up. Max had put him off with a partial payment. But not before the brutish man knocked him across the room with his meaty fist.

Callie had thrown herself at the man's mercy, begging him to stop, but he'd thoughtlessly pushed her to the side then jammed a boot firmly on Max's heaving chest. Threatening far more than that if he didn't pay the rest by week's end.

Max had paid up, all right. With his very own baby girl.

A small moan escaped her lips. A quiver ran down her spine as she stumbled out the door. To know that her husband had given their precious baby into the hands of a man like that weighted her heart with such sorrow she couldn't help but release a strangled cry.

At the same time, anger, deep and penetrating, sprang to life within her like a choking weed as she made her way to the horse she'd tethered near the tree line. Her entire body shook. It scared her, the feelings that kind of rage invoked, because, had Max not been dead already, and had he been standing here with her, she would've killed him.

And she'd hate herself for it, too.

She could write a book of regrets and give it to Max, signed and sealed just for him, but even that wouldn't release the anger and regret that barraged her soul.

She could fight. Fight to get her child back, wherever the little girl was. But what did she have to fight with? Her daughter had been signed away with a contract, however malevolent and unfair. The fact that Callie hadn't given her consent would mean nothing in a court of law. She could do nothing. At least not now. Maybe when she was back on her feet again, after she'd paid back the debt to Whiteside.

Callie untied her mount and swung up into the saddle just as two riders made their way around the bend. She edged her horse into the cover of trees, watching as two men with badges dismounted and stalked toward the cabin.

Glancing down at the photograph again, she realized that God might exact punishment on her for her mistakes, but she'd never understand how He could allow an innocent child to fall into the hands of a man like Thomas Blanchard.

She struggled to hold back the emotions that tore through her like some hungry tornado raking across the plains. Her fingers quivered as she worked the photograph free from the frame and tucked it inside her cloak, tossing the broken frame aside. In spite of the fact that that horrible man was in the picture, looking as mean as she remembered him being, she wanted to keep the photograph. If this was the one and only visual memory she had of her baby then she'd treasure it. Until the day she died. Though it was tattered and she couldn't see her baby's face for the bundle of blankets, Callie just knew that the little baby, cradled in another mother's arms, was her little girl.

Chapter Fifteen

Callie barely remembered the ride back to Boulder. It was probably close to ten o'clock when she trotted the horse into town and returned him to the livery.

When she walked the few blocks home from the livery, she stared up at the stars that studded the dark night sky. How could a God who lavished such brilliance and glory in His creation seem to be so finicky and vengeful with His children?

As low as she felt right now, she was desperate to believe something more pleasant and hopeful, but she was afraid. Afraid that if she opened her heart and soul enough to see if God was more than that, she'd be sorely disappointed. She just didn't think she could take that kind of disappointment, again.

Arriving home, she was surprised to find the lamps burning in the office. Ben must've gotten home from his trip already and was probably tending to a patient, since he wasn't normally at the office this time of night. Likely, he wondered where she'd gone off to. He did say that she was free to do whatever she pleased while he was away, but still…

She quietly unlatched the door and moved inside.

When her gaze collided with Ben's, her heart faltered for a moment at the tender, gleaming look in his eyes. He sat before the fireplace in a rocking chair, holding a child in his lap.

He motioned her closer with a crooked finger. "Callie, you have to see her." His comforting voice was almost a whisper.

Callie shed her cloak, fingering the doll again, then stepped closer, concern mounting for the young child in Ben's arms. "What can I do?" she whispered so as not to disturb the patient. "Is the child fevered? Would you like me to get a cool compress?"

"She's fine." He grasped Callie's hand. "She's yours, Callie."

Her gaze darted to the child in his lap.

Then to Ben.

Her stomach surged to her throat. Her brow beaded with perspiration. And her pulse swished through her head with bright clarity. Smoothing her free hand down her dress, she grappled for her bearings as the words echoed through her soul.

Had she heard him right? Did he just say—

"Yes. I said she's yours." The warm smile tipping his lips made her heart skip several urgent beats. "This is your little girl."

"Wh-what?" Her vision narrowed as she pulled in a thin gasp of air. When her legs grew watery beneath her, she sank to her knees at Ben's feet.

He snuggled the little girl closer and scooted to the edge of the chair, his hand still firmly locked on Callie's.

"Just look at her." Ben's voice quavered as he crooked a finger beneath her chin and raised her gaze. His eyes shone through a glimmer of tears, and she was certain she'd never seen such visible, magnificent, powerful pride before. As if the little girl in his arms was his very own.

"She's beautiful." When he trailed the back of his fingers down Callie's face, a warm rushing sensation cascaded all the way down to her toes. "She looks just like you."

Disbelieving, she studied him for a long moment, searching his face for any hint that this was some sick and horribly cruel joke. But she knew, even as the thought crossed her mind, that he would never, ever do something like that. He was just too good. Too honorable. Too noble.

He was Ben.

A far cry from the man Max had been.

Time skidded to a halt as she inched forward. She leaned over the little girl in his arms, her lungs craving just one full breath of air. With a trembling hand, she edged the thick quilt away from the little girl's face. Peered at the child—her child. She could barely see the cherublike face through the hot, wet tears clouding her vision.

Choking back a sob, she pulled her hand from Ben's grasp. Set it to her mouth as she watched the little girl's pink lips pucker. Her breath catch. Her petite brow furrow then smooth out in a distinct expression of...

Peace.

Security.

And of comfort.

For six years her arms had ached—a real, tangible ache—to hold her little girl. She'd longed for the feel of her little girl's soft skin against her cheek. Longed for the fresh baby scent and sweet voice to hang in the air around her, like some eternal and blessed tribute to motherhood.

But now that her child was here within her reach, she felt clumsy, awkward. As if she had no idea what to do.

She'd faced an angry father with grief and suspicions that ran deep.

She'd faced a husband who drank, gambled and had fallen into long months where his personality changed so dramatically, Callie wondered if he was the same man she'd married.

She'd faced a man like Lyle Whiteside, who'd seemed to delight in holding the threat of her wicked demise over her head like some noose.

But she'd never felt as afraid as she did right now. Facing her daughter. Knowing that this little girl was dependent upon her now for food, care, love. And for hope.

Callie trailed a finger, featherlight, over her child's brow, scared to death that she might fail her daughter. What if the mistakes of her past trickled down to her little girl, bestowing a legacy of pain and hardship?

"How?" she finally asked, the word buried in a ragged whisper. She willed her hand to stop trembling. "How? I just came from there and the place was in shambles."

"You were there?" He peered at her, his brows creased in a look that had her feeling suddenly ashamed.

Callie dipped her head to the side. "I'm sorry. I just wanted to see her. That's all. I shouldn't have left, and I—"

"Don't be sorry." Ben smoothed her hair from her face. "It doesn't surprise me that you tried to find her—

you're determined like that, Callie. I'm just glad you're home, safe and sound."

Was this her home?

Deep inside, she wanted to be able to call someplace home. Her daughter needed a place to call home. But if Callie allowed her heart to get too attached to this place and this man, she might lose herself once again. She might end up right where she'd been seven years ago, with a man who'd stood before her as a valiant hero, when in reality he'd been more like a shameless villain.

Ben related the events of the day to her, his voice like some quiet, serene lullaby echoing in the room.

And all the while, Callie kept her frantic gaze clasped to the little girl in his arms, frightened that she wouldn't be able to make up for the significant years she'd lost with her daughter. And desperately afraid that if she looked away, even for a moment, her child would be gone. Again.

Ben had saved lives. He'd been an instrument of healing in God's hands for many townsfolk. He'd been a source of comfort for those who passed on to their eternal reward.

But he didn't know if he'd ever felt quite as good as he did right now, holding Callie's daughter—Max's daughter.

Just hours ago he'd ridden away from Thomas Blanchard's farm, his pocketbook empty and his arms full of a precious little girl.

He couldn't help but smile down at the child as she slept. Her breathing even and deep as she dreamed, her sweet face passing from an expression of peace to stubbornness to moments of apprehension that made his heart surge with protectiveness.

Ben saw Callie, through and through.

Callie…a welcome breath of fresh air in his stale life. Callie…a beautiful young woman with courage that made his heart hurt. Callie…an uncharted treasure with walls so thick he wondered if he'd ever get through.

If ever he thought he might be falling in love with Callie, it was now. He glanced at the woman who'd shown up on his doorstep just four short weeks ago. Her big blue eyes were suspended in pools of unshed tears as she peered almost reverently at her daughter.

Her face contorted with emotion, real and raw. As if she didn't know what to feel. How to feel. Or whether to trust that this little girl was really hers.

Ben had thought Callie would've scooped the child up in her arms and hugged her till she could hug no more. But instead, she threaded her hands nervously at her waist, as if holding her own child would break some kind of magical spell.

It'd been no small task getting her child back, and over the past hours Ben had thanked God plenty for blanketing him with favor and protection.

It was another matter altogether to break through the mistrust and reserve ruling Callie's every move. That loomed before him as an even bigger undertaking. He had to trust that God was big enough to handle a slight young woman like her, because Ben didn't know if he could gain control over the way his heart beat a sure and steady rhythm for Callie.

But finding just the right moment when he could confront her about the truth of her past, the truth of her present and her plans for her future seemed a difficult undertaking. There was the child now…little Libby.

And Ben had no intention of letting the auburn-haired, delicate-boned, flesh-and-blood remnant of Max go.

A few days ago, when Callie had discovered the paper, signing the child over to Blanchard, Ben had wondered if Max hadn't wanted the child because the baby had been a product of some other man's lust. But once Ben had the little one safe in his arms and several hundred feet away from Blanchard's stingy grasp, he'd looked at the little girl closely. The moment she'd flashed him even a hint of a smile, he knew that this child belonged to Max.

Along with all of the perfect and utterly feminine physical attributes that clearly pointed to Callie as her mother, the child had the distinct, telltale dimples bracketing her rosebud lips. Just like Max.

"Who's the girl?" Luke furrowed his brow, his questioning gaze nearly lost behind a thick sweep of blond hair. He folded his arms against his chest in such an adult manner that Ben fought to hide his grin.

"Her name is Libby," Ben answered when he heard Luke shift his boots impatiently against the wood floor.

The little girl sat in front of the crackling fireplace, her attention fixed on the picture book in her lap. She'd been in Boulder for almost two days now, and had taken to following him around whenever he wasn't out on a call, chattering on and on, just as Luke often did.

She'd won his heart, just like her mama had won his heart.

But Ben couldn't ignore the awkwardness that seemed apparent whenever Callie was with her daughter. She'd watch her mama with a keen, studying gaze, the warmth and openness she readily showed with Ben turning up missing with her mama, as if she hadn't decided whether to trust her as she had Ben.

Both Callie and Ben had talked with Libby the morning after she'd arrived. The little girl had planted herself on Ben's lap, clinging to his neck as they told her that this was her new home now. That Ben was her uncle. Callie, her mama.

He'd been hard-pressed not to tear up when she'd flashed him a bright grin and hugged him so tight, he thought she might never let him go. But the pained vulnerability apparent on Callie's face when her daughter draped her arms around her neck in a loose-fitting and hesitant hug was hard to ignore.

Luke gave a curt snort. "So…where's *she* from?"

"She came from down around Golden. She's Miss Callie's daughter." Hunkering down a bit, he settled a hand on Luke's shoulder. "And she's come to live with her."

The boy's eyes grew wide with surprise as he slid his gaze to where Callie walked into the room. He'd fallen over himself to please her, and suddenly his surly expression turned congenial. Just like that. "Yer daughter?"

Callie gave Luke a quick hug. "Yes."

"Maybe I could bring my kittens by to show yer girl. You know how girls like them kinda things."

Before Ben or Callie could get out one word of response, Luke marched over to Libby and plunked down beside her.

"Hi." He stuck out his hand. "Name's Luke."

The shy smile Libby gave him brightened the room, just like Callie's did when she smiled. "Hello."

Luke roped his lanky arms around his raised knees. "I got me some kittens."

Shrugging, the little girl glanced back at Ben. "Uncle Ben's got kitties, too."

"Molly and Smudge? I know them cats." With a sorry shake of his head, Luke acted as though the felines that he'd painstakingly helped Ben care for were suddenly old news. "My cats…they're kittens. They're babies," he added, dragging out the word *babies,* as if Libby was ignorant of the English language.

Ben turned and caught a forlorn smile pass momentarily across Callie's face. She fingered the locket at her neck.

"Oh, I love little kitties," Libby cooed, as if he'd opened a treasure box of brilliant baubles. "Are they fluffy? What color are they? Can I see them?"

Luke rolled his eyes. "You can see 'em. But ya gotta promise me somethin' first."

Libby scrambled to her knees, clapping her hands together. "I promise. I promise."

Inching away, Luke's brow furrowed in an exaggerated look of alarm, but beneath the apprehension Ben felt sure a tender smile lay in wait. "Ya cain't make a promise when ya don' know what yer promisin'." He threw a determined gaze over to Ben. "Can she, Ben?"

He chuckled, pulling his hand over his freshly shaved jaw. "Well, I—"

"Ya hafta' be real careful with my kittens, cuz they're still young'uns." Fumbling with the new leather strings Ben had laced through his boots the other day, Luke set his focus on his new charge, drawing his chin up a notch. "But they're gonna grow up to be real good hunters. Prolly the best in town, I'm thinkin'. I'll be a doctor jest like Ben, *and* I might even be a cat trainer, too."

Libby's mouth dropped open. "Are *you* teachin' 'em how to hunt?"

"Not yet, silly." He gave a long, loud sigh. "They're still babies. Won't be long 'fore I start learnin' 'em, though."

"Teaching them," Ben corrected with a chuckle.

"Yep. Teachin' 'em." With one slim finger, he tapped the correction into his head. "I been figurin' it all out, how I'm gonna do that."

"Oh, maybe I can help." Libby wriggled her dainty fingers beneath her chin. "I'd be real good at it. I just know."

Ben turned to Callie, fully expecting to see her face beaming with pride. But the troubled expression marring her beautiful features took him aback. When she caught him staring at her, he tried for a half grin and nodded to the children. "I'd say they're doing just fine together, wouldn't you?" he whispered.

"It looks that way." The too-quick, bleak smile plastered on her face hit him like a heavy weight against his chest. "I'm glad she'll have a friend like Luke."

He would've thought she'd be beside herself with joy. Her daughter was alive—very much so—and back with Callie where she belonged. Libby seemed to be adjusting so well, as if coming here to live had been a wonderful gift.

There were so many reasons to smile. To rejoice.

So why the long face?

Luke shoved himself up from the floor, jammed one stray tail of his shirt back into his britches. "Well, I'm not sayin' one way or t'other yet. Gotta see how ya fair with 'em. If'n they take to ya, then maybe."

Libby sprang up and grabbed his arm on a muffled shriek.

"Maybe," he reiterated with direct firmness.

Libby clamped her hands down to her sides, bunching her fists around the new pink dress Ben had bought for her yesterday. "My mama always told me I was good at everything."

"Miss Callie?" Luke cocked his head.

"No." She shook her head. "My mama back at my old home. She died right b'fore summertime."

Luke shoved a hand in his coat pocket. He raised his eyebrows and peered at her in the most honest and earnest expression Ben had ever seen on the boy. And Ben was proud. Darn proud of the way Luke seemed to consider a six-year-old little girl's feelings.

"You still sad 'bout that?"

"Yes. 'Specially when I go to bed." She turned and met Ben's gaze, and when she gave him a shy smile, he was sure his heart would swell right through his rib cage. "But Uncle Ben came and got me. And he's real nice."

Ben's throat suddenly burned with a thick, raw lump. Seeing the adoring smile on Libby's face, he'd do it all again—paying the thick wad of money he had to bring the little girl home. She was worth every last cent.

So was Callie. He'd gone after the girl for Callie. How could he not? When he'd heard the torture in Callie's cry? Seen the anguish in her crumpled features? Felt the agony in her rigid form?

The wrenching emotions had seemed to pour from some deep well that she'd stopped up for a long time— and they'd been there because of Max. Had Max not done something so cruel in the first place, Callie wouldn't have had to endure the past six years of grief.

As much as he hated to see her hurt like that, it was a relief knowing that she'd been freed of some of the secrets of her past. But looking at her now, the way her eyes were shuttered, and the way she couldn't seem to manage much more than a wane expression, he wondered what had happened. Just a week ago, she'd been much softer toward him. But she'd closed herself off almost as firmly as before.

What secrets did she still hold?

Ben eased from his contemplation when he heard Luke clomping over to stand beside him.

"You better believe Ben's nice. Ben and me, we been friends fer a while." Luke nudged Ben's arm like a puppy begging for attention. Folding his arms at his chest, he peered down his slightly crooked nose at Libby and added, "Actually, a long, *long* time. Prolly longer than you can even count."

Ben laughed and set his hand on Luke's shoulder. "You're definitely my helper, aren't you, Luke?"

"Yep." He worked his way into the crook of Ben's arm. "I'm his helper."

Holding his free hand out to the little girl, Ben added, "And Libby can be my helper, too. A fella can never have enough helpers, now can he?"

With wary optimism, Luke peered at the girl. "S'pose not."

She promptly took her place at Ben's other side, seemingly oblivious to the fact that her mama stood there, too.

Ben tried not to take notice, but the way Callie wrapped herself in a strangled hug, and the way she slid anxious glances to her daughter, she appeared as nervous as a cat in a room full of stomping boots. He didn't know how to help her. Didn't know what to do to ease her discomfort.

After Ben sent Luke and Libby off to traipse around

outside in the barn, he walked into the exam room where Callie was busily organizing an already perfectly ordered supply shelf.

"Is there something wrong?" He came to a halt behind her.

Her fingers stilled on the small tins she'd been moving. "No. I'm fine."

Resting a hand on her shoulder, he released a sigh. "I can't claim to know you all that well, but if you don't mind me saying so, you look nowhere near fine." Grasping her upper arms, he turned her around to face him. "Are things not going well with you and Libby?"

"We'll be just fine." She shrugged, as if to remove his touch.

He refused to let her spurn his concern. He caught her gaze, wanting to find the same softness he'd seen there when they'd danced. When she'd softened to his gentleness. Melted to his touch. She'd felt so right in his arms, as if she'd been created just for him, and he for her. At that very moment he'd all but convinced himself that God had been masterful in the way He'd turned a very tragic, traumatic and tricky situation for good.

"Callie, what happened in the last few days?" He angled a concerned look down at her. "I mean, I know you've faced some big changes, but something is different."

She set her focus just past him. "I don't know what you mean."

"You were softening. I was hoping that maybe you were starting to trust me." He ducked his head to meet her blank stare. "What happened to that vulnerability?"

What could he have possibly done to push her away? He'd gone to great lengths to make her happy.

But why was he so determined to earn her trust when he was still a long way from trusting her?

Just yesterday he'd discovered his small weight scale missing. A large item like that certainly wasn't something he'd just misplace. The stethoscope, the tweezers, the roll of gauze and even the bottle of iodine were items he could misplace. But a scale?

He wouldn't have drawn his conclusion to Callie taking them, if not for the fact that these things hadn't started disappearing until days after her arrival.

And then there hung the constant question about her past. Aaron had made enough crude remarks as to her morality. Then there was Pete's testimony. And she had shown up wearing a dress not fit for any kind of upstanding company. She hadn't even seemed ashamed, or embarrassed. As though the dress was part of her... just Callie.

But every time he allowed his thoughts to wander to that precarious edge of suspicion, he'd turn tail and flee the other direction. Nothing—*nothing* about Callie would point to that being some murky part of her history. She didn't flaunt herself as a harlot would. She didn't hold herself with that self-protection-dripping arrogance. She didn't look at men with that sultry, half-lidded gaze meant to reel in prey.

She was just Callie.

And regardless of the way things looked with the dress and the missing items and the eyewitness testimony, he wanted to believe she was innocent.

When he looked down at Callie again and saw the way she hiked her chin up a notch, in that sweet way he'd marveled at from the beginning, he felt his heart snagged again. The desire to take care of her overwhelmed him. He wanted to see her free—really free from the pain and anguish of her past. To see her dream again. Because she'd likely not done any dreaming from the day she'd married Max.

"I don't know what's wrong with me, Ben." Closing her eyes, she gave a slow, disheartened sigh. "I'm trying. Really I am."

When he attempted to pull her close, his heart sank at the way she stiffened. "It's going to take some time for Libby to adjust. This is a big change for her, Callie. For you, too."

She shook her head. "I'm so afraid I won't be enough for Libby."

"You'll be more than enough," he said, smoothing a hand down her arm. "You'll be a wonderful mother for her."

"I don't know…" When Callie nibbled on her lower lip, Ben had to force his gaze elsewhere. "She doesn't seem to notice I'm around—not like she notices you, or Luke, or even Katie and Joseph."

"I'm the one who brought her here, so she probably does feel that way, at least for now."

She threaded her fingers at her chest. "I know that she loved her mother, Blanchard's wife…"

"She might be struggling with feeling disloyal if she gets too close to you." He wished he had the words that would take away all of her apprehension. Especially when her brow furrowed even more, and she stepped away from his touch. "Just you watch, Callie. She'll be drawn to you soon enough. She'll be at your elbow wanting to bake bread with you or help you make supper."

For a long time she stood there, close enough to reach out and touch, yet hundreds of miles away. She hugged her arms to her chest as she turned her head and stared at the freshly cleaned exam table.

"She said something yesterday when she was playing with her doll." Wary indecision shadowed her fair, delicate features. "She didn't realize I was there listening, but I heard her."

Ben pictured the doll that Callie had brought with her when she'd returned from Blanchard's place. He'd almost suggested discarding it. But Callie had gone to great lengths to repair the ragged doll that first night, when, instead of turning Libby in to an unfamiliar bed with another unfamiliar face, Ben had held the little girl for the entire night in the rocking chair by the woodstove, while Callie cleaned and repaired the doll. She'd painstakingly added stuffing by the dim lamp's glow, and had even replaced two of the doll's tattered limbs.

Her instant resolve to take care of her child in some way had been a wonder to watch, had warmed his heart from the inside out. When Libby had spotted the rag doll resting in the crook of her arm the next morning, her eyes had lit with wonder and amazement.

"What did you hear her say?"

Callie touched the dainty lace trimming the neckline of her dress. "Apparently—apparently he told her that her real mama and papa didn't want a girl like her." The strangled sound in Callie's voice broke his heart. "She said that's why she had to live with him and her other mama…because her real mama didn't want her."

Chapter Sixteen

Callie swiped a solitary tear from her eye. It seemed that in the past few days she couldn't help herself from tearing up now and then. Watching the tender way Ben tucked Libby into bed even now, the way he'd read to her from the Bible...the story of David and Goliath just minutes ago. These things made Callie's heart and throat swell with ready emotion.

Truly, Max had missed out.

She'd missed out, too.

And she might continue to miss out if she stayed here. But every bit of her wanted to stay put in Boulder. In the safety of a family who'd been good to her. A man who'd been so very good to her.

"She's all tucked in." Ben winked, setting her pulse off-kilter.

He shut the door behind him, his nearness commissioning a flurry of activity in her stomach.

She tried for a relaxed smile, but the expression felt forced. "Good."

"Care to join me on the back stoop before I go home for the night?" The brush of Ben's arm as he edged past her in the hallway's close proximity sent a shiver of delight inching through her veins.

She knotted her hands in front of her. "For what?"

He gave a long, lingering glance into the exam room, the way he usually did each night, in his silent and perceptive way, making sure all was as it should be. "Oh, just because it's a beautiful night." He turned to settle his half-shuttered gaze upon her. "A little chilly, but beautiful, nonetheless."

"Sure, let me get my cloak."

After Callie secured the front door lock and grabbed her cloak from the wood peg, she peeked in on Libby one last time. Struck again by the sweet way her little girl slept, her arm cradled around her doll.

Prying herself away from the peaceful scene, she made her way out the back door and sat down next to Ben. Though she'd left a good foot between them, she could feel his body heat permeating her in an unseen wave of glorious comfort.

She was so aware of his presence—whenever he was around. She'd even go so far as to say she craved it.

Without a doubt, she'd become far too comfortable around him.

Sighing at her irrational, wandering thoughts, she watched her breath puff into the cool night air in tiny clouds. "I've never really appreciated the cold months."

"Why's that?"

"I suppose because there was never enough wood for burning. I was always cold." Always uncomfortable. Always seemed to be a breath away from freezing.

"Max should've taken better care of you. The way you deserve," he breathed, his voice thick.

"It's not your fault." She wished Max, even once,

would've taken responsibility, but for some reason he always blamed her for everything. For their lack of money, comfort, and general peace and solitude.

Ben's gaze lingered with hers, his eyes searching, looking deep into that part of her that she'd tried so hard to protect. Then he shifted his focus and stared up at the sky, his silken eyes shimmering in the moon's pearly light. "It always amazes me how much more stunning the sky seems on a cold, clear night."

She tipped her head back to witness the breathtaking way radiant stars soaked the midnight-blue sky. "It is spectacular, isn't it?"

He settled a hand at her back. "Things are as clear as they've ever been." The husky timber of his voice infused the placid night air with tangible intensity.

For some reason, she didn't think he was referring to the night sky. When he turned and settled that deep, searching look on her, she felt it every bit as much as if he'd pulled her into his embrace. Her pulse raced. Her cheeks warmed with an unwelcome blush. She averted her gaze, but not for long.

With tender affection, he set a hand to her chin and coaxed her focus back to him, her control rapidly—she swallowed hard—slipping away.

Desperate for a way out of this spiral of innate emotion, she jerked her attention back to the door. "Is that Libby I hear?"

She made to rise.

He set a hand on her shoulder, keeping her beside him. The low chuckle he gave swirled her nerve endings into a reverberating hum. "Either you're more innocent than I thought, I'm really bad at dropping subtle hints, or you're downright nervous about now."

"What?" She gulped.

"Callie…" He cradled her cold hands in his. Hands that had gentled newborn babies, eased the passing of a patient and brightened the face of a cold and needy child with readily bestowed gifts. The warm, work-worn strength of his hands had been healing medicine to her. "You don't have to be afraid."

He imprisoned her total attention. In fact, she felt as if some unseen force held her firmly, right there, a breath away from the man she'd tried so desperately to avoid.

Yet felt such a compelling draw to know.

"When you showed up here," he began, rubbing the pad of his thumbs gently over her hand as if to still her wild, racing heart.

It didn't work.

"I didn't know what I was getting into, taking you in like I did."

"Probably more than you bargained for," she sputtered nervously.

"Oh, *definitely* more than I bargained for. But you were worth it." Setting his hand under her chin, he drew her nearer. His gaze fixed on her lips, sending a quiver straight through her that had nothing to do with the cool night. "You *are* worth it."

"Ben, I—"

"For the first time in a long time I'm seeing things clearly." Like a whispered word of care, he brushed a finger across her lower lip. "I want to kiss you, Callie."

She struggled to take in the thick air caught between them.

He inched closer, a half breath away. "So if you have any objections, you better let me know now."

Her breath hitched. Held. Her pulse whooshed like

steady waves through her head in an innate and age-old rhythm.

He settled his mouth against hers, a warm and tender claim.

Closing her eyes, she reveled in the moment. In the heady, cherished feeling.

His breath passed through her parted lips as if to infuse her vulnerable heart with hope and promise and whatever else he had to give her. His trembling hands rose to frame her face. She heard the breath catch at the back of his throat. Felt the rapid beat of his heart as he pressed his lips to hers in a soft kiss that threatened to be her undoing.

"I think I'm falling in love with you, Callie." His words filtered through her like warm fire.

Her eyes snapped open. "Ben…"

He drew just slightly away from her and stared down into her eyes with a deep, poignant look that had her quaking from the inside out. "I never thought I'd hear myself say that. I was content being a bachelor."

Bracing an arm around her shoulders, he pulled her close to his side. "I want to take care of you."

The mellow, soothing cadence of his voice and his inspiring presence roused her long-forgotten dreams. Dreams of a shared love that could boldly withstand the winds of change, the storms of life and the drought that could strip a life bare. Love that could convey a thousand heartfelt sentiments without uttering a word.

He pressed a slow, warm kiss to her head. "I want to make sure you don't ever lack for anything, ever again, Callie."

It was too much to withstand.

When he brushed his cheek against her forehead, her

heart slammed against her chest. "I want your daughter to be raised in a good, solid home."

And would be way too much for her daughter or for Callie to ignore.

She hugged her arms tight to her chest, trying desperately to maintain control, but it was nearly impossible. His loving words, his gentle touch and his passion called to some long-ago, buried desire deep within her heart.

He was so good. Too good.

Too nice.

Too gentle.

Too strong.

Too willing to love Callie and her little girl. Too willing to promise things she'd dreamed of, but never had.

"I want to give you the world." His whispered words against her head set her hair on end.

Max—he'd said that... *I want to give you the world*.

She could barely breathe as she remembered how he'd waxed eloquent with all of his talk of adventure and love and lifelong devotion, and at the first hint of challenge a few months after they'd married, he'd abandoned every pledge.

And now Ben, Max's flesh and blood, made the exact same pledge.

She'd vowed never to make herself vulnerable again, and here she was, lapping up Ben's nurturing words as if she were some hungry kitten lapping up a bowl of rich cream.

Before she lost any more of her heart and resolve, she sprang up from the step and darted back inside. Closing the door, she locked it, wishing she could just as easily lock out the wholly consuming feelings that rocked her entire being.

Making her way to where her daughter slept soundly, she tiptoed across the room, berating herself that she'd so easily fallen prey to Ben's intoxicating presence, just as she had with Max. While she stared down at the peaceful, content way Libby slept she felt desperate to escape the compelling draw before he so completely won over Libby that the girl would never want to leave. Before he snatched away Callie's freedom—just like Max had done.

"Looky what we have here." The sound of Lyle Whiteside's low, gravelly voice coming from the alley-way brought Callie to a faltering stop.

And immediately blocked out the sun's warmth.

"You're looking real nice, Callie. All gussied up. You didn't go working for somebody else, did you?"

She made a slow turn, bracing herself for the man's snapping black eyes to land on her like a vulture's sharp talons to prey. She'd never met anyone who could wound so with a mere look. It was his way—with the girls back at the brothel and with any other poor soul who dared cross him or owe him.

"But I'm disappointed." He lunged out of the shadows. Crowded her close. "You walked out on our agreement."

Callie willed her hands to stop trembling, her stomach churning at the scent of his stale breath. "No. Of course I didn't."

She wished now that she hadn't parted ways with Ben and Libby a block back. While Libby had shadowed Ben into the mercantile, Callie strolled down the street to the milliner's shop. After what had happened last night, when Ben had kissed her and made the declaration he had, she'd jumped at any chance to be as far away from him as possible.

Whiteside drew a hand up to her face and snagged a lock of her freshly washed hair between his thumb and forefinger. He rubbed it as if inspecting it for some clue.

She half expected him to sniff it.

His thin lips tipped in a sardonic smile. "Sure you made an agreement. Remember?"

She refused to let him intimidate her. "I didn't agree to anything more than paying back the debt. And I intend on doing that."

"But we agreed that you could get that done faster on your back." He trailed his meaty hand down her cheek to her arm. "And then I come to find out that you up and left."

Callie clutched her reticule tight to her chest, mentally tallying the amount she'd saved so far. She could give him what she had, but the amount was still not enough. And if she was going to leave Boulder as she'd decided last night, then she'd have nothing with which to make her way.

She slid back a step. "I left you a note."

"I didn't find a note." He nailed her with one of his deceptively nice, understanding kind of looks.

Callie struggled to stay composed instead of flinching as she often had in his presence. She forced herself not to run. "I wrote you a note explaining everything."

"Notes aren't my way, Callie. You should know that I perform most of my business with my mouth." He laughed at his own sick sense of humor while she fought off the urge to vomit all over his shiny shoes.

She'd never do what he asked. Even if a girl stooped to that low a level and paid him back by sacrificing herself, she'd never find her way back to freedom. And Callie would never, ever allow that. She had Libby now, and would do whatever it took to keep her daughter safe from the likes of Lyle Whiteside.

She forced her gaze to meet his. "I'll have the rest for you by the beginning of December."

Shaking his head, his large jowls jiggled.

"I will." She grabbed the sleeve of his expensive coat before she thought better of it. "I'll have the whole debt paid off by then. I promise."

He looked down at where she held his coat then seized her hand and squeezed so hard that Callie stumbled forward against him. "Why would I want to wait when I could be getting my money's worth by having you pay on your back now? You'd have that debt paid off in no time, Callie. Just think, you'd be free to do whatever you wanted."

"Please." She pried his fingers loose from her hand, trying to hide her discomfort from an older couple passing by. Not wanting to be any kind of embarrassment for Ben, she smiled as though she was enjoying the present conversation. "You'll have the rest soon."

"The men might even front a good sum for you, the way you're looking." He raised his bushy brows. His beady eyes sank into his thick, red-blotched face as he held her hands out to the side, looking her up and down in a leering perusal. "If you do well, I might even throw in a bonus. Maybe a fancy new dress or two, instead of this awful get-up you're wearing."

"I like the dress I have on just fine."

"Come now." With stealthy precision, his hands slithered up to part the cloak Ben had purchased. "You can't be serious."

"Of course I am. This dress is lovely. And appropriate." Forcing the bile back down her throat, she met his gaze. "And I won't do what you're asking. I'll have your money for you, but not like that."

The way he shoved her away from him, as if he were done playing with a toy, almost sent her into a wild frenzy. He'd do that to his *girls,* toying with them then leaving them unsure of their status with him. It was his way.

But Callie refused to let him see that, deep down, her insides churned with raw fear. Not for herself, but for Ben and for her daughter.

"You have two days."

"Two days? But I'll never be able to—"

The smile he gave her stopped her midsentence, and sent an ominous chill down her back.

Would God allow another tragedy to befall her? Did He even hear her when she called to Him?

Would she ever truly be free from the stain of her husband's past?

Two days? There'd be no way she'd have the rest of the money for Whiteside by then. And she couldn't— wouldn't—ask Ben for an advance on her salary. She couldn't imagine staying in Boulder after the proclamations Ben had made. Doing so could risk repeating history, and she didn't know if she could withstand the trauma of that again.

In spite of her vow never to make herself vulnerable to another man again, her feelings for Ben were so strong and real. Whiteside's appearance today only secured her future for her, leaving her with no choice. Either she could flee with her daughter in tow and her integrity intact, or she could stay and risk losing everything she'd struggled so hard to gain.

Tipping his hat to her, Whiteside pinned her with a

grave and biting glare. "I'll see you in two days. If you don't have the rest by then, you'll be doing far more than just talking."

Seeing is believing.

Only this was one thing Ben hadn't wanted to believe.

Was she turning a trick right here under his nose? Or was this some nefarious brute from her past trying to bag her now? She certainly hadn't seemed as if she'd minded the interchange.

His heart sank low. His stomach dipped to meet it.

Furious, he turned and stalked back toward the mercantile to retrieve his packages and little Libby, whom he'd left in the care of Mrs. Heath, trying to decide which flavor of candy stick she wanted.

Five minutes ago he'd felt about as confident as he could about the future. Sure Callie had run inside last night after the kiss, but he could understand her wariness, and was determined to give her plenty of understanding. But now he had serious reservations about the next few minutes, let alone the upcoming day.

Moments ago, he'd stepped outside to make sure Callie didn't need anything from the mercantile, when he'd been brought to a heartbreaking halt in his tracks.

The way his blood still pulsed with hot energy through his veins made it clear that he'd seen enough, all right. He'd stared in stunned disbelief at where Callie had stood near an alleyway a good block away, in front of some man Ben didn't recognize.

All of this time Ben hadn't wanted to believe that she had a sordid, secret past.

Striding up the stairs to the mercantile platform, he

clenched his jaw in a silent admission...he'd been fooling himself. That had been made painfully apparent to him when the man had reached out to touch Callie, and she didn't move away. Didn't even seem to flinch when he'd stroked her face and arm in a very forthright manner, as if they'd shared some kind of long-standing, intimate past.

As soon as Ben had spotted the two of them clustered together as if they were lovers, the hair on the back of his neck had stood on end. He'd been close enough to notice she didn't rebuff the well-dressed man's touch.

As she had Ben's.

His gut churned with outrage and sadness.

Aaron was right. His brother had tried to warn him, several times in fact, but Ben had refused to believe Callie capable of living that kind of life. Pure and simple, Ben was just too trusting. And now, it seemed, he'd been burned.

Just last night, he'd embraced her. He'd relished the feel of her petite frame protected in the shelter of his arms. He'd kissed her, cherishing the way her soft lips melted to his. And he'd fallen over himself, declaring the things he had. Thank goodness she'd run back inside before he could ask her to marry him.

She had secrets, all right. Secrets that he'd be darned if she'd keep from him even one more day. Her little girl deserved more. Callie deserved more. But as long as she consorted with her secretive past, she'd never know how it could feel to step boldly into the future.

He forced down the thick lump searing his throat, trying to calm himself before he stepped foot in the mercantile. Libby didn't need to find him on the edge of rage. She was a sweet child with a past that begged for stability and security.

Just like her mama.

That sobering little fact sliced straight through to the very center of his heart. He had to figure out what he was going to do. He still wanted to take care of Callie and her daughter. But he'd find out about Callie's past, all right. Everything. Because if he ever meant to build a solid future with her, then he'd have to lay some kind of groundwork for trust in the present.

Right now, the whole thing lay in sinking sand.

Callie had to leave Boulder. Between Whiteside's threat and Ben's promises, she had no choice.

She touched the wrinkled and yellowed telegram in her pocket, silently reciting the words her father had conveyed some time ago. That he wanted her to come home.

She could only hope that he still felt the same way now as he did when he'd sent this to her. Had Max not hidden it from her, would she have gone to her father before?

It was useless to guess. The important thing was what she had to do now. Gathering the ends of an old sheet, she secured it with a knot, mentally recounting the items she'd packed into the roll. She didn't feel right taking the new things Ben had gotten for her daughter, but Libby had nothing else. And just as soon as she could, Callie would send money to pay Ben back.

She might never get her head above the swirl of debts that threatened to eat her alive, but at least she'd be in control of what happened to her and to those she loved.

Love… Did she love Ben?

She hadn't even considered it until now. Or maybe she had chosen to ignore the glaring facts. How could it be that she could find love with a man like Ben Drake? Max's flesh and blood?

She couldn't ruminate on such things now. It was useless.

Thankfully, he'd been out for most of the day and evening on calls, so she'd been able to get her things together to leave as soon as night fell.

Stepping over to the bureau, she picked up the letter she'd written earlier and skimmed her heavy gaze over it one last time. The paper still felt faintly damp from her tears as she'd penned the words. The note wasn't long, but it conveyed her sincere appreciation. That would have to be enough for Ben because if she let on as to what her plans were, he'd locate her whereabouts. She didn't want to put him in jeopardy. Herself in jeopardy. Or her child in jeopardy.

Whiteside was not one to mince words. When he said something, he meant it. And if Ben was privy to what the man intended to do, she had a very real and grave sense that in order to thwart Whiteside's plans, Ben would risk his own safety.

It was like some lavish gift, thinking that someone was looking out for her like that. She'd surely never experienced something so wonderful with Max. It was within her grasp now, but she'd never be able to know the warm and tender embrace of that kind of security. Her past…her husband's past had come back to haunt her and until she rectified the situation she'd never truly be free.

But she feared that if freedom hinged on everything being all ordered in her life, she might never be free.

Chapter Seventeen

"She's gone." Ben choked out the words as Aaron walked into the room where Callie and her daughter had slept, his hands jammed on his hips, his lips pulled taut in disgust.

"No sign of her or the girl?" he asked, scanning the room.

Ben shook his head, feeling more alone than he'd ever felt before. And angry. "No. I've checked everywhere and all of their things are missing. It's as if they'd never lived here."

"I'm sorry, Ben. Really I am. I'd hoped it wasn't Callie and her daughter I saw climbing into that wagon earlier."

"Why didn't you stop her?" Ben paced out to the hallway, frustrated, angry and scared.

"I should have. I'm sorry." Aaron followed, a few steps behind.

He imagined her leaving town, head held high, face set with steady resolve toward what, he had no earthly idea. "Well, I'm glad that you at least came to get me."

"I had a feeling she'd do something like this to you. I just didn't think it would be so soon. I tried to tell—"

"Are you trying to make me feel better?" he spat.

"The truth usually doesn't feel good."

Ben had tried to ignore the gut-wrenching feeling that had eaten at him the past twenty-four hours, that Callie would do something like this. This evening he'd ridden hard all the way home from his last house call because of it, and when Aaron had met him on the edge of town, Ben's heart had ceased beating for several seconds.

When he'd kissed Callie last night, she'd seemed so receptive. But just like strays he'd taken in, just as soon as he'd shown love and affection, she'd run off. Usually strays returned, as if giving in to a deep down need for care and love.

But not this time. Not this stray.

"We still don't know she left for good," he muttered, hoping that he was flat-out wrong.

Though he feared his suspicions were true, for some reason he couldn't seem to reveal that deep-seated dread with Aaron. Aaron had had it out for Callie from the day she'd shown up in Boulder.

Ben had no doubt that the man he'd seen her talking with yesterday had as much to do with her disappearance as her desire to run from love. And the idea that she might be in danger sent his pulse stampeding through his veins.

"For Pete's sake, Ben, are you still holdin' to your claim that she's innocent? That her life as a harlot might not be true?"

"Innocent until proven guilty." He stalked toward the front door, grabbing his bag and an extra blanket. On the way out to saddle his horse and ride out, he held his hand near the stove. "They couldn't have gone far. The woodstove is still hot."

Aaron followed him out the door and matched Ben's

long strides. "How much more proof do you need to call her guilty? Seven years ago Max said he'd hooked up with some harlot."

Ben jerked his brother to a stop. "Don't say that."

"That she's a harlot?"

He tightened his fist around Aaron's coat. "You know how Max would say things just to shock all of us. For some reason he enjoyed seeing us flinch."

Aaron brushed Ben's hand away. "Believe what you will. She showed up in a harlot's slinky dress four weeks ago. Remember? You showed it to me. And then with everything else…well, what more do you need for proof?"

Ben turned and strode toward the barn, thankful he hadn't told Aaron about the man he'd seen Callie talking with this morning. Something had kept him tight-lipped. Aaron already had plenty of ammunition against Callie. Ben didn't need to offer him more for his stockpile.

"You just don't want to believe it's true. That Callie could actually sell herself."

"Enough," he bellowed, entering the barn. He immediately regretted his outburst upon hearing his mare's anxious snort. "I don't want to hear another word about this."

Ben stepped up to the stall and spoke in low, soothing tones to his mare as he opened the gate and led her out.

While Aaron hung back, clearly and appropriately wary, Ben had to wonder what had gone through Callie's mind to leave so abruptly. Though the weather conditions weren't bad, in his estimation it was nowhere near fit for traveling at night with a young child.

She had not only herself to think about, but her child, too. And if their departure had anything to do with the man he'd seen with Callie this morning, then Ben would be dead in his grave before he'd allow his brother's child to be raised in some hole of a brothel.

He hauled his saddle up on his horse and cinched it almost as tight as the cord of betrayal that nearly cut off the feeling in his heart.

"I'm heading out." He loosened the cinch a couple of notches and set his focus on his brother. "You can ride along if you want. But if you choose to ride, I'll not have you saying one more thing like that about Callie. Do you hear?"

Aaron spoke not another word as he mounted his mare and spurred his horse alongside Ben in a fast gallop south.

Within an hour, they'd located Callie and her daughter riding in the back of a wagon driven by a traveling salesman. To Ben's great relief, both Callie and Libby seemed sound. To his almost equaled relief, she didn't fight him when he gave her no option but to come back to Boulder.

It almost broke his heart that some of the stubborn tilt to her chin had gone missing. As if some of the fight and determination that defined Callie had been lost between home and the road south. Hesitation, and maybe even a small sense of relief, had hung heavy in her gaze when he lifted her up to ride sidesaddle in front of him.

With little more than a few complacent words said for the sake of Libby, Ben returned in silence with Callie. Her little girl perched in front of her uncle Aaron, stealing sweet, almost worshipful glances in the moon's light over at Ben every minute or so, as if to make sure he was heading the same way. His throat grew raw with the effect that had on him—to know that Callie's little girl looked at him with such awe. He'd be hard-pressed to ever live up to the appreciation he saw in her eyes. He'd failed those he loved more than once, and all he could do was trust that God would work it all out.

When Callie shifted against him, he struggled to ignore the way every nerve ending hummed with instant attraction. Had Ben not been angry with the petite little woman in front of him, he'd have been driven to distraction by the way her body molded to his in the saddle. The way an errant lock of her hair whispered against his cheek. The way her eyes seemed to pool with unshed tears as she gazed with vacant sadness across the milky, moonlit horizon.

After they returned to Boulder, Aaron continued on alone to his cabin outside of town. Ben felt an overwhelming sense of relief when he tucked Libby into bed—not in the room she'd been sleeping in with her mama, but in the extra bedroom in his home.

He found Callie standing in front of his fireplace. As he advanced closer, she trembled slightly as she hugged her arms tight to her chest. Her gaze flickered between shame, stubbornness, sorrow and resolve.

"Why?" He stood back from the fire, irritation still running with heated energy through his veins. "What were you thinking?"

She met his gaze with the same kind of bravery he'd seen in her that very first night. "I didn't have a choice, Ben."

He shook his head, noticing for the first time that the heirloom locket didn't hang there against her creamy white skin, as it had every other time he'd been with her. Had she left it for him?

"You had a choice." He couldn't let that kind of sentimental musing affect his mood. Misplaced mercy wouldn't do him or Callie any good. "We all make choices. Only yours happen to border on irresponsible."

She pinned him with an insolent glare.

He raised his brows. "Well, far be it from me to say… I mean, I am just your brother-in-law, your daughter's uncle, and your employer—"

"Not anymore."

On a frustrated sigh, he jammed a hand through his hair. "What I'm saying is that I care, Callie. I care what happens to you and Libby, and exposing your child to the kind of lifestyle you might lead isn't wise. Or healthy. Or right."

She furrowed her brow, her perfect features crinkling in bewilderment. "What do you mean…the kind of *lifestyle* I might lead?"

"You're single." He took a step closer. "And alone. Do you think there will be many options for you out there?"

"I'd make it just fine," she retorted with sharp precision. Grabbing her cloak from the chair, she whipped it around her shoulders. "I can do all kinds of work."

"I'm sure you can." He shoved his hands into his pockets and gave his head a slow, sorrowful shake.

Just like that, her stubborn streak had barged in on her vulnerability, taking it over by force. Ben would have to be more forthright if he hoped to get through to Callie. Though he may be a fool, he cared for this woman. Deeply. And if he planned on enjoying any kind of future with her, then he'd have to be up-front about his suspicions.

As irritated as he was with Callie, he also felt sick thinking about how lost he'd feel if something happened to her or her daughter. And how he'd blame himself, too. No matter what her past, he'd hold himself directly responsible for any ill fate that would come their way. The fact that he hadn't been able to keep her here and turn the situation around would only add to the shaming regret eating at his sense of trust in God and himself. It would be the final nail in his coffin.

"How do you think I made it the past seven years?" she asked through clenched teeth, her spirited gaze narrowing.

"I'm afraid I already have an idea." He thought about the medical items that had come up missing along with the other evidence that was piling up against her. "What about your daughter? What will you do with her?"

She glanced down the hallway to where Ben had tucked Libby into bed, her gaze suddenly filling with doubt and apprehension. "She'll attend school, of course."

Though a small part of him wanted to come right out and accuse her, something else, something bigger and unexplainable, stood like some thick barrier against the accusing thoughts as they made their way to his tongue.

Was he just like those who'd accused her in the past?

He remembered how timid she'd been when he'd taken her to church that first time. She'd feared judgment as though it had already been measured out for her in large doses, and she had only to take it. Sadness had gripped his heart at how petty those in the church could be, and now he wondered if he was being the very same way.

But she'd betrayed him. She'd never been forthright about her past. This whole time he'd felt like maybe he was breaking through, now he wondered if he'd even begun to crack the thick layers.

But she'd been betrayed, too. In the worst way possible, and maybe because of all of that, she was so set on protecting herself that she would walk away from all he could offer.

"Did you like the life you shared with Max?" he finally asked, trying for a more reasoned approach. "Was it anything like you've had here?"

"No." She gave a snort, her gaze briefly sliding to the flames that licked at the dry wood. "But I made the best of it. I had to."

"And I suppose you'll make the best of it again." He sighed, frustrated by her inability to see things for the way they really were. "You're just going to strike out on your own…with no more than a month's wages to your name. *And* with a child."

Taking a step nearer, he rested his hand on the sturdy, beautifully crafted mantel Joseph had made when Ben had the house built three years ago. "Do you forget how you showed up here?" He dipped his head to get her attention as her long lashes whispered down over her eyes. Ben lowered his voice. "You were half-dead, Callie. If I hadn't come along when I did, you'd be buried in some unmarked grave up on a lonely hillside."

"And I thank you for your care." With an earnest gaze, she peered at him. "But that won't happen again."

"How can you be so sure of that?" More, how could she be so careless with herself or her daughter? Either she was more naive than he'd ever imagined or she had well-laid-out plans. "Is it because you already have a safe, warm place to go where you'll have your meals prepared for you, a wardrobe for your evenings," he bit off, picturing her in the ruby-red dress she'd shown up in, and remembering how his stomach had turned seeing his mother's locket framed in such gaudiness. "Well, I'm sure you'll get *plenty* of attention where you're going."

She shrugged, as though belittling the words he'd just spoken. Words that had come hard, tasting like some bitter draught on his tongue. "Your implication is harsh. Surely you can't believe—"

"I want to believe that the shoe won't fit." He stood to his full height, watching for any kind of remorse or indecision or regret to flit across her face. He really wanted to see at least an inkling of those emotions in her gaze, not because he wanted her to hurt, but because he wanted a reason, a good, solid reason not to believe all of the things he'd questioned in his heart were true.

She looked at him with that blank, unconcerned stare of hers. That stubborn wordless expression that shut off all vulnerability.

Something snapped inside him, the worst of his suspicions now ricocheting through his head with conscience-numbing force.

"I can't stop you from making a bad decision for yourself, but I'll do whatever I have to, to keep you from dragging Libby into a life that no child should have to witness. Or live in." He crossed to the front door and held it open for her. "If you want to go and sell yourself, then you'll do it without your daughter."

Had she stayed in his house a minute longer last night, Callie would've rained down on him like some wild woman on the loose. He'd insulted her dignity, her character, and he'd made himself some self-imposed guardian over her daughter.

Ben was trying to control her life. Just like her father. Just like Max. Just like Mr. Whiteside. The insulting jabs, the questioning of her decision making, the I-know-what's-best-for-you attitude…she'd heard it all before. And until last night she hadn't really believed that Ben was capable of the same kind of behavior.

How could he question her integrity like that? The very thought made her skin crawl.

Last night she'd walked out on him, leaving with those disgusting words resonating in her head like some dread dirge. Even now she felt mad enough to spit. And she was a lady!

Determined to tamp down her irritation before she sought out her daughter at Ben's, she sat out on the front porch of the office. Where she'd huddled, sick and weary, against a blinding snowstorm just four weeks earlier.

Had she known then what she did now, she wouldn't have come anywhere near this place. She would've run as far and as fast as her legs could take her in the opposite direction, staying clear of his control.

Unwanted images of the gentle and tender way he'd cared for her when she'd been sick flashed through her mind. His big, strong hands had sheltered her so that she could breathe and rest for the first time in a long time. His warm, endearing grin had lit her days with promise and hope and anticipation for something more. And his arms had opened like some wonderful refuge when she'd been at her lowest.

But she knew well how people could change. Her kind and patient father had changed dramatically after her mother had died. And wonderful, adventurous Max had changed within a few short months of marrying.

At least she'd found out sooner rather than later with Ben.

When a wagon rolled by the office, she glanced up to

see Mrs. Duncan craning her neck, staring at her with that ever-watchful gaze of hers.

Callie forced a smile to her face and waved as though it was a daily occurrence for her to sit outside every November morning. She was unwilling to give the woman one morsel, or even a crumb, to gossip about. If she looked forlorn or angry or irritated, the woman would take that to the bank, invest and build on it before the sun went down.

Callie had to figure out what she would do. There was no way she'd leave Boulder without her daughter, but in less than two days Whiteside would be back. If she didn't have the full amount then he'd make good on his claim and muscle Callie back with him to Denver to live as one of his *girls*.

Her skin crawled with repulsion.

And that Ben had insinuated that she'd already lived some compromised life selling herself sent bile from her stomach burning all the way to her throat, just like his words had burned all the way to her heart. She'd desperately wanted to defend herself, but why would he believe her? Furthermore, she in no way wanted to elicit sympathy from Ben. And if he knew the way she'd had to work in a brothel just to pay off Max's gambling debt, he was sure to treat her with pity. And he was sure to feel worse about what kind of life Max had led. When she'd shown up on Ben's doorstep four weeks ago, she'd been backed into a corner. She'd had nowhere else to turn and had been forced to follow her dying husband's last words back home. To his home.

To Ben.

To comfort.

To a family who really seemed to care.

She couldn't drag Ben or anyone else into the mess

she faced. And no matter how unfair it seemed, she couldn't wriggle her way out of the debt Max owed. When she'd married him, it had been for better or worse.

With a heavy sigh, she wished once again that there'd been some *better* in the mix of it all.

Her silent musings were broken when she heard the awkward clump of boots on the boardwalk, racing this way.

Luke's blond head bobbed a good block down, his thick hair hanging in his eyes.

She rose, and as soon as she saw his frantic wave and heard his frenzied call for help she set off, running to meet the boy.

"Luke? What is it? What's wrong?" she asked when she was halfway down the block.

He almost ran right over her, but stumbled back at the very last moment. His breath came hard. Fast. "Fire. There's a fire."

Callie braced her hands on his shoulders. "Where?"

"My house. My ma—she's still in there." His sweet face contorted in an effort to hold back tears pooling in his wide, fearful gaze. His lower lip trembled. "And the kittens—I tried to get 'em, but the smoke…"

"Where is your ma, Luke? Where is she?" she implored, tugging the boy that direction as she set off at a run. She remembered what Ben had said about Luke's mama, that she was often drunk and had kept a steady stream of men coming and going from her house.

No way for a child to live.

"In the bedroom. I tried to get 'er, but she's too heavy when she's out cold."

"And the kittens?" Callie swallowed hard. She pictured

the way Luke would hold his fluffy little charges. Loving them and talking to them as though they were kin.

"I keep 'em up in the loft. So's they don' bother Ma."

Dread crawled up Callie's spine. She willed her expression to stay clear and focused for the boy, but all the while she prayed that God would spare the kittens and his mother.

"Is there anyone else there to help?" Remembering the way the sorry little house sat like some lonely survivor on a forgotten street, she doubted it.

Luke shook his head, his chin trembling.

She skidded to a stop, pulling in a long breath. "Go. Get help. Get Ben." She pushed him that way. "Run fast."

Sprinting toward Luke's house again, she hoped that some merciful soul had arrived. Before she reached the remote, heavily rutted street, she caught a whiff of acrid smoke hanging in the crisp, frosty air.

He'd said his mother was in there. And the kittens. When she turned the corner and saw smoke whispering from cracks in the walls into the morning, her throat seared with instant grief. She pulled up her skirts and ran as fast as she could, her heart faltering with each step when it was clear that no one else was around.

She opened the front door as a wave of thick, gray smoke hit her square in the face like some knock-out blow in a back-alley fight.

Callie pulled her skirt up and held it to her face, peering in vain through the smoke.

Luke's mama. She was in there.

She pulled in a long breath, held it and charged into the burning structure. "Mrs. Ortmeier...are you in here?" She searched frantically through the smoke for the bedroom. "Mrs. Ortmeier…"

The faint sound of a cough sounded to her right. She barged into the bedroom. The caustic air stung her eyes. She groped through billowing, choking smoke. "Are you in here…?"

When the woman grabbed her arm, Callie felt a surge of relief. "Come on, let's get you out of here."

She heaved her to her feet. Having had enough experience with Max when he would straggle home drunk, she couldn't miss the unmistakable scent of hard liquor even through the biting smell of smoke.

"The boy," the woman choked. Grabbed her blanket around her. Fell into Callie, nearly knocking her down.

"He's fine," Callie choked, struggling to pull Luke's mama to safety. "Come on. We need to get you out of here."

Stumbling out of the bedroom door, fear gripped her heart. She could hear the crackle and pop of the fire across the room.

She coughed, her lungs craving fresh air.

When she found the door to the outside, she felt a surge of relief. "Go. Far from the building—" She gave a harsh cough. "I'm going to get the kittens."

Confident that the woman could make it on her own from here, she nudged her outside. Heaved in a gulp of what little fresh air she could grab.

"God, if You're listening, please help me get Luke's kittens," she whispered then held her breath.

The smoke was thicker. She sank lower and felt for the ladder leading to the loft. She sprang up the ladder, taking the steps two at a time. She crawled forward and located the box of kittens near the thin pallet.

Panic raced through her veins. She'd never be able to manage the cumbersome box down the ladder. And the smoke—its blinding effect had her feeling her way back to the ladder.

Her mind searched frantically for a way as she gave a long, harsh cough. She had to get his kittens out.

Her pulse pounded harder at the crackle of flames.

Grabbing her skirt, she made a sling and scooped all five kittens out of their box, laying them in the make-shift hammock. She pulled it together. Held part of the thick wad in between her teeth to free both hands.

Her heart swelled when she heard small mewing sounds coming from her skirt as she made her way back down the ladder. When her foot reached the floor her legs threatened to buckle beneath her. She coughed hard. Her heartbeat fluttered wildly inside her chest. She was almost outside.

Her hope fell hard as she reached the doorway to find the heat of orange flames barring the way to safety. She had to get out. For the kittens. For Luke. For her daughter.

Libby… She couldn't leave her daughter motherless, again.

And Ben… She couldn't leave this world without him knowing the truth. She couldn't let him believe that she'd been some tramp who thought so little of herself that she'd sell her body.

Turning, she crawled toward the back of the house, groping around in the unfamiliar dwelling for another way out. When her hand touched the wall, she rose to her feet to find the morning's crystal light filtered in a faint, hopeful stream through dense smoke. She blinked hard against the sting burning her eyes, fumbling for a door handle. She tugged it open. Stepping into the fresh air where she was safe, she fell to her knees, coughing, sputtering and thanking God.

Chapter Eighteen

"Callie's in there?" Ben's heart fell hard as he locked his gaze on the bright orange flames leaping at the side of Luke's house. His pulse thundered through his veins at the dark, ominous smoke billowing into the sky like some ill-begotten sacrifice.

"Oh, no..." Luke's strained voice brought Ben's focus around. His face contorted with grief. "What if I kilt her, Ben? What if she died savin' my ma or my kittens?"

Ben took hold of the boy's shoulders and dipped down, eye to eye. "Callie's fine, Luke. We've got to believe that."

Ben ran headlong toward the house, spotting Luke's ma lying on the ground ahead of him, her slumped form barely clad in a flimsy nightdress. He pulled his coat off, rushing over with Luke close at his heels to lay it over her, even as his stinging gaze drifted to the burning structure.

Callie must've gone back in there for Luke's kittens. The thought sent a swell of emotion so deep through him that he had to struggle to catch his breath. "Luke, stay here. I'm going in for Callie."

When he felt a faint touch against his leg, he glanced

down to see Luke's ma peering up at him, her heavily painted eyes fluttering open as she let out a harsh, ragged cough. She struggled to pull him close. "T-take care of my boy, won't you?"

Her whispered, ragged words seized his heart. Luke had already suffered so much and now he could face the loss of his only kin. That wasn't fair. Not to Luke. And not to his ma. She'd miss out on raising a young boy with dreams and hopes and love. He wouldn't let her do that.

He braced her with a steady gaze. "You're not going anywhere. You'll see Luke grow up to be a fine, honorable man."

Pushing himself up, he sprinted to the burning dwelling. He broke a window and crawled inside. Glass scraped, shredding his shirt and arms as he lowered himself through the small window.

Flames snapped, angry. Ravenous.

"Callie?" he called above the fire's menacing roar. "Callie, where are you?"

Peering blindly through the thick smoke and searing hot air, his hope nearly caved.

He dropped to his knees to stay low. Inched forward. Braced himself against the heat and smoke. "Callie? Please answer me."

His heart thudded with frantic madness inside his chest.

"Callie, are you in here?"

A large crack sounded above him. He jerked back. Glanced up.

Something heavy cracked over his shoulder and neck. White-hot pain seared through him. He teetered on his hands and knees. Crumpled to the floor, the last glorious image drifting through his mind of Callie.

* * *

"Miss Callie!" Luke cried. "Ben found you!"

"Ben?" She coughed, staggering toward the boy.

Luke knelt beside his mama again. "I thought somethin' might'a happened to 'im just now when I heard that crash."

Callie turned and peered at the house, emotion piercing her already raw throat as she recalled hearing the sharp crack followed by a crash. Her breath came in desperate gasps as the boy's words hit her full force.

She blinked against the stinging pain in her eyes as she peered at the broken window. It hung like the mouth of some ravenous predator, poised and ready to devour another soul.

"B-Ben is in there?"

She turned to see Luke's eyes widen to twice their size. He nodded, thick tears springing to his eyes.

Callie knelt and carefully dumped out the kittens from her apron next to where Luke sat with his still, unconscious mother.

"Check your kittens over, Luke. And watch over your mama," she said, her voice sounding all raw and rough from the smoke. She set a hand to his shoulder. "But don't go near your house. Do you hear me?"

"Here, take my coat." Luke grabbed her arm and pulled her to a sudden halt. Tears streamed down his face as he shrugged out of the coat Ben had given him a couple of weeks ago.

"All right."

Spotting an old pan sitting in the yard with a generous melting of snow pooling in the bottom, she ran over and dipped the coat into the pan of icy water. Then dashed toward the broken window.

As she approached the burning building yet again,

a sick feeling crept through her at the thought of losing Ben. He'd been nothing but good to her. He'd taken her in, fed her, clothed her, cared for her when she was sick. He'd done more for her these past weeks than Max had done the entire seven years they'd been married.

Yet she'd spurned Ben. At every single turn, she'd spurned him. She'd held Max's reputation over Ben as though it were some instrument of torture passed through the family.

If something happened to him it'd surely be her fault. Had he not gone after her, he'd be safe from the flames and smoke.

Pulling a long breath into her already raw lungs, she climbed into the window, shielding her eyes from the heat and smoke and flames. She nearly landed on Ben. He lay facedown on the floor. Mere feet from where heated flames licked at him.

"Ben? Ben," she called, kneeling down beside him. Fear singed her bravery when he didn't move or speak.

She smothered the flames inching closer to him with Luke's coat. Then through the smoke saw a large beam lying over him. She reached down to lift it off, but the weight of the solid wood wouldn't even budge.

"I won't leave you," she choked out, coughing. "God, please help me…I can't leave him here."

Panic wrapped her tight and suddenly the flames loomed too much. Too hot. Too big a foe for just Callie to take on.

Desperate to free Ben from the weight of the crushing beam and burning flames, she heaved again. In vain.

"Callie…" The voice seemed to come out of nowhere. She started then found Aaron hovering near her shoulder.

Relief so great that she nearly cried washed over her in huge waves.

"Aaron. He's trapped." She coughed, her lungs desperate for a gasp of fresh air.

"I'll lift. You drag him toward the window," he yelled above the roar. Coughed. "Now. Move him now."

With a firm grip on his ankles, Callie tugged him back. Two seconds later, the beam crashed back down and Aaron was beside her lifting Ben in his arms.

"Is there another way out?" he yelled.

Callie motioned with her hand. "This way. There's a back door," she called over the angry fire's fierce roar.

Her face and skin burned. Pulling her skirts up from the fire, she led the way. Beating back flames with Luke's coat as they rushed headlong through the house, desperate for fresh air.

An eerie creaking resounded over the loud crackle and roar. Dread crept down her spine. She fought to stay on her feet, locking her gaze on the slim thread of light coming from the back doorway.

She crossed the threshold, tugging Aaron and Ben with her as a thundering roar sounded. Then a deep, haunting groan. Lunging forward away from the burning structure, Callie looked over her shoulder to see the middle of the house swell as if taking one last dying breath, then sag and cave in a spray of bright orange sparks.

She surged ahead, barely escaping the sparking roar of flames. Aaron followed and knelt next to her, struggling to pull in a gasp of fresh air. Callie's knees began to buckle. She sank to her knees next to Ben as Aaron laid him ever so carefully on the ground. Her burning, smoke-tinged eyes pooled with tears and her throat constricted tight as she peered down at Ben's unconscious form then glanced up at Aaron.

"Tha-thank you," she rasped on a harsh cough.

Her head swam. Chest tightened. She could barely hold a coherent thought as she willed herself to stay focused. Willed her burning eyes to stay open against the corrosive sting. Though her lungs burned and she struggled to capture a full, cleansing breath, she would manage. She had to. She had to make sure Ben was all right. The guilt and condemnation she already lived with would grow to insurmountable proportions. She'd never forgive herself if something happened to him.

"I couldn't have done it without you," she rasped.

On a bellowing cough, Aaron gave her a long, contemplative look. "You're the hero here, Callie. Ben was right about you all along."

It'd been a good six hours since the fire, but it may as well have been a day for the fatigue Callie felt. She peered at the thick bandages she'd wound around Ben's head, arms, and hands.

Those hands had touched her with such tenderness. With such care and concern. They'd healed her. They'd brought her comfort. And his hands had made her feel again. Made her yearn for his touch, his gentle caress calling to life dormant, yet fully innate and glorious, sensations.

She shifted on the padded chair Katie had placed next to Ben's bed. She'd cleaned his wounds, stitched and bandaged them, and all the while Ben had wafted in and out of consciousness, mumbling step-by-step directions that would've put him in the grave, had she followed them.

But since she'd patched him up, he'd been sound

asleep, the raspy sound of his breath on each inhale and exhale worrying her. Had he taken in too much smoke?

"He'll be all right, Callie." Joseph settled a hand on her shoulder. "He's too stubborn to die."

She gave a hiccupping chuckle that turned into a cough. She blinked hard against her red eyes. "That's what he said about me." Her voice still sounded and felt raw and scratchy. Her hands bore angry, red burns where she'd tried to lift the beam, and her skin felt stretched tight over her frame.

"I think he mentioned that," Katie added, smiling as she tucked a tendril of hair back from Callie's face. "It was a brave thing you did, going in for Luke's mama and his kittens. And then Ben."

"Very brave." Joseph's voice came out low and choked with emotion.

She smoothed a hand over the fresh, clean dress she'd donned after Katie had insisted she pull herself from Ben long enough to bathe and tend her wounds. "Aaron? How's he doing?"

"Just a few minor cuts and burns, but he'll be fine," Katie assured.

"Did he get some kind of medical attention for them?" Even though there'd been a kind of mutual appreciation after the incident, Callie grew immediately concerned that Aaron might forgo treatment just to stay clear of her.

"He said he did," Joseph remarked.

"And what about Mrs. Ortmeier?"

"She's very grateful to you." Katie grasped Callie's hand in hers. "She feels like she's been given a second chance to make things right. Isn't that wonderful?"

She nodded. Hot tears welled in her stinging eyes.

Anger, deep and grating, had thundered through her veins when she'd realized the woman was drunk. But to know that that same woman now saw this circumstance as a second chance somehow dispelled the anger. Mrs. Ortmeier had hope.

A second chance was all Callie wanted. Was it too much to ask for?

"Miss Callie?" Luke whispered as he peeked around the door. "Think I could come in there?"

"Of course, Luke." She motioned him over, noticing the way he snatched a tentative, worried glance at Ben. "Come on in here."

Luke inched into the room on his toes. When he reached the bed, he snuck a trembling hand out, fingering the quilt with an awkward kind of hesitance. "He gonna be all right?"

"I think he'll be fine." Sympathy pricked at Callie.

Ben had been everything to that boy. He'd been a mentor, a friend and a father. Luke's fragile world would likely cave without him.

Callie shuddered. Her world would likely cave, too, without Ben in it. She'd felt so horribly vulnerable after the fire that she'd almost been unable to calm her quaking hands as she'd stitched his head. She'd had to summon every single ounce of her concentration to do right by him.

Her own scrapes and cuts and aftereffects of inhaling so much smoke were the least of her worries after they'd gotten Ben back here.

"Think I could pray for 'im? I seen Ben do that for his patients lots of times…" He slid Callie a watery gaze. "I seen 'im do it fer you, Miss Callie."

Just knowing that Ben had beseeched God on her behalf made Callie's heart swell with indescribable hope. Like some lifeline lowered down inside a deep, dark pit.

But the idea that he'd prayed for her even as she'd eyed him with such suspicion, assuming him to be just like Max, sent shame slipping through her.

"I'm sure Ben would want you to pray for him." She felt the lifeline jerked out of her reach. She just didn't know—didn't trust that God would welcome her the way she knew He'd welcome Luke or Ben…or anyone else in this room.

Luke pulled in a long breath. "God…I'm prolly not real good at this," he began, his voice quavering, his blond hair hanging in his tightly squeezed eyes. "But Ben, he makes it look real easy, praying. He says it's jest like talkin' to a friend. Anyways, I guess what I'm askin' is that You'd take care of Ben." On a long pause, he sniffled, swiping his sleeve over his nose as Joseph settled a hand on the boy's back. "He's been a real good friend to me, God. Like a pa, even. And I know—well, I know You prolly like 'im, too, but maybe You could let 'im stay here longer. A lot longer."

Callie fought to gain some control over her ragged emotions. She watched as Luke reached out and touched his fingertips to the bandage covering Ben's head.

"That was very nice, Luke," Katie whispered.

"I think he's going to be fine," Joseph assured the boy. "He just needs to rest."

Luke suddenly turned and faced Callie, his earnest gaze a mix of childlike hope and adult caution. "Ma said she's gonna change, Miss Callie." He kept his voice low. "Said she's gonna start being a real good ma fer me after she gets better."

Callie slid her hand around his. "I'm so glad for you, Luke. You deserve that. She'll be so proud of you."

When she spotted Libby standing over by the doorway, peering at her with that hesitant gaze that cut Callie to the quick, sorrow pricked through her heart.

Maybe Ben was right. Maybe she was fooling herself to believe that she could make it on her own while raising a daughter. She didn't want to rely on others. She never again wanted to place herself in such a vulnerable, helpless position.

She had her fiery will. Stubbornness. She was a survivor.

But there was one element she felt sorely lacking deep in her heart…peace. Peace she could trust in. Rely upon. Rest in when her journey took her over rough spots. She could stand on her own two feet, insisting on carving out a new future, but the fact that Mr. Whiteside lurked a day away somehow sealed her bleak fate. As much as she wanted to believe in second chances, she had to wonder if there would ever be hope for her.

Luke stepped over toward Libby and took her by the hand. "I told yer girl here that yer a hero."

Callie's breath caught as Luke maneuvered Libby closer.

"You're right, Luke," Katie whispered. "Miss Callie is a hero."

"Yep." Nodding, he stood behind Libby, his hands perched protectively on her shoulders. "And then she went and asked me what a hero was, so I told 'er. 'Member what I said?" He craned his neck around to look at Libby, eye to eye.

Libby slowly nodded, her sweet innocent gaze flitting to the ceiling as if searching for Luke's definition there. With a determined nod, she fixed her enthusiastic gaze on Luke. "It's someone who's brave and cares 'nough about others that they do something big."

"And…" he prompted, twirling his finger in a wagon-wheel motion.

"And brave." Libby's long-lashed gaze rose to meet Callie's.

"Don't be shy, silly." Luke gave the girl a tender nudge. "She's yer ma."

Libby took another step closer. Then, as if breaching some wide, yawning gap in time, made a giant leap into Callie's lap. She wrapped her little arms around Callie's neck for a wonderful moment as Callie did the same, struggling to hold back a deep cry.

She barely worked a swallow past the thick lump in her throat. She hadn't allowed herself to feel for years, and in the past few weeks she'd fought to stay one step ahead of the emotions nipping at her heels. The fear, the sorrow, the anger and even the joy all made her feel horribly vulnerable, prey to anyone who'd choose to use it for their own gain.

Her eyes burned with the lingering effects of smoke and heat and unshed tears. Still, she risked crying in front of all of these people she'd come to care so much about, and pulled Libby close, pressing a gentle kiss on her silky, auburn hair. The emptiness that had filled her arms and heart for the past six years seemed to lessen some.

She stroked a trembling hand down her daughter's petite frame, closing her eyes and breathing in the fresh, little girl scent she'd been deprived of for so long.

What would happen tomorrow, when Lyle Whiteside returned for his money?

Libby pulled back, peering intently at Callie. "You're brave, Mama." She carefully settled her hands at Callie's cheeks. "Luke thinks so. And I think so."

"And I think so…" came Ben's smoke-rasped voice.

Callie whipped her focus over to see him, his searching gaze locked on hers. The unmistakable love she'd seen in his eyes that night at the dance was there again, and sent a tremor shimmying all the way up her spine.

His mouth drew up in that heart-stopping half grin of his. "You were very brave, you know," he rasped with a lazy wink. Then he gave his head a long, slow shake. "But don't *ever* scare me like that again."

"I—I... You'd gone in—" She shifted in her chair to face him, drinking in his easy smile, the way his eyes sparkled, the way a faint shadow already hinted at his strong, masculine jaw. "I couldn't leave you there."

"Thank you." His quietly uttered words whispered over her like the gentle way he trailed his fingertips down her cheek.

It was useless to try and tame the wild beat of her heart.

"How are you feeling?" Joseph stepped closer to the bed.

"Are you havin' pain?" Luke edged his watchful gaze from Ben's head to his quilt-covered toes.

"Not enough to be stuck in this bed." Ben threw back the covers.

Callie yanked her focus to the sturdy pine headboard. "What are you doing?" She craved a small peek at his bare chest, but instead, pinned him to the feather-down mattress with a wide-eyed stare, settled directly on his face. "You need to stay in bed. At least for the time being."

With a sigh, he conceded, lying back as Luke rustled the covers over him and smoothed them back into place again. The creased brow and innocent look Ben flicked to her couldn't have been more than puddle-deep. "Look at what happens…I'm out of commission for a few hours and you've gone from *just* Callie to Doctor Callie?"

"Apparently you can give orders better than you can take them," Katie retorted, sidling down to the end of the bed and nudging his foot.

"Yes, and believe me," Joseph added. "With the instructions you mumbled to Callie as she patched you up, you ought to be glad she knew enough on her own about what she was doing."

The slightest of winces wafted over his face as he held his arms out, surveying the thick, gauze wraps. "I must not have been very coherent. Huh?"

Callie grinned wide. "Umm…not exactly."

"I taught you everything you know. Right?" He gave Callie a pulse-quickening wink then reached out to touch a fingertip to Libby's nose. "How are you, sweetie?"

"Jest fine." Libby scurried to sit on the bed, perching quietly next to Ben, her dainty fingers edging over the bandage wrapped around his head. "Are you gonna be good again?"

"Thanks to your mama and uncle Aaron, I'm going to be fine. I'll probably be up and going before the day's out."

Luke frowned at Ben. "But I thought you said…"

"Yes, what was it that Ben said?" Callie put in, raising her brows and encouraging Luke to continue.

As soon as Luke caught on, he gave his head a single nod then looked down at Ben with eager dedication. "You said that when a body's sick they gotta rest. So they don' get worse. That's what you say all the time. I heard it with my own ears," he added, plucking his ears for effect.

"Luke's right," Joseph added, chuckling.

Ben huffed. "But I—"

"You got a banged up head, Ben." With great conviction, Luke folded his arms at his chest. "I heard the crash all the way from outside. Scairt me half t'death."

"You've been through quite a lot today," Katie added.

Callie breathed a sigh of relief at that uniquely Ben kind of warm, comforting light that had settled into his gray-blue eyes.

"Why don't I take Libby and Luke home with me?" Katie smoothed a hand over Callie's back as she leaned close. "We'll take care of the kittens and then bake some cookies."

"The kittens are all right, then?" Callie pulled her head around, noticing that Katie's eyes pooled with tears. "They're all healthy?"

"They seem fit to me." Joseph settled his hat back on his head. "Though, as little as they are, they probably wouldn't have made it much longer had you not gotten them out when you did."

Relief washed over her. "I'm so glad they're doing all right."

"Thanks for savin' my kittens, Miss Callie." Luke wrapped her in one huge hug. "Mr. Joseph found me another box to put 'em in, and after Miss Katie warmed up some milk and gave 'em some food they went right t'sleep."

"They did." Libby nodded her vigorous agreement. "They're sleeping now."

"No wakin' 'em this time, Libby." Luke angled a squinty-eyed look at her. "Like Ben says, when ya been through somethin' bad, ya need yer sleep. And the kittens went through somethin' real bad this mornin'. Fact, they're prolly the only kittens who survived a fire like that, I'd think."

With a solemn shake of her head, Libby threaded her little hands together beneath her chin. "Promise. I won't even touch the box."

After Katie and Joseph ushered the children out of the room, Callie was left alone with Ben.

She should be overjoyed right now. Luke's mama had her sights set on the right path, the kittens were safe, Ben was alive and things with her daughter had just taken a miraculous turn for the better.

Deep inside, though, she felt strangely empty. She craved peace as much as she did her next breath. But it seemed so elusive.

Without being able to reconcile her past, the painful history that followed her like some stealthy predator, she'd never fully enjoy the bright outlook of each new day.

But no matter how much Ben would protest and insist otherwise, she'd never leave Boulder without Libby. And she couldn't—wouldn't ask Ben for money to pay off the rest of the debt. He'd already given her so much. As wily as Thomas Blanchard was, Ben had to have paid a generous sum to bring Libby home with him. Scoundrels like Blanchard didn't make gestures like that out of the goodness of their hearts.

Likely, the man didn't even have a heart.

Trapped once again by the decision she faced, she pulled in a long, slow breath. She raised her head to find Ben's crystalline gaze settled on her, the effect penetrating all the way to her core.

"Thank you again, Callie. You did something today that most people wouldn't have considered."

"I'm just glad you're all right," she breathed, slumping in the chair and cradling her head in her hands. Thoughts of how horribly different circumstances could've been rushed through her head, scavenging almost all of the emotional reserve she had left. "I wasn't sure we were going to make it out."

When she felt his hand settle like some warm claim at her back, she fumbled about for control. But as she turned and saw the way his eyes shone with care and unmistakable love, she barely bit off a small cry.

"You came after me. All alone, didn't you?"

Callie threaded her hands together in her lap. "You risked your life, Ben. For me," she breathed, gulping down the sense of shame she felt as her gaze inched from his bandaged hands, to his arms, to his head. "I don't know what I would've done if something had happened to you." She shuddered at the thought that he could've died trying to save her. How could he risk his life, ransom his own fulfilling life to the flames like that? Just for Callie.

Chapter Nineteen

"And I don't know what I would do if you'd been hurt. Or killed," he said, his voice low and choked.

Regret at the caustic words Ben had said to her last night filled his mind. How could he have been so callous? How could he have so easily allowed his frustration to rule his words?

He'd so much as called her a harlot.

Just seeing the vulnerability that weighed her down, the suspicions didn't matter. None of it mattered. Whatever her past, whatever her present, it just didn't matter.

He needed her.

He wanted her.

He loved her.

And if she had some things to overcome, then so be it. Didn't everyone have some kind of secret that loomed too difficult to face?

He'd seen the way God had been softening her heart. The three times she'd been to church with him, and when she'd sat and listened with rapt attention while he'd read to Libby from the Bible, his heart had swelled at the hunger he'd seen in her eyes. As though she wanted so badly to reach out and partake of God's goodness and mercy and unconditional love.

But something always held her at bay.

"I felt so helpless when I called and you didn't answer, and when I couldn't see to find you through the smoke." His breath hitched at the awful memory as he moved a hand to the side of his head where bandages hid a deep, long gash. He blinked against the stinging moisture crowding his eyes. "When I felt the beam hit me, I thought for sure you and I were as good as dead."

Slamming his eyes shut, the same old, haunting regret shook the chains that had held him hostage for so long. He'd failed those dearest to him. He couldn't seem to rescue those he loved the most. What he did, the grand efforts he made, just weren't enough.

"What, Ben? What's wrong?" Callie leaned over him, her hand resting against his cheek. Her light breath whispered feather-light over his face.

He grasped her hand. "In those seconds before I lost consciousness, it was you that I thought of, Callie. And how I wished I could go back and do things differently."

She gave his shoulder a gentle squeeze. "You don't need to do anything differently. You've been good to me, Ben. It's time you let others take care of you for a change."

The way she touched him with such tenderness, and the way she looked at him, as if pleading with him to rescue her from her silent pain, sent his heart into a shuddering frenzy inside his chest.

He'd often pondered that she was much like the strays he'd rescued. Had God really meant all along for him to rescue her? Not just from the here and now with a job and a warm home, but from the pain of her past?

It would be just like God to defy all of Ben's thoughts and plans and assumptions. It would be just like God to bring a woman whose history intertwined his with such delicate force that it would be an undeniable connection. A forever and always bond marked by providential design.

"Your arms and head and hands...do you think they'll heal?" Her concern penetrated his heart.

He nodded, taking in the beautiful, faint way her fingertips trembled against his cheek. "I'm sure they will."

She turned his hand over in hers and stared down at the bandages. "You'll have scars."

"Probably," he agreed, raising her chin with a crooked finger. "But everybody has a scar or two, somewhere."

He couldn't miss the way her hand strayed as if by some involuntary force to her side. And the protective way shame shuttered her vulnerable gaze, leaving him feeling as if she'd stood up and swept out of the room.

If he was going to help her and free her, then he'd have to take a risk. "I know about your scars, Callie."

"What?" She threaded her hands, white-knuckle tight.

"Katie told me about them after she'd helped you with that bath. At first I couldn't imagine the scars were from Max, but now I know. They had to be from him. And I'm sorry." He lifted her gleaming auburn hair from her forehead. When he lightly brushed his fingertips along the red puffy scar marring her hairline, he struggled to reconcile how a man—how Max—could be so cruel. "So sorry you had to endure that kind of treatment."

Her eyes shimmered with unshed tears as she tugged his hand away from the scar. "That's in the past. It's all in the past. And it's surely no fault of yours."

He pushed up to sitting, not quite able to take the words to heart. "Well, I'm not likely to believe that anytime soon. I'm sorry for the things I said last night. I care about you, Callie, and I want to spend every minute I can showing you just how much I care."

He desperately wanted to reach that part of her, the area of her heart held back by some powerful, unseen force. "When I look in your eyes I see things that make me hurt. Right here." He pointed to his heart.

The look she gave him, that look that begged to be rescued, was like some pleading cry he could never, ever ignore.

"I want to help, but I can't if you won't let me," he said, his voice low and tight.

He wondered if he might never be able to unlock that prison. That maybe he had to trust God to reach her and free her from the chains that held her so firmly.

He settled his searching gaze on hers, looked deep enough to see the longing in her eyes, a desire that was meant just for him. He loved Callie. Not because deep down she yearned for love. Not because she was Max's poor, mistreated widow. Not because she needed to be loved.

But because God had led her straight to Ben's heart.

Because she was perfect for him.

Because she was just Callie.

"You're right…the scars are in the past. And Max did plenty wrong, but one thing he did right…he sent you to me."

"What is all of that?" Ben asked, catching the distinct stench of smoke as he peered down into the bag Aaron had dragged in with him. "It smells like you've been digging around in the fire rubble."

"I have." Aaron settled his hat on the back of the chair with a bandaged hand.

"Why would you do something like that? There couldn't have been much worth saving in that house."

From the burlap bag, Aaron pulled the charred remains of a stethoscope and the blackened skeleton of a medicine bottle.

Ben's face flamed hot. And when Aaron hefted out the small scale that had come up missing just last week, his heart skidded to a halt inside his chest.

"These things were in the rubble?" He knelt down across from Aaron, taking the stethoscope in hand.

"Yep. There were other things, too, but some of it was too burned to even recognize." He plucked out the warped remains of tweezers. "The fire was so hot. Even a day out, and some areas were still smoldering."

Ben touched the heat-deformed pan to the scale. "I can't believe it," he whispered.

He'd always seemed to give others the benefit of the doubt, but in this instance he'd listened to whisperings of accusation.

"How did you know to look there?" he asked, perplexed. "I've never said anything to you about the missing items."

"Actually, Luke came to see me." Aaron fiddled with the iodine bottle. "He's been feeling mighty bad, because he'd only borrowed the items."

Ben sighed, sickened at how easy it had been to accuse and condemn—and how very unlike God that was. "Here I thought Callie had taken them."

Aaron met his shame-filled gaze with one of his own. "We've both been guilty of accusing her, Ben."

He gave his head a disgusted shake. "I should've been more trusting. I accused her—silently, but still, I accused her."

"Well, if it's any consolation, you've never done anything but defend her honor—to me, anyway," Aaron said, bracing a hand on Ben's good shoulder. "Luke wanted to tell you himself. But he wouldn't come in here. He thought you'd be mad at him."

Ben eased himself into a chair, his shoulder throbbing. "Please, would you mind getting him for me?"

"Sure." Stashing the items back into the bag, Aaron stood. "Ben, I'm sorry. I was way out of line in the things I said about Callie. It doesn't matter what her past was."

"Her past was with Max. And as far as I'm concerned, that makes her one courageous woman. I just know that she couldn't do what seemed obvious—no matter what proof points that way. She doesn't have it in her."

"She showed more bravery than most men." Aaron cleared his throat. "I don't know why I was so determined to bring her down. I guess maybe she represented Max. And, well…I have some things to take care of as far as that goes."

"Believe me, I think we all probably have a bitter root or two stemming from our last couple of years with Max." He eased a hand over his eyes, feeling the pull of the tight red skin. When he glanced up at his brother, he saw deep regret in Aaron's repentant gaze. "Now that you know that, you can deal with it. And I know you will. You're a good man."

"Thanks." Aaron nodded. "For everything."

Everything? Regret and failure snapped at him as he remembered how incompetent he'd felt, how horrible he'd felt at not being able to turn the events for Aaron's wife and baby. "I wish I could've done more for Ellie and the baby. I wish I could've saved them. For you."

"I know you do." Aaron's mouth formed a tight line. "You did everything you could. I don't blame you, Ben."

Swallowing hard, Ben's eyes filled with hot tears. "Thanks," he ground out, his voice tight and strained with emotion. "Thanks."

Pulling in a slow breath, Aaron's knuckles whitened as he grasped the bag. "Someday, maybe, I'll figure out why God thought it was best to take them when He did. Or maybe someday I'll just finally accept that they're gone."

Ben nodded, astonished at his brother's dignity. "You're going to make it. It's going to be all right."

With the locket cradled in her hand, and purposeful strides, Callie walked over to Ben's house where Libby had been keeping him company. She had to return the locket. And if worse came to worst, she'd have to humble herself enough to ask him for help. She didn't have a choice.

Maybe if she'd made it back home to her father, he might have loaned her the money, but that was a risk she couldn't take. With Libby in her care now, she wouldn't take off for her father's home and risk Whiteside tracking her down and hauling her back with him.

Since the fire yesterday, Callie had felt as if she'd been moving through life in slow motion. The entire Drake family and then some had been together at lunch today—a celebration of sorts. Even Aaron...

He'd taken her by complete surprise and apologized. For being so harsh toward her. For assuming the worst. For hoping to sway Ben's opinion regarding her. She'd felt oddly vindicated, yet still without the peace she craved.

She was surrounded by all of the things she'd ever longed for…a loving family, her beautiful daughter and friends who cared.

But she didn't have peace.

"Your time's up," came Lyle Whiteside's voice.

Steadying herself, Callie turned to find him slinking a heartbeat behind her.

"Did you hear me, girl?" He caught her arm in a meaty fist hold. "I've waited long enough. Either pay up what you owe now or you're comin' with me."

Callie blinked hard, trying to calm the racing beat of her heart. Intimidation snaked around her, threatening to suffocate her will and hope. For a moment, she couldn't seem to grasp a single, coherent thought. When her frantic thoughts settled on her little girl, a fierce sense of protection rose within her. "I don't have all of it—yet. But I won't go with you."

God, please…I need Your help. Would God hear her this time? Would He help her? All morning long she'd prayed that He would turn the tide. Give her a second chance, just like He'd given Luke's mama a second chance, because Callie would never sell herself. Never that.

"I'm sure you don't want me getting the law involved in this," he cautioned, wrenching her arm so hard she barely bit off a cry. "You wouldn't stand a snowman's chance in a hot box with all the cheatin' that husband of yours did."

"Please, I'll have the rest for you soon," she assured, struggling to keep the fear from her voice.

Feeling the locket in the palm of her hand, she stuffed it inside the pocket on her dress. If Whiteside got his hands on it, she likely would never see it again, and she had every intention of returning it to Ben.

"I have a good job now and the pay is good. I'm doing everything I can to make right on what Max owed you."

He yanked her toward the street. "Not everything. There's plenty more you could *do* for me."

She fought to wrench her arm free. "If you'll just give me another hour…"

"Not another minute." Whiteside tugged her toward the carriage that sat in the street like some fancy, black coffin. "You know me, Callie. I don't like being put off. With the way you ran out on me like you did, you should consider yourself lucky I gave you an extra two days."

"Back away from her." Ben's strong, authoritative voice broke through the nightmare. "Now."

Whiteside glanced over his shoulder and pivoted. "This isn't your concern."

Ben caught Callie's eye with a reassuring look. "She is my concern. And I'm telling you now…you better release your hold and back away."

Whiteside tightened his grip on her arm. "It's not that easy. She's coming with me."

She shook her head. "I won't go with you. I can't."

Ben moved in closer. "As far as I'm concerned, you're taking her against her will. And that could get you into trouble with more than just me."

"That's right." Aaron strode out from behind the house. "You'll be in hot water with me, too. And probably the rest of this town."

"Let her go," Ben commanded.

"I'm telling you. She owes me." Whiteside edged back a step. "And I intend to collect."

Ben stalked up to stand nose to nose with Whiteside.

He placed a hand on her arm, like some warm, wonderful claim as he stared the man down. "Get your hands off her. Now."

Callie's eyes grew wide as she shifted her gaze from Ben's calm, collected look to Whiteside's red face and his flaring nostrils. Ben obviously didn't know how vengeful Lyle Whiteside could get—especially when someone dared to cross him.

Ben drew a fistful of Whiteside's crisp white shirt in a bandaged hand. "If you know what's good for you, you'll step away and leave her alone."

Looping an arm around her waist, Whiteside hauled her against his side. "I'm not going anywhere without my money. And if she can't pay up then she's as good as money to me."

Ben advanced another step. "What are you talking about?"

"He's talking about a gambling debt, Ben," she managed, her voice betraying her with a quaver.

Ben sent her a confused glance.

"It's a long story. But Max…before he died, he'd stacked up a mountain of debt with gambling losses."

"And he's making *you* pay?" Ben nodded toward Whiteside.

She boldly met Ben's gaze. "I was working at his saloon and brothel as a cook and housekeeper to try and pay it off before I came here. But then I—"

"She was lucky I let her do that. I shouldn't have gone easy on her. She could've made me a fortune."

Ben's calm slipped away. She could see it in the way his jaw tensed. His eyes suddenly grew sharp with anger. He drew his grip tighter around Whiteside's shirt. "Is this how you always do business? Swooping down on widows when they're still grieving?"

"She had a roof over her head and decent meals," Whiteside barked, the words causing her stomach to churn.

The tiny closet she slept in and the pitiful, half-eaten leftovers she was allowed were a far cry from decent. That he spoke of them as though he'd let her live in the lap of luxury stirred anger from deep within.

"I suppose you gave her a clothing allotment, too?" Ben's voice was so even and hard, Callie almost didn't want to look at him.

"Why, yes. She could have the best if she'd come back and work for me." Whiteside tugged his head to the side in a useless effort to free himself from Ben's grip. "I'm offering more than that sorry husband of hers ever gave her."

Aaron joined Ben beside the man. Callie didn't think Whiteside stood a chance, but if he had a gun on him, then they were the ones without a chance.

"You're a sick man," Ben confirmed.

Her skin crawled thinking of all the girls back at Whiteside's brothel, and how he'd convinced them that he was doing them a favor in taking care of them.

Aaron gave a derisive snort. "Taking advantage of this situation for your own gain…"

"Let her go," Ben commanded.

"He owed me plenty and I'm going to collect." He hissed a breath through his clenched teeth. "He promised to pay up with her, but he backed out."

She jerked her head around to peer at him, her heart thudding in her throat. "What did you say?"

In spite of his bandaged, injured hands, Ben locked a crushing grip on Whiteside's hand and yanked it free from Callie.

"He must not have thought much of you, girl,"

Whiteside chided as he stumbled back a step. "'Cause he was willing to pay off his debt with you."

"No… Oh, no…" Bright splotches of light embedded in darkness bombarded her vision. Her head spun. She tried to steady herself. "He w-wouldn't do that."

But even as she uttered the words, she knew that Max could. And probably did. He'd done it with his own daughter.

"Said so himself," he spat with a derisive snort. "Drunk as all get-out when he made the offer, but the idea was very tempting. Too tempting to pass on."

Ben hauled his arm back and pummeled Whiteside's face, sending him toppling backward. An instant later, Ben was straddling him as he seized his coat so tight, Callie was sure Whiteside would suffocate.

Aaron knelt over them, his hands clenched into fists. "You said the wrong thing," he muttered. "I wouldn't want to be you about now."

Through the tears clouding her eyes, Callie noticed Whiteside struggling to edge a hand to his side, under his coat.

Dread shot up her spine. "He's got a gun, Ben!"

In a flash Aaron snatched Whiteside's hand and held it tight as she pulled the gun from the holster and held it in her hands.

"Get the sheriff, Callie," Ben breathed, the pained look he gave her piercing her heart.

He had to be about ready to collapse in his weakened condition. But mostly, he'd said more than once how responsible he felt for Max's failings. This must've come as a horrible shock, as much for him as it was for her, to know that his brother would suggest such a thing.

"If Max wasn't such a white-bellied chicken and gone through with it, he might still be alive." Whiteside angled an intimidating, beady-eyed stare her way. "I may have felt generous enough to let him have a stab at you. For a reduced rate."

She held her breath. Stared at the man. Max had offered her as payment for a gambling debt, just like he'd offered his own child.

But if he hadn't had second thoughts...maybe he'd still be alive.

She peered at the cold, heartless look in Whiteside's eyes. "You killed him, didn't you?" she heard herself say.

"Surely you don't think I would do that." He raised his bushy eyebrows. "I will say, though...my establishment's a better place without him."

Chapter Twenty

Unless Whiteside was more forthcoming with the truth, Callie realized that she might never know for sure if Max had been shot because he'd refused to go through with his agreement.

But this was certain…Max had betrayed her more than she probably knew.

And—she swallowed hard—with his dying breath, he'd implored her to find Ben.

Even if the sting of seven years of betrayals never fully waned, she could find comfort in knowing he'd tried to do what was right before his life slipped away.

After the confrontation with Whiteside, Callie had sat for an hour in Ben's office with Sheriff Goodwin and Brodie Lockhart, answering more questions than she'd heard both Libby and Luke ask, combined. Ben had been beside her for most of the questioning, offering her his good arm for support even when he had to be cringing with the information she'd disclosed. About the last few months with Max, the night he was shot, the way Whiteside threatened her if she didn't work for him as a harlot.

Pulling her cloak tighter, she walked next door, the

crisp, early evening air invigorating her tired eyes a little. The sheriff had said that with as much time as had gone by since the murder, it might be hard to pin it on him. But the fact that he'd reached for his gun would be enough to put him behind bars for a while, anyway. Maybe with a little encouragement, the right people, those who knew the truth, would be brave enough to come forward and expose Whiteside.

There was no guarantee. But for some reason, Callie didn't have it in her to fret about that. She'd been through so much over the past days, she was spent.

And the debt…well, Whiteside wouldn't need it for a while. Maybe if he managed to wriggle free from the charges, she'd have enough to pay him back by then.

Opening the front door of Ben's house, she quietly entered. She could hear the faint sound of her daughter's sweet voice coming from down the hall.

She tiptoed in that direction and pecked through a crack in the door into the spare bedroom, where Libby had slept that night Ben and Aaron had found them on the roadway south.

Her little girl sat on Ben's lap in the sturdy, walnut rocking chair. She peered up at him, her eyes big and gaze earnest. "And what if someone does something *really* bad?"

"Like…" Ben prompted.

Callie set a hand to her lips, her heart warmed by Ben's show of patience. As though he had all the time in the world to answer her endless questions, even when he had to be exhausted.

"Well, Luke, he told me he took some doctor stuff of yours." She traced a finger around the top button of Ben's white shirt.

"He told you that?"

She nodded. "He took 'em without asking. And then they burned. That's bad, isn't it?" Her delicate, perfectly shaped eyebrows creased in a sorry frown. Holding one of his hands up, she pressed her small palm to his. "Are you mad at him?"

"No. Luke and I...we got that cleared up a little bit ago. I understand that he was just trying to help his kittens. He knows now that he needs to ask before he borrows something."

"And is God mad at him?" Libby tapped the toes of her new black boots together—boots Ben had insisted on purchasing. "Does He still like Lukey?"

Her throat grew tight at her daughter's heartfelt and innocent questions.

"Of course He does. He loves Luke." Ben held Libby's chin, urging her focus up to him. "And He loves you. There's nothing you can do that will make God love you any less."

Her big blue eyes grew even wider. "Really?"

"No matter how bad you are, no matter how good you are, no matter how old or young you are, God loves you. He loves you, Libby. His love and forgiveness is like a great big blanket that covers over every bad thing." Ben stretched a leg out in front of him. "His love is what leads us to Him."

She shifted to peer at him, eye to eye. "Do you think He's leading me?" She slid a serious gaze around the room. "I don't see Him."

"I'm sure He is."

A fleeting memory flashed through Callie's mind. Of when her own father would look at her, way back before her mama died and grief had turned Callie's happy world upside down. Death had a way of stripping life from more than just the one who passed.

"You'll know He's leading you because you'll feel it right here," Ben promised, tapping on her chest. "In your heart."

Tugging her dress taut, Libby angled her focus to where Ben had pointed. "Is God in there?"

He chuckled, touching a fingertip to her nose. "Only if you ask Him to live there." Tucking a wisp of hair behind her ear, he added, "He wants to live in your heart and be your friend."

Libby gasped. "Oh…I wanna be God's friend. Then I'll have two friends…Luke and God." She threaded her fingers together beneath her chin, looking as if she might burst with delight. After that Ben led her in a prayer that filtered beyond Callie's ears, all the way to her heart.

"I wanna go tell Luke, then he can make God his friend, too." Libby's giggle filled the room. Her little feet bounced with joy.

The warm look of contentment and the undeniable glow of peace coming from Ben's face shook Callie to the core.

Was that it? Could peace be that simple?

As simple as receiving God's forgiveness and love?

"I believe Luke's out in the barn with Aaron," she heard Ben say. "Maybe you should go tell him right now."

Libby jumped down from Ben's lap and bolted to the door, coming to a sliding halt when she found Callie standing on the other side. "Mama…guess what? God's my friend."

"I'm so glad, honey." Before Callie got the words out of her mouth, Libby was already halfway to the front door.

"Is it true?" she whispered in a strangled voice as

Ben walked out of the bedroom and stood beside her. "Is all that you told her true? About God's love and forgiveness?"

He ushered her to the living room sofa. "It's true."

Callie stared at him as he sat beside her. "Do you believe that?"

"With all my heart." He grasped one of her hands in his and peered at her. The peace blanketing his face was so tangible she was sure she could almost touch it. "You can't mistake God's love and forgiveness for the ways of His people. Sometimes they're as different as night and day. We all make mistakes," he breathed, his eyes closing for a brief moment before he looked at her again with a reassuring intensity that nearly took her breath away. "We all react wrongly at times, but that doesn't change the way God loves us. Ever."

Her mouth pulled tight in a quiet cry as she wondered how she could've been so wrong for so long. "For years I've thought that because I disobeyed my father and married Max, that all of the bad things that happened were because of that." Struggling to steady the quaver in her voice, she pulled in a deep breath.

"That's not true." He edged closer, settling an arm behind her shoulders.

She pulled the locket from her pocket, remembering how devastated she'd felt when she'd found out that Max had stolen the heirloom from his own brother. "I thought I'd never get free from paying back for the mistake, because one bad thing after another after another kept happening."

Ben shook his head. "There's no paying back to it, Callie. We make mistakes, but there's nothing you can do to pay back for the mistake. You can only ask forgiveness—and that is free."

"But my father's words? That God's fierce wrath is exacted upon those who disobey..." She willed her heart to slow its rapid-fire beat. "When I came here, it seemed like things started changing for me, but then the fire happened and Luke almost lost his mama and his kittens. And I almost lost you..."

"You didn't lose me, Callie. I'm right here." He tugged her closer, his strong, capable arms around her like some mighty fortress. "And I'm not going anywhere."

She pushed away. "Ben, what if all of that happened because I'm here?"

He steadied her quivering chin. "No, Callie. You're stubborn. You're a fighter. You're strong. But—"

"But—" She fought back a cry, hot tears stinging her eyes.

"But you are *not* that powerful." He gave an adamant shake of his head, conviction cloaking every single word.

But could she trust them?

"All of the things you went through with Max were because of his choices. And I'm so sorry that he put you through that. You are far more valuable than that. You have to know it's true. God loves you, Callie."

"His love covers you," he encouraged as he watched one lone tear trickle down her cheek. She was so strong, even when she faced lies and betrayals that were as wounding as anything he'd ever seen. Ben thumbed away the tear, his heart clenching inside his chest. "It's unconditional. It's real. And it's for you."

"Ben..." Uncurling her tightly fisted hand, she revealed the locket. Held it out to him. "I want you to have this back."

"What?" He furrowed his brow.

She pulled her lovely, full lips into a determined line. "I can never repay you. But at least I can give this back."

"No." He held his hand over hers. "This is yours, and you don't have to worry about paying anything back."

Callie's long lashes fluttered momentarily over her eyes. "But—"

"That debt's been paid," he said, catching her gaze in his.

"What?" She gasped then, as if she'd been holding her breath. "What do you mean?"

"Whiteside won't be bothering you for his money again."

The vulnerability he saw there in her wide-eyed gaze, as if she was not fully understanding his meaning, made his heart ache. He'd take care of her for the rest of his days if Callie would have him. And if he was moving too fast for her, then he'd wait. As long as she needed.

"I took care of it," he breathed, his voice catching. "Maybe not in the way Whiteside wanted, but I've arranged to have the money owed him put toward getting those ladies out of there. Getting them some decent clothes. And maybe a place to live."

Her brow rose in shock. She slumped against him, as if a huge weight had been removed. "Y-you did?"

"Yes." With a slow nod, he drew her close and pressed a kiss to her head, breathing in the wonderful, beautiful scent of Callie. "You don't have to worry about the debt."

"You shouldn't have," she squeaked, sniffing. Squaring her shoulders.

"Yes. I should have." He couldn't help but smile at her stubborn insistence even in the face of insurmountable odds. He didn't even want to think about the way things could've turned out had Whiteside gotten to her first. "And I'm glad I did."

"I'll pay you back." Callie wrenched free from his embrace. "I'll work as long as I need to, to pay back every cent, Ben. I promise."

"You don't understand, do you?" He held her cheeks between his hands. "I'd pay that ten million times over, then again and again and again, if it meant freeing you."

"But, Ben—"

He settled a finger to her lips, to stop the willful protests. "I care for you, Callie. And I've learned that I can never go back and change the past. I can't change the loss of Aaron's wife and baby, or the loss of Joseph's sight. I can't change what I did or didn't do right in raising Max. I can't change the way he treated you…but I can trust God to work things out," he breathed, tracing the full pout of her lower lip. "And I can tell you just how much I love you."

He drew in a ragged sigh. "I love you, Callie."

"But, Ben, I—" She stopped herself short and stared at him, as if seeing him for the first time. "You what?"

"I said, I love you. I think I did from the moment I found you on my porch."

The soft, new glow in Callie's face was all the confirmation he needed to know that she believed him. She really believed him. And she trusted him. She was opening her heart to trust God, as well.

Ben's heart swelled with that knowledge. The softness and vulnerability in her gaze was fresh and new and wholly attractive.

"I'm crazy about you. I love you and want you to be my wife." That wonderfully innocent, warmly beckoning look could melt his heart. "I love you. And I'm not going anywhere. I'm going to be here for you, Callie. I'll rejoice when you rejoice and when you're sad, I'll be a shoulder for you to cry on."

"You would do that? For me?"

"Aww, darlin'…I'd do that and so much more. And if this is all too quick for you, then I'll wait. I'll wait however long until you're ready. Because there's no one I'd rather spend the rest of my days with than you."

"Why? Why would you give so much for me? You ransomed me—my life and my daughter's life, too, and you've done it with no thought of return."

"Let me show you." He gently took the locket from her hand and opened it.

Through bright tears, she stared down at the engraving: *All for love*.

"Oh, Ben…I love you. I do. I love you."

The new, tender look of peace growing on her face seemed as if to come from the inside out. As if she had finally grasped not just his love, but the higher revelation of God's love.

With his bandaged hands, he fumbled to clasp the locket around her neck once again, moved by the glowing look of love and tranquility in her unshuttered gaze.

"All for love, Callie. All for love."

Epilogue

"Slow down, Libby," Luke whispered, his voice echoing in the packed church. "Yer goin' too fast."

Callie looked on from the back of the sanctuary, smiling as her little girl came to a stop five rows down the aisle.

Libby peered, with charming devotion, at where Luke stood proudly next to his mama, at the end of the very first pew. She took two slow steps forward as if trying out her feet for the first time. "How's this, Lukey?"

"That's better." He rewarded Libby with a decided wink as he struggled to tuck something inside the new jacket Ben had purchased for him. "Jest remember what I showed ya."

An errant giggle escaped Libby's lips as she clasped one hand to her mouth. "A kitty," she squealed, glancing over her shoulder at Callie. "Mama, look. Lukey brought Beauty to yer wedding."

"I had to," Luke tossed in Callie's direction then swung his focus back to Libby. "She *is* named after yer mama."

"Yep. For Mama," Libby echoed.

Sliding his hand into his coat, Luke withdrew the

fluffy kitten. "'Sides…she wanted to come. She told me so, herself."

The trickle of laughter streaming through the sanctuary was more meaningful and pleasant than a hundred bouquets of fresh flowers to celebrate Callie's trip down the aisle.

"Aww…that's very sweet of you, Luke." Callie glanced to where Ben waited for her at the front of the church, her heart taking flight at the look of complete adoration he'd aimed directly at her.

You're sweet, he mouthed, his affectionate gaze like some gentle caress.

A fresh blush warmed her face. He'd made her cheeks rosy more often that not over the past month with his endearing compliments and oh-so-tender touch. It was as if he knew just what to say and just what to do to coax the last little bits of reservation from her heart.

With the newfound freedom she'd discovered, her smile had been next to impossible to wipe off. All the years of pain and regret had seemed to crumble away since Callie had found true peace with God. The experience had made her feel alive again.

Breathing deeply, Callie slid her gaze over the faces of everyone in attendance. She was surrounded by those she loved. And by a town that had gone out of its way to make sure this wedding was perfect: with a reception hosted by Mrs. Duncan, a lovely wedding dress made by Katie and a hope chest packed as full of gifts as this church was packed with well-wishers.

Gratefulness welled up inside of her, seeing Joseph and Katie, Zach and Aaron positioned there in the first pew, in a show of unconditional, loyal support. She didn't even want to think about how different her life would be had she not finally and desperately sought out her last resort. But Ben and his family…they were so much more than her last resort…they were her only resort.

Yes, this day was perfect.

Callie took it all in as Libby made her way to the front of the church, pausing long enough to pet the kitten Luke held out like some prized possession.

"Come on, Mama," she whispered, motioning Callie forward.

Callie took her first step down the aisle then, glancing at where her father had secured her arm in his. His presence here at her side was yet another testament to Ben's goodness and thoughtfulness. Even though she'd assumed her father had long since written her off, Ben had contacted him two weeks ago about the wedding, and her father had booked passage immediately.

The tears of joy Callie and her father had shed when they embraced far outweighed the tears of regret about so many lost years.

"You look so pretty, honey." The low crack of emotion in his voice belied the steadying comfort she felt as he patted her hand. "Just like your mama."

"Oh, thank you, Daddy," she whispered, her throat growing tight. "Thank you for being here with me."

"I'm just glad I can give you away…." As he pressed a kiss to the top of her head, tears crowded her gaze. "And to the man of your dreams."

She squeezed his hand, her heart swelling with deep, pure love as she continued down the aisle, shifting her attention forward and locking gazes with Ben. He was so handsome in his dark gray suit. So noble in the way he treated each and every person.

And he was hers.

The man of her dreams.

He'd been waiting for her all along—that's what he'd told her. And she believed him.

Not in her wildest dreams did she imagine she'd find such love and comfort in his arms, at least not that night when she'd shown up half-frozen on his doorstep.

Had Max somehow known that, with his last breath, he was sending her straight into Ben's arms?

Callie's heart stirred with a poignant awareness as she neared the front of the church where Ben stood, his hand outstretched to meet hers with the pledge of protection. And his ardent gaze…penetrating and capturing her completely, drawing her to his side.

She willed her feet to slow down. Willed her heart to slow its rapid beat inside her chest, but it was useless.

Her head and heart rushed with the glorious promises of today and every single tomorrow she'd share with Ben.

When her daddy placed her hand in Ben's, blissful peace infused straight through her hand to every part of her being.

"I'll take good care of her, sir," Ben breathed, his voice so true and steady as he entwined his fingers in hers and pulled her a little closer.

"You're beautiful," he whispered. "I'm a blessed man."

"I love you, Ben," Callie responded on a contented sigh. Peering up at him, she was humbled by the powerful love she could see in his gaze…for her. And she knew, just as sure as the sun's rising, that she would forever and ever be safe, secure and loved in Ben's arms.

* * * * *

Dear Reader,

I hope you enjoyed Ben and Callie's story and were touched by the message of redemption. This story depicts a very special love…the beauty of two lives woven together through heartache.

Life's journey can take painful twists and turns, and our response can vary from faith to fear and everything in between. Whether we like it or not, it is in these times that we often discover our greatest weakness and enduring strength. I'm a planner, and as much as I'd love to know the end of a trial from the beginning, life just doesn't work that way. But God's promise is that He will be with us through our trials, and that He will work all things together for good for those who love Him. I am learning to trust Him in this.

It is my hope that as you lean on Him, you will discover resilient aspects about yourself that were yet unseen. And that, like Callie and Ben, you will find God's beauty in the midst of the storm.

Thank you so much for taking the time to read *Rocky Mountain Redemption*. Please check out the first book in the Drake Brothers series, *Rocky Mountain Match*, and watch for the third book, *Rocky Mountain Proposal*, due out in May. I'd love to hear from you. Visit my website at pamelanissen.com.

With Love,

Pamela Nissen

QUESTIONS FOR DISCUSSION

1. Callie boldly faces her nemesis, Ben. Have you ever faced a situation expecting one thing, only to experience the opposite? If so, what was your response?

2. Ben bows to his strong pull of compassion and takes Callie in. Do you think he responded foolishly?

3. If you were Callie, how would you have responded to Ben's kindness and gentle demeanor?

4. Aaron's suspicion of Callie forces Ben to choose between his brother and a woman he knows little about. Have you ever made a difficult decision that could alienate someone you loved?

5. Ben's brothers want only the best for him. How do they show they care?

6. Betrayal cuts Callie deep when she discovers the truth about her daughter. How would you have dealt with such a painful discovery?

7. In spite of her bold show of strength, Callie is very vulnerable and is yearning for love and safety. Have you ever found yourself fighting against the very thing you need? If so, what was your breaking point?

8. As the oldest brother, Ben feels a strong sense of responsibility for the wayward path Max had

traveled. Do you feel that his responsibility is misplaced?

9. Callie wants to trust God as a forgiving and loving Father, but her own father had drilled a warped view of God being harsh into her head. Have you ever had to work beyond a distorted view of God to find the truth of his love?

10. Heartbreak has carved the noble, yet sometimes overbearing, need to control a situation into Ben's soul. How does he finally release this to God?

HISTORICAL

TITLES AVAILABLE NEXT MONTH

Available March 8, 2011

A GENTLEMAN'S HOMECOMING
Ruth Axtell Morren

PRAIRIE COWBOY
Linda Ford

THE PROPER WIFE
Winnie Griggs

WANTED: A FAMILY
Janet Dean

REQUEST YOUR FREE BOOKS!

2 FREE INSPIRATIONAL NOVELS

PLUS 2

FREE

MYSTERY GIFTS

Love Inspired

HISTORICAL

INSPIRATIONAL HISTORICAL ROMANCE

YES! Please send me 2 FREE Love Inspired® Historical novels and my 2 FREE mystery gifts (gifts are worth about $10). After receiving them, if I don't wish to receive any more books, I can return the shipping statement marked "cancel." If I don't cancel, I will receive 4 brand-new novels every month and be billed just $4.24 per book in the U.S. or $4.74 per book in Canada. That's a saving of at least 23% off the cover price. It's quite a bargain! Shipping and handling is just 50¢ per book in the U.S. and 75¢ per book in Canada.* I understand that accepting the 2 free books and gifts places me under no obligation to buy anything. I can always return a shipment and cancel at any time. Even if I never buy another book, the two free books and gifts are mine to keep forever.

102/302 IDN FDCH

Name	(PLEASE PRINT)
Address	Apt. #
City	State/Prov.	Zip/Postal Code

Signature (if under 18, a parent or guardian must sign)

Mail to the **Reader Service:**
IN U.S.A.: P.O. Box 1867, Buffalo, NY 14240-1867
IN CANADA: P.O. Box 609, Fort Erie, Ontario L2A 5X3

Not valid for current subscribers to Love Inspired Historical books.

Want to try two free books from another series?
Call 1-800-873-8635 or visit www.ReaderService.com.

* Terms and prices subject to change without notice. Prices do not include applicable taxes. Sales tax applicable in N.Y. Canadian residents will be charged applicable taxes. Offer not valid in Quebec. This offer is limited to one order per household. All orders subject to credit approval. Credit or debit balances in a customer's account(s) may be offset by any other outstanding balance owed by or to the customer. Please allow 4 to 6 weeks for delivery. Offer available while quantities last.

Your Privacy—The Reader Service is committed to protecting your privacy. Our Privacy Policy is available online at www.ReaderService.com or upon request from the Reader Service.

We make a portion of our mailing list available to reputable third parties that offer products we believe may interest you. If you prefer that we not exchange your name with third parties, or if you wish to clarify or modify your communication preferences, please visit us at www.ReaderService.com/consumerchoice or write to us at Reader Service Preference Service, P.O. Box 9062, Buffalo, NY 14269. Include your complete name and address.

LIH11

Conor Russell knows what prairie living can do to a delicate female—that's why he's raising his daughter, Rachael, to be tough. But can the new schoolteacher, Virnie, look beyond his hard exterior and help both Conor and his daughter experience a family once and for all?

Find out in PRAIRIE COWBOY by Linda Ford, available March 2011 from Love Inspired Historical.

"You wanted to speak to me?" Virnie kept her voice admirably calm despite the way her insides vibrated at speaking to Conor, who had inadvertently opened an unwelcome door in her heart.

Conor seemed very interested in the reins draped across his palm. "I have to go to Gabe's farm and help him with his harvest. Rae can't go with me."

"Of course not. She has to attend school."

Conor's gaze rested on Rachael standing near the school watching them. He loved her so much it seemed to almost hurt him.

"I will miss her." His voice was low, edged with roughness. "But out here we do what has to be done without complaining."

She nodded, not understanding the warning note in his voice any more than she understood why she ached inside.

He jerked his gaze away as if aware of the tension lacing the air between them. "She needs someone to stay with her. Would you?"

Her mouth fell open. Was this God's answer for a way to spend more time with Rachael? He'd certainly found a unique way of doing it.

"Why, I'd love to stay with her. On one condition. You allow me to teach her a few skills around the house."

They did silent battle with their eyes and then he nodded. "So long as you don't teach her to be a silly, weak female."

"Female doesn't necessarily equate with weak and silly." She'd tried to prove it to her father. She pushed the hurt of her former life back into the shadows. This was not about her. It was about Rachael.

"I have to leave immediately. Take good care of her." He waved Rachael over.

Virnie thought he looked as if he regretted it already. As she walked away she overheard him say, "Don't expect her to stay when things get hard."

Virnie grinned. If he thought she'd turn tail and run at the first challenge she encountered, he didn't know the things she'd faced in the past.

Don't miss PRAIRIE COWBOY by Linda Ford,
available March 2011 from Love Inspired Historical.

Love Inspired®
SUSPENSE
RIVETING INSPIRATIONAL ROMANCE

TEXAS RANGER JUSTICE

Keeping the Lone Star State safe

Follow the men and women of the Texas Rangers,
as they risk their lives to help save others,
with

DAUGHTER OF TEXAS by **Terri Reed**
January 2011

BODY OF EVIDENCE by **Lenora Worth**
February 2011

FACE OF DANGER by **Valerie Hansen**
March 2011

TRAIL OF LIES by **Margaret Daley**
April 2011

THREAT OF EXPOSURE by **Lynette Eason**
May 2011

OUT OF TIME by **Shirlee McCoy**
June 2011

Available wherever books are sold.

www.SteepleHill.com

Steeple
Hill®